# Happy Campers

## Book III of the Commitment Series

BADGER BLISS BOOKS

# DEDICATION

I dedicate this book to my older brother, Steve Dusablon, who we lost to cancer at the age of 58. Steve had a very dry wit and would have very much appreciated the humor in this book. In fact, he is credited with at least one of the scenes that happened on a camping trip to Cape May, NJ many moons ago (i.e., 'tent poles'). Steve was a gentle soul with an immense capacity to love. He was taken from us way too soon. I will miss you forever, Bro. Say hi to Boonie for us all and don't let him drop the F-bomb too often in front of the Big Guy, okay? I love you, Stevie! Your sister, Karen (who can still grow a better mustache than you! LOL!).

ALSO WRITTEN BY KAREN D. BADGER AND
AVAILABLE FROM BADGER BLISS BOOKS:


ON A WING AND A PRAYER
YESTERDAY ONCE MORE
THE BLUE FEATHER
ALL MY TOMORROWS
1140 RUE ROYALE

The Billie/Cat Commitment Series:
 IN A FAMILY WAY
 UNCHAINED MEMORIES
 HAPPY CAMPERS
 COLLECTIVE IDENTITY
 SWEET ANGEL
 RELATIVE-LY SPEAKING

www.badgerblissbooks.com

# Happy Campers

## Book III of the Commitment Series

$\mathcal{B}$

A BADGER BLISS BOOK

By

*Karen D. Badger*

This is a work of fiction. All characters, locales and events are either products of the author's imagination or are used fictitiously.

HAPPY CAMPERS – BOOK III OF THE COMMITMENT SERIES

Copyright © 2013 by Karen D. Badger
www.karendbadger.com

Cover photograph by Kacie L. Badger
Cover design by Ann Phillips

A Badger Bliss Book
Published by Badger Bliss Books
Georgia, VT  05468

www.badgerblissbooks.com

ISBN 13: 978-1-945761-07-2
ISBN 10: 1-945761-07-5

1st Edition published by Blue Feather Books, Ltd, June, 2013
2nd Edition, published by Badger Bliss Books, September 2014
3rd Edition published by Badger Blis Books, August, 2016

Printed in the United States of America and in the United Kingdom

# ACKNOWLEDGMENTS

To my beta readers who helped to make this book as good as it could be: Mom, Kacie, Donna, and Barb. You guys rock! To my editor, Day Peterson for not pulling any punches or sugarcoating the edits. Every edit is a learning experience for me, so I appreciate your inputs. I hope to work with you again on future books. To Emily Reed of Blue Feather Books for believing in me and for continuing to support my writing. To my wife, B for unscrewing me from the ceiling every time I disagreed with an edit, and for her unwavering support and advice during the writing of this book. Finally, to my sons, Heath and Dane, their ladies, Kacie and Daisy, and to our grandkids, Kyren, Ari and Ellie for providing so much of the fodder that fueled this story.

# Prologue

Billie and Cat sat side by side in stiff, faux-leather chairs. Cat thumbed through a fashion magazine while Billie looked around impatiently.

"I wonder what's taking so long. We're the only ones in the waiting room," Billie said.

Cat laid the magazine in her lap. "Are you nervous, love?"

"Not especially. Why do you ask?"

"Because your leg is jiggling up and down."

Billie massaged her thigh. "Force of habit, I guess."

Their attention was drawn by a door opening on the other side of the room. "Ms. Charland, the doctor will see you now," the receptionist said.

Billie stood and offered her hand to Cat, who remained seated.

"Are you sure you don't want to talk to her alone?" Cat asked.

"I'm sure," Billie said. "After all, this is our life we're going to be talking about here, not just mine."

Cat slipped her hand into Billie's and accompanied her into the doctor's office. Doctor Connor was on the phone when they entered.

She motioned for them to sit in the two chairs in front of her desk. "All right, then. Call the front desk, and they'll schedule an appointment for you. Okay. I'll see you soon. Bye." Doctor Connor hung up the phone and turned to Billie and Cat. "I'm sorry, ladies. Please make yourselves comfortable. Can I offer you something to drink?"

"No, I'm good," Billie said.

Cat nodded. "Me, too."

Doctor Connor sat back in her chair. "Okay. So let me

see… it's been about a month since your last appointment," she said as she paged through Billie's file. "How have things been going?"

Cat motioned for Billie to speak first.

"Things have been good," Billie said.

"Then why is your leg bouncing up and down?" Doctor Connor asked.

"See," Cat said.

Billie lowered her chin to her chest and rubbed her forehead. She sighed deeply.

Cat placed her hand on Billie's shoulder. "Are you okay?"

Billie wiped a tear from the corner of her eye. "I'm okay. It's just that I can't shake this feeling."

"What feeling is that, Billie? Can you describe it to me?" Doctor Connor asked.

"I have this overwhelming sense that things are out of control in my life."

"Really? After the emotional roller coaster we've lived through over the last several months, I thought things were finally settling down," Cat said.

Billie took Cat's hand in her own. "They are, love, but not a day goes by that I don't have this anxious feeling in my chest when I think back over the events of the past year—brain surgery, the months of recovery during which I had no sense of self or belonging. Cat, I didn't remember you or the girls when I came to after surgery. Do you have any idea how terrifying it was to be told I was married with children and not remember any of it?"

"The anxious feeling, Billie, tell me about it," Doctor Connor requested.

"It's always there, under the surface, but sometimes when I dwell on what happened, my heart skips in my chest and I get a sick feeling in my stomach."

"Does it happen only when you're remembering the past year?"

"Most often, yes. I don't have any control over when it happens. I can be sitting behind my desk at work, and suddenly it hits me."

"How has work been lately?"

"I'm a lawyer, Doctor Connor. Things can get pretty intense, depending on the nature of the case I'm working on."

"Billie, you never told me your heart was skipping," Cat said. "I'm a doctor, love; you need to tell me these things. If that's the case, we should be monitoring your blood pressure and providing treatment as necessary."

Billie nodded. "Why is this happening, Doctor Connor?"

"It's a form of Post Traumatic Stress Disorder, or PTSD. You've been through a lot over the past year, both of you. How is the memory recall coming along?"

"Much better than it was right after the surgery. I never felt so lost and alone as I did for those few months, despite the fact that I was surrounded by people who loved me. It was frustrating not to remember. That's all behind us now."

"We certainly don't want to dwell on the past, but it's important for all of us to understand where you are in your recovery," Doctor Connor said. "Are you still having recall moments? Are there details of your past that are still missing?"

"Occasionally I experience the beginnings of a recall, and then it flits away just beyond my grasp. That's pretty frustrating, but it's happening less and less these days," Billie said.

Doctor Connor leaned forward. "We've done an exercise before, actively recalling the timeline of your life, starting with the last memory you had before the injury. It allows us to gauge how much more you remember since the last time we talked, and it may trigger a memory that's been tucked away in your brain. Do you want to give it a try again today?"

Billie glanced at Cat, who nodded her head enthusiastically.

"Go ahead, Billie. I'll fill in the blanks if you need me to," Cat said.

"Okay. Let's see... Seth just turned eleven, so that means we met a little more than five years ago. You joined the aerobics class I was teaching and proceeded to fall flat on your face during the first class."

"Of course you would recall my most embarrassing moment! Feel free to forget that one again, okay?" Cat said.

"Not a chance," Billie teased.

"Obviously, Cat's clumsiness didn't scare you away, Billie. Just how did your relationship develop from there?" Doctor Connor asked.

"I began giving her personal one-on-one aerobics lessons, and it wasn't long before I found myself falling in love with her." Billie turned to Cat. "It was then I found out you were keeping a secret from me."

"Tara," Cat said.

"Yes, Tara. I never dreamed you had a four-year-old daughter."

"Not fair," Cat said. "You didn't tell me about Seth right away, either. Imagine my surprise when you escorted me to his hospital bed where he had been lying in a coma for six months."

"I had no choice but to take you to see him. You were accusing me of cheating on you."

"Do you blame me? You were disappearing every evening and wouldn't tell me where you were going. I never dreamed you were visiting your son in the hospital."

Billie picked up Cat's hand and kissed the back of it. "I was worried Seth's condition would overwhelm you. I should have trusted you more."

"Yes, you should have, but that's water under the bridge now."

"How is she doing so far, Cat?" Doctor Connor asked.

"Pretty good," Cat said.

Doctor Connor looked at Billie. "Go on, please."

"All right. So as soon as you learned about Seth and his condition, you took right over, just like you always do." Billie grinned evilly.

"Hey, what's that supposed to mean?" Cat objected.

"I'm not complaining. If you hadn't jumped in, God knows what might have happened with Seth. Anyway, you contacted your dad, who, as luck would have it, is a neurosurgeon. To make a long story short, he was instrumental in bringing Seth back to us. Not long after that, we decided to move in together." She frowned.

"Billie, are you struggling with a memory?" Doctor Connor asked.

Billie shook her head. "Yes, I am, but not with a recall. I'm remembering what happened not long after Cat and I moved in together."

Cat squeezed Billie's hand. "The rape?"

"Yes. I'll never forget rushing home after your frantic phone call and finding my ex-husband had assaulted you. I wanted to kill him, Cat."

Cat rested her palm on Billie's cheek. "I know. At least he went to jail for his crime."

"That must have been a very trying time for you," Doctor Connor observed.

Billie's eyes filled with tears. "You don't know the half of it.

Cat was withdrawn for such a long time. The only thing good that came from that event was Skylar, our beautiful baby girl. She looks just like Cat, you know."

Cat smiled at Billie. "Yes, but she's her mommy's girl."

Billie looked sheepish. "I guess I do kind of spoil her."

"You spoil all three of the kids, you big softy," Cat said.

"Anyway," Billie continued, "we bought a house together not long after Sky was born."

Doctor Connor tapped her pen on her notepad. "I imagine it was hard to live in the same apartment where the rape occurred. Buying a house was undoubtedly a good move."

"It was the best decision we ever made, at least I thought it was at the time. I remember how hard it was in the new house at first. The neighbors didn't take kindly to lesbians living in their back yards. It wasn't until Jen and Fred's house caught fire one night, in the middle of winter, no less, that the neighbors came around."

"Do you remember what you did that night, Billie?" Cat asked.

"I did what anyone else would have done, Cat. I would never have been able to live with myself if I hadn't gone into that house to get Fred, Karissa, and Stevie out. As it was, Stevie almost died of smoke inhalation."

"But he didn't, and now we have the most amazing lifelong

friends in Jen and Fred," Cat said.

Billie grinned. "They're more than just friends, they're family."

Cat bumped Billie's shoulder with her own. "I love the relationship we have with them, especially Jen."

"I'm glad they're our friends. I can't imagine life without them."

"Neither can I." Billie wiped a nostalgic tear from her eye. "I digress. Where was I?"

Doctor Connor glanced at her notepad. "House fire."

"Right." Billie's gaze became distant.

"Another bad memory, Billie?" Doctor Connor asked softly.

"Yeah." Billie rubbed her forehead. "A couple of months after the Swenson's house burned, we learned my ex-husband bought himself an early release from jail. The man is a lunatic. While I was at work, he broke into the house and took Cat and the kids hostage."

"He held them hostage?" Doctor Connor asked. "Why?"

"Because he thought he had something to gain. He wanted money, pure and simple, and he didn't care if he had to hurt his son and daughter to get it."

The doctor jotted a note. "And what happened next?"

"I snuck into the house through a basement window and managed to get into the kitchen, where I introduced his head to the food processor, but not before he managed to get a shot off. It lodged in the front part of my brain."

"It all happened right in front of me," Cat said. "My medical training kicked in and, between myself and the paramedics, we were able to keep her stable." She looked at Billie. "We almost lost you, love. I would not have been able to bear that."

"It's amazing how much the two of you have been through in your relationship," Doctor Connor observed.

"You're telling me!" Cat replied. "Sometimes I think we're cursed. Bad stuff happens to us all the time."

"There's a school of thought out there that people bring on

their own bad luck," the doctor said.

"Like karma or bad juju?" Cat asked.

"Kind of, but we can save that discussion for another time. Please continue, Billie."

"Okay. So, what's next... Oh yeah. The next summer, we decided to get married. Who would have guessed that we'd have to fight City Hall to do it?"

"Billie, I was so proud of you. You established your reputation as a civil rights lawyer with that trial."

"I couldn't have done it without you."

"You couldn't have done it without Art's help. He and Marge have become good friends."

"Yes, they have. He was also a big help when we went through the adoption proceedings for Seth and Tara." Billie rubbed her forehead again.

Cat touched her arm. "Billie, are you okay?"

"Just a little headachy, that's all."

"Maybe we should stop for today," Doctor Connor suggested.

"No, I want to continue. I'm okay."

"All right then. Please, go on."

"So that takes us up to the McBride case," Billie said.

"The McBride case?" Doctor Connor prompted.

"Yes. It was a domestic abuse case I was dealing with at work. You may have heard of it, it was all over the papers. The victim was a chronically abused wife and mother. Her husband was very controlling and emotionally unstable. I tried to convince her to leave him, but she wouldn't listen to me." Billie began to cry. "I'm so sorry, Cat."

She rubbed Billie's back. "It's okay, love. I understand."

"Billie, why are you so upset?" Doctor Connor asked.

Billie looked at the doctor. "Why am I upset? Cat and I came to you for couple's counseling after it happened, Doctor Connor, so I think you already know."

"Yes, and I apologize for putting you through this, but I need to know how much of it you remember," Doctor Connor explained patiently.

"You want to know what I remember? I remember grabbing Cat by the neck and threatening to hurt her. I remember the memories of my ex-husband beating me when Seth was just a baby. All of this happened to me because that rat bastard McBride beat his wife to death and triggered horrific memories of my own marriage to Seth's father."

"What happened next, Billie?" Doctor Connor asked.

"I don't know. My next memory was of waking up in the operating room and not remembering the last five years of my life, including Cat. Apparently the scar tissue from the gunshot wound to my head two years earlier had thickened to the point that it was obstructing blood flow in my brain. All my memories from the previous five years were lost. I couldn't walk. I could barely feed myself. It took months of physical therapy before I could take care of myself again."

"I have to admit, Billie, I wasn't sure our relationship would survive, especially when you thought Jen and I were having an affair."

"Well, what did you expect me to think? You were all lovey-dovey with her at the hospital."

"True, but that's how she's always been with both of us. You just didn't remember that. I guess all of that jealousy stuff could have been avoided if I had thought to tell you she bats for the other team."

"Ya think?"

"Jen was a real life saver during all of that, Billie. She was there for me and the kids, and she was there for you, too. She's a good friend."

"I know that now, but at the time, all I could see was her being affectionate with you and you not opposing it."

"So, how are you feeling now, Billie?" Doctor Connor asked.

"It's taken Cat and me the better part of the last year to rebuild our lives."

"How are the kids dealing with things?" Doctor Connor asked.

"Pretty well for the most part," Cat replied. "They love their mom unconditionally."

"Seth was a little freaked out by the whole thing, but he's

old enough to understand what happened," Billie added.

"You said Seth was eleven now?" Doctor Connor asked.

"Yes. Tara is nine, and Sky just turned five. It amazes me how fast time flies. It seems like yesterday that Skylar was born," Billie replied.

Doctor Connor looked at her watch. "Our time is almost up for today. Cat, do you have anything you would like to add?"

"Not really. This past year has been pretty stressful. Sometimes I wish we could just put everything on hold for a while and focus on ourselves."

"Why can't you?"

"I... I..." Cat looked at Billie. "She's right. Why can't we?"

Doctor Connor rose to her feet. "The PTSD symptoms concern me. If we don't identify and reduce the sources of anxiety, it could lead to longer term health problems. Here's what I recommend—take some time to do something fun. Get away for a while, by yourselves, or even as a family. Throw caution to the winds and just let loose. You'll be better grounded for it and more able to deal with the day-to-day stress when you return. In the meantime, I think you're right to monitor her blood pressure, Cat."

Cat and Billie stood and shook hands with the doctor. "Thank you, Doctor Connor. That sounds like a great idea," Cat said.

"I think you're making good progress, Billie. Let's schedule your next appointment for three weeks from now."

# Happy Campers

# Chapter 1

## Lazy Days

Billie yawned as she walked into the kitchen early on Saturday morning, catching a glimpse of herself in the stainless steel refrigerator as she passed it. "Holy shit, my hair looks like I stuck my finger in a light socket." She tried to smooth down the errant locks to no avail. "Oh well, it's Saturday. A girl's got a right to enjoy a down day once in a while. Right now, I need a coffee."

Billie clicked the coffee pot on, silently congratulating herself for setting it up the night before. While she waited for her coffee to brew, she slipped her feet into the Mud-Cats that sat on a tray by the kitchen door and went out to the fetch the morning paper. Billie paused on the front porch and breathed fresh air into her lungs. Summer was rapidly approaching, and the last vestiges of the chilly spring morning were being chased away by the warm sunshine. A feeling of euphoria filled her as she looked around at the trees and bright green grass. She stepped into the path of a sunbeam and stood there for several long moments, allowing the warmth of the sun's rays to wash over her.

Billie loved summer. Everything was green and the flowers were in bloom. The Fourth of July was just around the corner, and she had ample reason to celebrate all the good things in life with her family and friends. What a beautiful day! she thought.

Dressed only in a football jersey, boxer shorts, oversized socks, and her mud boots, and uncaring of what passersby might think, Billie descended the porch steps and strolled across the road to the mailbox. It wasn't unusual for the other ladies of the neighborhood to retrieve the morning paper while wearing a robe and curlers, and she felt that her attire was just as acceptable as theirs. A car drove by and the driver tooted the horn. She waved as she recognized the neighbor who lived one house down from Jen and Fred.

Billie picked up the paper and scanned the front page as she walked back to the house. Nothing of real interest caught her eye. Back in the kitchen, she kicked off her boots, tossed the paper onto the table, and then reached into the cupboard for a coffee mug. The fresh-perked aroma scented the air as she filled her cup and took that first anticipated sip. Through the window above the kitchen sink, she looked out over the back yard, smiling as her gaze rested on the freshly painted tree house. Seth insisted Billie wait until school was out for the summer so he could help paint it. They had applied a new coat of paint just days before Cat, Tara and Skylar planted flowers around the base of the tree. Billie shook her head. She couldn't believe how fast time passed. It seemed like yesterday that Seth had started the fifth grade, and here it was almost the middle of summer already.

Billie loved this time of the morning, especially on the weekends. An early riser, she generally had the house to herself while everyone else slept. She paused to listen to the sounds around her, or more precisely, to the absence of sound around her. Lately it seemed as if the early morning was the only time of day the house was quiet. In a household usually dominated by the sounds of children playing and the TV blaring in the background, she listened intently to the silence and took a mental check of how she was feeling. No anxiety yet today. That's a good sign. Billie took a long flavorful sip of coffee, then unfolded the newspaper and spread it out on the table in front of her. Legs crossed under the table, she cradled her coffee cup in both hands. For the next half hour, she immersed herself in the news and utterly enjoyed the uninterrupted solitude.

A sudden noise and movement to her right drew her attention toward the living room. Billie turned and saw her youngest daughter in the doorway, holding her blanket in one hand and a stuffed puppy dog in the other. Skylar yawned. Billie put her coffee mug on the table and opened her arms. Skylar happily climbed into them, curled up on her mother's lap, then pulled her knees into her chest and tucked her head against Billie's shoulder. Billie wrapped her arms around the child and held her close as she placed a tender kiss on Skylar's head. "Good morning, pumpkin. Did you sleep well last night?"

Skylar nodded and snuggled closer.

"Good." Billie marveled at the unfathomable sense of peace and happiness in her heart at that moment. She rocked back and forth and hummed as she continued to scan the morning paper.

After several moments, Skylar uncurled in Billie's lap and placed both hand on Billie's cheeks. "Mommy, I'm hungry. Will you make me some breakfast?"

"You know Mommy's not a very good cook. Do you want risk it?"

Skylar smiled a toothy grin and nodded. "Can I help?"

"You sure can, lovebug." Billie slid Skylar onto her feet, then went to the cupboard to take a look at the boxed breakfast selections. "Let's see what we have. Okay, I see Cheerios, Mini-Wheats, oatmeal, Pop Tarts–"

"Pop Tarts! Pop Tarts!" Skylar jumped up and down and clapped her hands in excitement.

"Pop Tarts it is." She held the box open for Skylar to select the one she wanted.

Skylar handed a package to Billie. "What one is this, Mommy?"

"Let me see. It says strawberry. Is that the one you want?"

Skylar nodded.

Billie tore open the package and handed it back to Skylar, then lifted the girl and sat her on the edge of the counter near the toaster. "Okay, put the Pop Tarts into the first two slots." She watched as Skylar extracted the pastries from the package and carefully dropped them into the toaster. Billie put two for herself in the remaining two slots, then helped Skylar push both levers down.

Skylar watched in fascination as the heating elements began to glow, and Billie suddenly realized the dangers associated with showing a five-year-old how to use a toaster. She placed her palm on Skylar's cheek to get the little girl's attention. "Sky, the toaster gets very hot when it is cooking something. You can't ever touch it, or you'll get burned, understand?"

Skylar stared at the glowing elements. "Are those red things on fire?"

"No, sweetheart, they're not on fire, but they are very, very hot. Here, put your hand way up here, above the toaster, and you'll feel the heat. Can you feel it?"

Skylar nodded vigorously.

"It gets a lot hotter as your hand moves closer, so hot it could burn you. That would not be good," Billie cautioned. "So don't ever touch it, okay?"

"Okay, Mommy," Skylar promised solemnly. Just then the Pop Tarts nearly jumped out of the toaster, and Skylar squealed with delight.

Billie placed two pastries each on small plates. She lowered Skylar to the floor and gave her a plate to carry to the table while she poured a glass of apple juice and refilled her own coffee mug. Soon, mother and daughter were enjoying their breakfast together.

"Mommy, guess what."

"What, love?"

"Missy wants to be my best friend."

Billie raised her eyebrows. "She does? That's wonderful, Sky."

"Uh-huh. I'm glad she moved here."

Billie tweaked Skylar's nose. "Me, too." Billie was thrilled to learn the new family across the street had a child Skylar's age and was even more pleased to learn it was a girl. Seth and Tara were relatively patient with Sky, but they preferred not to have her tag along all the time.

"We want to sit in the same seat on the school bus when we go to kinnergarden."

"That's kindergarten, and you've got a while before that happens. Summer's just begun. When it's over, it'll be time for you to go to school."

"I can't wait."

"Don't be in too much of a hurry to wish the summer away. Summer is a time for having fun and spending time outdoors."

"And swimmin'," Skylar added.

"Yes indeed." Billie tousled Skylar's hair, then drained the last of her coffee. "How are the Pop Tarts?"

"Yummy. I'm almost done."

"Almost finished," Billie corrected automatically.

"Mommy, can you watch cartoons with me when I'm done eating?"

Billie couldn't resist the beseeching look in her daughter's deep blue eyes. Cat must have looked just like that as a child... except with green eyes. "Of course, dumpling. I'll just take care of these dishes while you eat your last bite and finish your juice."

Billie put the dirty dishes in the dishwasher and followed Skylar into the living room where she stretched out on the couch with her head propped against the armrest. Skylar climbed up and lay down directly on top of her, using Billie's ample breasts as a pillow. Billie threw her arm over Skylar to keep her from falling, then punched the remote to flip through the channels until they found the program Skylar was looking for. In no time, Billie fell asleep with the child lying comfortably on her chest.

# Chapter 2

## Pillow Talk

Cat lumbered down the stairs into the living room. "Coffee... coffee," she murmured as she walked zombie-like through the living room toward the kitchen, her focus solely on her first cup of coffee. She poured a cup from the pot and rested her backside against the counter. Eyes closed, she inhaled the rich scent of coffee as the steam rose from her cup. A broad smile appeared as she sighed blissfully and then sipped the rich dark brew. "Oh, that's good," she said. It was then that she noticed the paper on the kitchen table. Ah, nothing better in the morning than a hot cup of coffee and the daily news. She picked up the paper and carried it into the living room to relax in the overstuffed chair.

As she passed the couch, she saw her wife and daughter lying there. She crouched down in front of them and realized Billie was sleeping. "Morning, sweet pea. You look comfortable."

"Mommy has soft boobies," Skylar said innocently.

Cat laughed. "You're right. They are soft. They make good pillows, wouldn't you say?"

Skylar smiled and poked Billie's breasts. "Yeah, they do."

Cat kissed her forehead. "Well, make yourself comfortable on your mommy-pillow and enjoy your cartoons, okay, honey?"

Skylar went back to watching TV, while Cat set her coffee down on the side table and curled her legs beneath her in her easy chair. She smiled at her wife and daughter on the couch, thinking about how different life would be if Billie's memory hadn't returned. When Billie awoke after brain surgery, she didn't know who she was and insisted she wasn't gay. Cat's world fell apart in a moment, as everything she and Billie had worked for over the previous five years evaporated. Every day was a struggle to hang on to hope. Cat was filled with gratitude that it was all behind them. No wonder she's having anxiety attacks. This past year has been hell on all of us, but especially hard for her.

Cat sipped her coffee, enjoying the flavor as sounds of the household rousing from sleep wafted down the stairs from the second story. Soon, all three children were sprawled out on top of Billie in one fashion or another while they watched TV. Cat was amazed that Billie was able to sleep through it.

When Cat finished her paper and coffee, she stood up and stretched. "French toast and bacon for breakfast?" Three nodding heads sent her into the kitchen to start cooking.

Billie woke to the smell of bacon and the sensation of a heavy weight on her chest and legs. She lifted her head and saw all three children piled on top of her. Skylar lay on her chest, Tara sat on her thighs, and Seth lay across her shins. "Looks like you guys are holding me prisoner here. What's the charge, Sheriff?"

Cat returned to the living room and approached the couch. "Sleeping on the job, varmint," she said to Billie. "Deputies, what do we do with outlaws?"

"Tickle them!" all three children sang out at once as they pounced on their mother. The couch was a frenzy of arms and legs climbing over each other. Suddenly the entire tangle of bodies rolled onto the floor into a heap.

Seth was nearly as big as Cat. In the face of that, combined with Tara's agility and limberness and Skylar's size that allowed her to get into tight spaces, Billie was helpless. The trio soon overpowered her.

"I give! I give! You win. Please stop!" Seth helped her to her feet. "You guys play dirty. Three against one is not fair."

"Hey, we were only following orders," Seth protested.

Billie raised an eyebrow at her wife and advanced toward her menacingly.

"Uh-oh." Cat turned and hightailed it back into the kitchen, with Billie right on her heels.

Billie chased her into a corner and pressed against her, forcing Cat to lean back against the counter. She lowered her nose to within an inch of Cat's and drawled, "Well, Sheriff, whaddaya think I oughta do with ya?"

Cat smiled wickedly. "You could always tie me up." She wiggled her eyebrows suggestively.

Billie's eyes widened. "Do you mean it?"

Cat's eyes narrowed seductively, prompting a growl from Billie, who leaned in closer. "Keep teasing me like that and I'll take you up on that offer, right here, right now—in front of the kids."

"You wouldn't dare."

Billie slipped her hands inside Cat's panties and grabbed two handfuls of butt. She squeezed hard and pulled Cat toward her. "Wouldn't I?"

"Where's the rope?" Cat asked.

Billie's growl deepened. Suddenly a noise from the living room reminded her they were not alone. She released her grasp on Cat's buttocks and took Cat's face firmly between her palms. "You will pay for this later, my love. That's a promise."

"I'll hold you to that, outlaw."

Billie kissed her long and hard before she released her. "I think the bacon is burning."

Cat squealed and ran to rescue their breakfast.

# Chapter 3

## You Can Choose Your Friends, But...

The kids ate quickly and went to their rooms to get dressed. Cat and Billie sat down to eat their own breakfast and to enjoy the opportunity to spend time together without the children demanding their attention. Just then the door opened, and Jen popped in.

"Morning, ladies." Jen helped herself to the last of the coffee and then set up a new pot to brew.

Cat and Billie looked at each other and smiled as their friend made herself at home.

"Good morning, Jen," Billie said.

"Want some breakfast?" Cat offered.

"No. Just ate." Jen dropped a kiss on Cat's cheek and nabbed a piece of bacon. She circled around Billie, deposited a kiss on her cheek, as well, then sat down between the pair and lifted a piece of toast from Billie's plate.

"Are you sure you don't want to eat?" Billie asked.

"No. Really, I just ate," she replied around a bite of toast. "What are you two up to today?"

Billie and Cat looked at each other. "Don't know." Cat shrugged. "We haven't really thought about it."

Jen looked at Billie, who also shrugged. "Boy, you two are a bundle of fun."

"What are you doing today, Jen?" asked Cat.

Billie placed her elbow on the table and rested her chin in her hand. "Yeah, what are you doing today?"

Jen grinned. "Same thing you are—don't know."

"Boy, are we in a rut, or what?" Cat commented with a shake of her head.

"What's Fred doing today?" Billie asked.

The three women looked at one another. "Don't know," they all exclaimed together, then broke into peals of laughter.

"Hey, I've got a thought," Jen said. "Last fall, didn't we agree to do something fun when the weather got nice?"

"I don't remember agreeing to anything."

Jen punched Billie lightly in the shoulder. "You did too, Big Guy. After the cookout you hosted last fall we talked about doing something fun together in the spring. Well, spring has come and gone."

"Cookout?"

"Yes. Right after your memory returned."

"Memory? What memory. I don't remember a memory?"

Jen slapped Billie gently on the back of the head. "Cut the shit. Don't you remember playing with our heads about what a wonderful cook you thought you were? Like we would actually believe that."

Billie grinned. "Oh, yeah, that memory. I really had you going about me doing the cooking, didn't I?"

"I could have kicked your ass when you admitted to setting us up."

"You're going to have to get a lot tougher before you can kick my ass, Blondie," Billie said.

"I'm plenty tough," Jen replied, bristling.

"Time out," Cat interrupted. "Enough of the Alpha Girl posturing. Sheesh, you'd think you were teenagers."

"She started it," Billie whined.

"Did not," Jen said.

"Did too."

"Did not."

"Enough, or I'll kick both your asses," Cat warned.

Billie raised her hands in surrender. "I know when I'm licked."

"Whipped is more like it," Jen teased.

"Don't knock it until you've tried it." Billie wiggled her eyebrows. "Licked, whipped—same church, different pew."

"You are such a pig," Jen said.

"Oink, oink."

Cat stood and picked up all three coffee cups. "No more coffee until you two can behave."

Billie and Jen looked at each other in mock dismay. "Yikes," Billie said.

"Double yikes," Jen added. "Okay, we'll behave."

"Good," Cat said. "Now, back to our earlier conversation."

"I forget what we were talking about," Billie said. "I think it was residual memory loss."

Just then, the back door opened, admitting Fred, Stevie, and Karissa. "Seth and Tara are upstairs, sweeties. Go on up," Cat said to the children.

Stevie and Karissa immediately took off into the living room as Fred helped himself to a cup of the fresh coffee. "Morning," he said to everyone. "What's up?"

"Don't know," all three women said at once, dissolving into laughter.

Fred looked at the three of them as though they were nuts. "Okay, what did you put in the coffee?"

# Chapter 4

## The Attack of the Killer Ennui

Billie pushed a chair out with her foot. "Have a seat, Fred."

He joined the women at the table. "So, really, what's up?" he asked.

"We're just sitting here discussing how exciting our lives are these days," Cat said.

"Boring is more like it," Jen piped in. "We really need to do something to get out of this rut."

"What do you mean boring?" Fred said.

"What do I mean?" Jen exclaimed. "Hell, Fred, its Saturday night and none of us has a date," she said pointedly.

"Huh?"

Jen kissed her husband's forehead indulgently. "Sometimes you are so dense, Fred. Why do I keep you around?"

"'Cause you can't resist my good looks and charm?"

"Oh, please." Jen groaned. "Look, here we are, four healthy adults, five healthy children, and what are we doing? Sitting around pulling lint out of our belly buttons! How boring is that? We need some excitement in our lives."

Fred cocked his head. "Last fall, didn't we talk about doing something together?"

"We were talking about that very thing just before you came in," Cat said.

"I wouldn't say our lives have been boring lately," Billie objected. "I mean, brain surgery and memory loss are anything but boring."

"It's not all about you, Billie. Why do you have to be so contrary?" Jen asked.

Billie grinned, "Because you're so easy to bait."

"Fu—"

"Jen, there are little ears around," Cat interrupted.

"Okay, okay."

So, Jen, what do you have in mind?" Billie asked.

"I don't know. Let's go somewhere... do something," she said, frustration clear in her voice.

"That's a great idea, Jen. In fact, our counselor recommended that to us just yesterday."

"You two are still seeing a shrink?" Jen asked.

"Yes. We go every few weeks," Billie said.

"Are you guys okay?" Jen said. "I mean, I thought things were going pretty well lately."

"For the most part, things are going well, but Billie's been having anxiety attacks. Doctor Connor thinks they're stress related, so she recommended we get away for a while," Cat said.

"Well, it's settled then," Jen said. "Let's do a trip together. Question is, what kind of trip?"

"How about camping?" Cat suggested. "The Fourth of July is coming up. Maybe we can schedule it for then."

"That could be a lot of fun," Jen said. "Yeah, we can rough it in tents. The kids would absolutely love it. No work, no stress, it should be relaxing. What do you all think?"

Billie opened her mouth, but was interrupted by Fred. "I'm in. Some of my best childhood memories are of camping with my dad. Did I ever tell you I was a Boy Scout?"

"Save it, Fred." Jen looked at Billie. "So, what do you think?"

Billie looked at Cat, and then at Jen. "I'm not so sure about camping."

"Come on, Billie. Doctor Connor did say we need to get away from it all," Cat pointed out. "You won't have to do anything. Jen and I can cook, you and Fred can go fishing. Doesn't that sound like fun?"

Billie sighed. *Shit, I hate camping. I know I'll regret going, but how can I say so without hurting Cat's feelings?*

"Billie?" Cat prompted.

"Sure," she heard herself say as she tried to put a smile on her face. "Sounds like fun." *I guess I can sacrifice one weekend*

# Happy Campers

*for Cat.*

# Chapter 5

## Timing is Everything

"Two weeks? You made reservations for two weeks?" Billie ranted as she paced back and forth across the kitchen. "Cat, are you out of your mind? Two weeks?"

Cat sat calmly at the table, both hands wrapped around her coffee mug, a travel brochure for the Happy Trails Campground on the table in front of her. "Calm down, Billie. Remember your blood pressure," she said evenly. "The time will fly by. You'll have so much fun you'll wonder where the time went." She tapped the brochure. "Look, there's a lot to do at this campground."

Billie realized she wasn't going to sway Cat with a tirade, so she sat down on the chair adjacent to her and reached out for her wife's hands. "Cat... honey," she began, "I have a confession to make. I really don't like camping. I only agreed to go because you seemed so excited about it."

"What?" Cat said loudly. "Billie, how can you not like camping? That's un-American. Have you ever even been camping?"

"Yeah. When I was nine years old, I went to Girl Scout camp. I hated it. I was taller than the other girls, and they all made fun of me. It was a nightmare," Billie recalled.

Cat grinned. "You must have been cute in a Girl Scout uniform."

"Cat, we're not talking about how cute I was as a Girl Scout." Billie threw up her hands in frustration. "Damn it, will you take this seriously for a moment?"

Cat wasn't going to let Billie's mood deter her. "Calm

down, love. You aren't nine anymore. Leave that to Tara. Heaven knows, I couldn't handle two of you."

"Stop changing the subject. Look, a few days, I could deal with... maybe even a week, but two weeks? I don't understand why anyone who lives in a home with electricity and running water and toilets would want to sleep in a nylon cave that heaves with every gust of wind." She was desperate to make Cat see how unreasonable her expectations were.

Cat placed a palm on Billie's cheek. "Sweetheart, don't be such a baby. Being one with nature is a great way to relax. You'll have fun. We'll bring the fireworks and sparklers. The kids will love it. Just give it a chance, okay?" She fluttered her eyelashes seductively at her wife.

"Cat—"

"Yesssss?" Cat stood up and leaned down over the table. When their faces were within a hair's breadth from each other, Cat nibbled butterfly kisses around Billie's mouth.

"I... ah... Cat..."

"I'm listening," Cat said as butterflies flitted across Billie's chin and neck.

"Cat," Billie moaned, the damned butterflies on her collarbone now.

"Hmm?"

"Oh, God. Ah, about this camping trip?"

"Yes?"

"Do we get our own tent?"

# Chapter 6

# If the Mountain Won't Come to Mohammed...

Billie and Cat stood in front of the display of camp stoves and cookware. "Okay, what's on the list?" Billie asked.

"Stove, pots and pans, utensils, propane, coffee pot, paper plates and cups, sleeping bags, air mattresses, tents, lanterns, canopy, rain gear, fire sticks, matches, trash bags, porta-potty, bug spray, sunscreen, first aid kit," Cat replied.

"Whoa! Slow down. That's a pretty long list. There's no way I'll remember everything."

"Well, we're basically starting with nothing."

"Why can't we use the cookware we have in the house?" Billie asked.

"I'm not going to drag our good cookware into the wild. I don't want to ruin it."

"The wild? It's a campground, right? Don't tell me we're roughing it out in the middle of nowhere."

Cat hip-bumped Billie. "Of course not, silly. This vacation is all about relaxing, and I want to make sure we're as comfortable as possible. The last thing I want is for this trip to be a disaster. If that happens, I'll never get you to go camping again."

"You got that right!"

"Okay, so where were we? Oh, yes, we need a stove."

Several hours later, Billie, Cat, and their three kids were standing outside their car in the parking lot with three shopping carts of camping gear waiting to be loaded.

"Where are we going to sit?" Seth asked.

Billie shook her head. "What am I getting myself into?"

"Why don't you leave us here and take the gear home, then come back to get us," Cat suggested.

"I guess we don't have many options, do we? I have a bad feeling about this, Cat."

"Don't be so pessimistic, love. Think positively. You'll see, it'll be fun."

"Define fun."

"Waking up in the morning to the sounds of birds chirping, sharing breakfast cooked in the open air with our friends and family, kayaking, swimming, hiking. Come on, admit it. You're looking forward to it as much as we are."

"Yeah, about as much as I'd look forward to a root canal."

"Don't be such a grump."

"Grrr."

"The kids and I will go back into the store and browse, while you take our purchases home. We'll see you in a few."

Billie grumbled to herself the entire way home. *God, I hate shopping. I hate shopping even more than I hate camping. What was I thinking when I agreed to go on this camping trip anyway? Damn Cat for hitting me below the belt! She knows my weak spots, and she isn't afraid to exploit them.* Billie felt her heart skip a beat, followed by a rush of heat. *So much for avoiding anxious situations.*

Cat and the children returned to the store, and the kids immediately scattered to the four winds. Seth went directly to the baseball equipment, Tara found the bicycles, and Skylar ran headlong into a very tall display of tennis balls—literally. The display folded in on itself like a perfectly planned demolition, and what seemed like an infinite number of tubes of tennis balls tumbled to the floor and rolled inconceivable distances down aisles and under racks of sportswear. Powerless to stop the implosion that was just beyond her reach, Cat shrieked, and Seth and Tara ran back to see what the ruckus was all about.

"Sky! Why did you do that?" Tara shouted.

Skylar immediately began to cry loudly.

"Tara, don't yell at your sister," Cat scolded.

"Look at what she did, Mama," Tara said in her own

defense.

Skylar howled louder.

"I can see what she did, but you've hurt her feelings. Skylar, please!" Cat said, a little more sternly than she intended.

Skylar threw herself on the floor and bawled. Seth ran down the aisle to collect the tubes of balls that were still rolling away.

Tara crossed her arms and pouted. Cat turned several shades of red.

"Oh my!" said a store attendant from over Cat's shoulder.

Billie returned to collect her family a short time later. As she pulled into the parking lot, she could see them waiting in front of the store. Cat sat on a bench with the girls. She had her arm around Skylar, who was crying. Tara was glaring at her sister, and Seth stood several feet away, as if to disassociate himself from the others.

"I don't want to sit next to her," Tara said as they climbed into the back seat.

Cat rubbed her brow. "Seth, would you mind switching seats with Tara so you're next to Skylar this time?"

"Then I have to sit in the middle. I don't want to sit in the middle," he replied.

"Seth, please. I'm not in the mood for this."

"Geesum!" he complained as he reluctantly belted himself into the middle seat.

"What happened?" Billie said.

Cat raised her hand to forestall any further enquiries. "Don't ask."

The ride home was tense and silent. Skylar whimpered nearly all the way, falling silent only when they pulled into the driveway. The kids piled out of the car and rapidly retreated into the family room. Her arms filled with the last of their purchases, Billie followed Cat into the house. When Cat stopped short, Billie almost ran into her. Cat's shoulders began to shake.

*Oh great. She's crying.* Billie put her packages on the closest countertop and placed her hands on Cat's shoulders, ready to apologize for her own sour mood. Suddenly Cat sank to the floor. It was only then that Billie realized Cat was laughing hysterically.

"Oh my God! Look at all this stuff," Cat exclaimed.

Billie looked at the mountain of equipment in the middle of the kitchen floor and had to admit it was pretty comical. Soon Cat's infectious mood spread, and Billie found herself on the floor next to her wife, holding her sides, which ached with laughter. She was suddenly aware of the light, happy feeling in the pit of her stomach. She also noted that her heart palpitations had stopped. The saying "laughter is the best medicine" sprang to mind. *Hmm, maybe this won't be so bad after all.*

# Chapter 7

## Is This What a Sardine Feels Like?

Jen, Fred, Cat, and Billie sat around Jen's dining room table looking at the food list they had prepared for their camping trip.

"How many of us are there?" Fred teased, and then groaned as Jen elbowed him in the ribs.

"We don't want to run out of food," Cat said.

"Yeah, but even our eating machines couldn't go through all that in two weeks," Billie observed. "There's enough on that list to feed an army for a month."

"Okay, okay," Cat said irritably. "Let's see what we can eliminate." Cat picked up the pencil and started making checkmarks next to the items that they absolutely had to have, Billie looking over her shoulder.

"You forgot to check the popcorn," Billie pointed out as Cat's pencil bypassed it. Cat went back and checked popcorn, then continued down the list.

"Wait, what about those dumplings you make with the red stuff in them?" Billie interrupted again. Cat shot Billie a sideways glare and went back and checked off the ingredients for raspberry turnovers.

"Don't forget—Hey!" Billie protested as Cat tossed the pencil and list at her.

"You take care of the food list Ms. 'I can't cook to save my soul.'"

Jen came to the rescue. "All right, give me the list." She grabbed it from a grateful Billie. "Let's see. Okay, we've decided to eat together, right? So all we have to do is plan a menu for two weeks, then put together a shopping list." The others nodded in agreement. "Okay, give me some suggestions."

"Pizza," said Fred.

"Pizza? How are we going to cook pizza around a campfire, Fred? We need an oven for that," Cat pointed out.

"Okay, how about tuna noodle casserole?" he suggested.

Jen rapped Fred's head with her knuckles. "Hello? Is there anyone in there? Fred, no more ideas that require an oven, okay?"

Fred shrugged. "What do you want from me? I'm a guy."

Cat looked at Billie. "Any requests?"

Billie looked thoughtfully at Cat for a moment then said, "I don't know. French fries, maybe. The kids like those."

Cat covered her face with both hands and shook her head. Finally, she said, "Billie, Fred, why don't the two of you go figure out how we're going to fit all the gear into the cars. Jen and I will work out the menu and food list, okay? Oh, and make sure there's room to take the kids along too."

Billie and Fred got up from the table and gave each other a high five before heading out to allot the space in the cars.

Jen looked at Cat with raised eyebrows. "Somehow, I think that was planned."

Two hours later, they had a comprehensive menu and food list.

"You know, it does look like a lot of food," Cat observed.

"Yeah, and that doesn't include the perishable stuff we'll pick up once we get there," Jen added.

"Oh well, at least we won't go hungry." Cat folded the list and pocketed it for that afternoon's grocery shopping. "Let's go see how the packing is coming along." She stood and led Jen toward the back door. When Cat stopped short, Jen plowed right into the back of her.

Jen peeled herself off Cat's backside. "Whoa, girl. If you wanted me to get that intimate, all you had to do was ask." When Cat didn't respond, Jen turned to see what her friend was staring at. "Holy shit!"

In the driveway were a station wagon and a van, each piled

so full of camping gear, daylight couldn't be seen from one side of the vehicle to the other. Bicycle racks full of children's bikes were mounted on the back of each. The van was sporting a large car-top carrier that looked like a giant hamburger container, and Billie and Cat's car had two tandem kayaks on top.

Cat pointed to the container on top of the van. "Tell me that isn't full too."

Billie smiled. "Nope, that's where the food's going."

"We couldn't possibly fill that big thing with food."

"A week's worth of massages says you do," Billie challenged.

"You're on."

"Hey, what about me?" Fred asked.

Billie and Cat both looked at Jen. She looked at them and frowned. "Oh, all right, you're on. A week's worth of massages for you, too, Fred, but Cat and I get to do the shopping."

"Fair enough," Billie said as she winked at Fred.

Three hours later, Billie and Fred worked together to force the car-top carrier closed. There was just barely enough room in the storage unit for the food and cooking supplies.

Billie latched the cover, dusted off her hands, and walked over to Cat. "I'll take my first massage tonight, sweetheart."

# Chapter 8

# The Midnight Ride of Billie Revere

To make the eight-hour ride easier on the kids, the adults decided to leave at midnight on the night prior to their reservations. Fred and Jen drove their fully loaded, hamburger box-topped van to Cat and Billie's to begin the trip. As soon as the van came to a stop, Stevie and Karissa hopped out and greeted their friends. The kids were excited about being allowed to stay up until midnight and vowed among them to stay awake all night.

"Okay, you guys, get into the cars. It's almost time to leave." Cat unfolded her list. "Now let's see if we have everything. Clothes—check. Food—check. Kayaks—check. Fireworks—check. Bicycles—check. GPS... Billie, did you program the GPS with the campground's address?"

"Yes, Sarge. It's all set," Billie replied dryly, rolling her eyes.

Fred and Jen sported identical amused looks as they watched the interaction between their friends.

"Did you program the sexy voice into it?" Cat asked.

"Sexy voice?" Jen inquired.

Cat grinned. "Oh yeah! Her name is Maeve, and she's Irish. Our GPS lets you choose the voice you want to give you verbal direction. We chose Maeve. Her voice is very sexy."

"How come ours doesn't have a sexy voice?" Fred asked.

Jen shook her head. "What? My voice isn't sexy enough for you?"

"Of course it is, but I'd rather have her tell me where to go. You already do that all the time."

Jen sighed. "Well, that's true enough." Fred looked pained.

"We probably should program ours to the same route, in case we get separated for some reason."

"That's a good idea," Cat agreed.

Fred and Billie huddled together, comparing routes and making modifications. It took a bit of effort and some cursing from Billie to ensure both GPSs had the same route. Billie walked Fred back to their car.

"Eww! That's gross!" she said when he licked the mounting suction cup before sticking the GPS to the windshield.

"If I don't do that, it falls off," he replied.

Cat refolded her list. "Okay. It looks like we have everything. Pile in and let's hit the road."

\* \* \*

Despite determined efforts to stay awake all night, by 12:30 a.m. the Charland kids were out cold, lulled by the motion of the car and the steady hum of tires on the asphalt. One by one, they dozed and leaned against each other and the pillows they brought with them. As the last one drifted off, Cat turned to Billie. "It worked," she whispered and was rewarded with a smile from her wife.

"What time is check-in tomorrow, Cat?"

"11 a.m. I figure we'll get there around 9:30, just in time to stop for breakfast, and then we'll find the campground."

"We're going to be pretty tired, you know."

Cat smiled at Billie. "You're probably right, but it'll be so worth it to not have to hear 'are we there yet?' every few minutes."

"Amen to that."

"Don't forget to stop at the next rest area we come to. We can use the facilities and get coffee to help us stay awake."

"Yes, ma'am."

Cat rubbed Billie's thigh. "Thanks for agreeing to this trip, Billie. I do think it will help with your anxiety. I mean, what can go wrong?"

"I hope you're right. I'm kind of looking forward to getting some fishing in. Our lives are so busy, we rarely have time to just enjoy the simple things in life. I know I haven't been easy to live with over the past several months."

"Well, I'll do my best to minimize the stress for you. I want you to just kick back and enjoy yourself."

"This vacation is for both of us. The past year has been just as stressful for you as it has for me. In a different way, maybe, but it hasn't been easy for you either."

"Just promise me you'll relax. Doctor Connor is right. If we don't get the anxiety under control it could lead to other medical issues, and I am not ready to lose you. I love you, even when you're being a royal pain in the 'you know what.'"

"I promise. Oh, and ditto on the love thing."

"You're such a romantic. I can hardly stand it."


Three hours into the trip, Fred drove his car into a rest area, followed closely by Billie. The four adults exited the vehicles and stretched. They went into the station in pairs to purchase coffee and snacks, the two who stayed behind standing guard over their sleeping cargo. Finally they were once again on their way, with Billie pulling out behind Fred.

Not five miles later, Billie felt a sudden tug at the steering wheel and had to fight to maintain control of the car as she guided it to the breakdown lane on the highway.

"What the hell?" Billie turned off the ignition and got out of the car. It was pitch black. There were no streetlights or oncoming traffic to light the way. Billie walked around the car, but it was too dark to see anything. She knocked on Cat's window and when it was opened, she ducked down and poked her head through. "Cat, I think there's a flashlight in the glove box. Could you hand it to me, please?"

Cat rummaged around until she found the flashlight. "Here you go. Want some help?"

"Not yet. I need to see what we're dealing with first." Billie walked around the car to see what could have caused the problem. She found that the right front tire had a flat. "Damn."

Cat leaned her head out the window. "What is it?"

"Flat tire. We're not going anywhere until I change the

damn thing."

Cat was immediately out of the car to lend a hand, following Billie around to the back of the car. Billie reached for the hatch release and suddenly remembered that the back of the car was jam-packed with camping gear. "Shit! Shit! Shit!" Billie stormed, stamping her feet and clenching her fists with each expletive.

Cat followed Billie's gaze into the back of the car and instantly realized what they would have to do to get to the spare tire, which was located under the rear cargo panel... and under sleeping bags, clothes, pillows, toys, cooking pots, tents, and on, and on.

"Oh groan," Cat said as she placed her forehead on the back window of the hatch.

"Back up, Cat. I need to open the tailgate." Billie's frustration got the best of her as she haphazardly pulled gear out of the back of the car and threw it everywhere.

Cat held the flashlight for her and cringed as each piece of gear hit the ground. "Billie, calm down. This isn't good for your blood pressure."

"Fuck my blood pressure. Goddamned camping trip. I knew it was a bad idea, but noooo... gotta go camping. I can't believe this is happening. You'd think the tire would be easier to get to. This is going to be one huge mess to repack. Goddamnit!" Finally, she retrieved the spare tire and jack from below the trunk panel and carried them to the front of the car.

Cat held the flashlight so Billie could see while she changed the tire. Several cars passed, but no one stopped to offer help. Cat could only imagine how they looked – two women broken down by the side of the road, in the dead of the night, with what appeared to be boxes and bags and general debris scattered all over the ground behind their car.

\* \* \*

Fred and Jen were far enough ahead that they didn't notice Billie's headlights were no longer in their rear-view mirror until several miles later.

"Uh-oh."

"What's wrong?" Jen asked.

"We've lost them."

"What do you mean?" Jen turned to look out the back window.

"I don't see their headlights."

"That's not good. Look, there's a sign for a rest area, one mile ahead. Let's pull in and call them."

"Yeah, you're right." Fred pulled into a parking space in the rest area and dialed Billie's number.

\* \* \*

"Goddamn, son of a..." Billie cursed. Her phone began to ring just as she applied torque to the first lug nut. The sudden sound startled her, and the wrench slipped off the nut when she jerked up.

She lost her balance and fell forward into the car, hitting her head on the quarter-panel and scraping her knuckles on the rough pavement. "Damn it! Cat, could you please answer my phone?"

Cat felt around inside Billie's pocket and found her phone. She looked at the name that was backlit on the flip cover. "It's Fred. Hello?"

"Hey. We've stopped at the next rest area. Where are you guys?"

"Damned if I know. We have a flat tire and had to pull over to the side. Billie is changing it right now."

"Do you want me to come help?"

Cat held the phone against her breast to muffle the sound of oncoming traffic. "Do you need Fred to come help?"

Billie applied additional torque to the last nut just as it broke its grip on the lug. The sudden release caused Billie to lurch forward and hit her face on the side of the car again. "Goddamnit!" she yelled.

Cat stifled her gasp. "Billie, are you all right?"

"I'm fine," Billie replied gruffly as she regained her composure.

"Do you need Fred's help?" Cat asked again.

Billie flashed an angry look in Cat's direction. "I don't need any goddamned help. I can change a fricking tire by myself, for Christ's sake."

"Okay." Into the phone, Cat said, "Billie said she really appreciates the offer, but she's almost finished changing it."

"Okay then. Will you be much longer?" he asked.

Cat watched as Billie kicked the hubcap across the road after she was unable to put it back on the car. "Uh... we should be there soon. Bye."

Cat stood on the side of the road and peered into the darkness, trying to see where the hubcap had landed while Billie threw the jack and lug-wrench into the compartment under the trunk panel. Finally, she gave up and returned to the rear of the car where Billie was in the process of reloading the camping gear. She handed Billie's phone back to her, which she set on the back bumper. The last thing Billie shoved into the car, on top of all the camping gear, was the flat tire. Moments later, they pulled back onto the highway.

Cat rode silently beside Billie, peering out the side window into the darkness.

"What?" Billie said.

Cat refused to look at Billie. "I didn't say anything."

"My point exactly. You haven't said anything since we got back on the road. What's wrong?"

"What's wrong? You're what's wrong."

"What the hell does that mean?" Billie asked.

"Never mind. Forget I said anything."

"Like hell I will. Out with it."

"You really want to know?"

"Yes."

"Okay. Sometimes you're a real pain in the ass, Billie, you know? I mean, we had a flat tire. Big deal. Why did you get so angry about it? You act like the world is conspiring against you or something."

"Sometimes it feels that way."

"Since when, Billie? Sometimes I wonder who you are, where the old Billie went. You never used to have such a hair-trigger temper before—"

"Before the shooting? Is that what you were going to say?" Cat looked into the darkness and refused to answer. "You can't spend the next two weeks not talking to me, Cat."

"I just want the old Billie back."

* * *

After what seemed like an eternity, Fred and Jen saw the station wagon limp in to the rest area on the undersized spare tire. A very angry Billie and obviously distraught Cat sat rigidly in the front seat. When the two women exited the car, Cat excused herself and rushed into the building to get coffee for her and Billie. Billie leaned back against the car, her arms folded across her chest. Fred looked at the doughnut tire, then at the mess in the cargo hold of the wagon. He opened his mouth.

"Don't even go there," Billie barked.

# Chapter 9

## Directionally Challenged

In the wee hours of the morning, Cat took over as driver while Billie tried to catch a few minutes of sleep. "Okay, Maeve, dear, lead the way."

"In two miles, exit right, then take the motorway," the GPS instructed.

"Maeve, you really do have a sexy voice. I'm tempted to ignore your instructions just to hear you say, 'turn 'round when possible.'" Two miles later, Cat merged onto the highway.

"Drive forty miles, then exit right."

Cat grinned. "You know, Maeve, it's not every woman I let boss me around. Even Billie can't get away with it, but whisper sweet nothings to me in that sexy voice of yours, and I'll follow you anywhere."

As Cat neared the forty mile distance, she approached a slow moving semi-truck. Believing she could pass the truck and pull back into her lane before her exit came up, she switched on her directional and made her move. Fred and Jen pulled out right behind her.

"In two miles, take the exit right."

"Yes, Maeve, that's what I intend to do, just as soon as I leave grandpa here in my dust." Cat glanced into her rearview mirror. "Come on, Fred. Keep up with me. This might be close." Cat pressed down on the accelerator and gained on the semi-truck.

"In one mile, take the exit right."

"Shit! Come on, girl," Cat said to the car as she pressed harder on the accelerator. Just as she turned on her directional to pull back into the right lane, the semi accelerated.

"No!" Cat rasped.

"In two hundred yards, take the exit right."

"I can't! Can't you see that? Jeez, Maeve, give me a break," Cat complained as the truck refused to yield ground. "Shit! Damn it!" Cat sputtered as she flew by her exit. "Now what am I going to do?"

"Recalculating," the GPS unit replied.

"Recalculating, my ass. I'm getting off at this exit coming up. There's got to be a way to turn around." Cat took the next exit and turned right. Fred and Jen followed.

"Turn 'round when possible," Maeve instructed.

Cat looked at the gas gauge and realized she was nearly empty. "Great, just great. There's no way I'm getting back on the highway until I find gas."

"Turn 'round when possible."

"Shut up, Maeve. I know what I'm doing."

"Recalculating."

"I said, shut up," Cat said loudly.

Billie stirred in the seat beside her. "Who are you talking to?"

"The GPS. I missed my exit," Cat replied. "Maeve wants me to get back onto the highway, but we're almost out of gas."

"Drive three miles, then turn right."

Billie sat up and looked around. "It looks like we're in the middle of Ass End, Egypt. Any idea where we are?"

"Beats the hell out of me. I think Maeve has been hitting the Irish whiskey or something. We appear to be lost."

"We can't be lost. Maeve is a GPS. Let's just follow her instructions and see what happens."

"See what happens? We might end up walking down a dark country road carrying a gas can if we don't find a station soon," Cat gritted out as she drove the required three miles. Fred and Jen followed dutifully, like mice behind the Pied Piper.

"Turn right."

'What the hell? It's a cornfield. I'm not turning into a goddamned cornfield. What have you been smoking, Maeve?"

"Turn right."

"No, you drunken Irish crack-whore."

"Shh… you're going to wake the kids," Billie chided. "Pull over."

Cat pulled over to the side of the road and turned off the ignition. Billie removed the GPS unit from its cradle and began searching the points of interest to find a gas station. A knock on the window startled both women.

"Ahh! You scared the shit out of me, Fred," Cat exclaimed as she rolled down her window.

"Sorry. Did we miss our exit? I tried calling Billie's phone, but it went to voicemail. Where the hell are we?"

"My phone went to voicemail?" Billie searched through the pockets of her jacket.

Cat ran her hand through her hair and released a sigh of frustration. "That's the problem, Fred, we don't know where we are and we're almost out of gas."

"What ever happened to Deep Throat? Did she lead you astray?" Fred teased.

"Where's my phone?"

"Forget your phone, Billie. We'll find it later. I gave it to you after you changed the tire. It's probably in that mess in the back of the car. Right now we need to find a gas station."

"No you didn't. I love my phone. And besides, we would have heard it ring."

Cat threw her hands into the air. "Yes, I did. Enough with the phone already. Gas?"

Billie returned her attention to the GPS. "It says here the closest gas station is 50.532 miles east."

"50.532 miles? She knows it's exactly 50.532 miles, and yet she wants me to turn right into a goddamned cornfield? She's on crack. Yep, definitely a crack whore," Cat said. "We'll never make it on what's left in our tank. How much gas do you have, Fred?"

Jen suddenly appeared by Fred's side. "Do you mean in the car or in bed at night? If it's the latter, you do not want to go there."

Fred glared at his wife. "Very funny. I've got between quarter and half a tank," he said to Cat.

"Are you out of gas?" Jen asked.

"Nearly, and I can't find my phone," Billie replied

forlornly.

"No wonder you didn't answer when we called."

\* \* \*

Fred rolled down his window and spat into the darkness.

"Fred, stop that. It's gross," Jen complained.

"You try having a mouthful of gasoline. It's not fun, you know. It's a good thing I don't smoke."

"Well, that would give a new meaning to the term 'hot lips.'"

# Chapter 10

## Flirting with Disaster

Thirty miles after filling up at a gas station, dawn began to grace the morning sky.

"Billie, look, the sky is beautiful. The sun is just cresting over the horizon."

Billie returned her seat to its upright position. "Wow. Look at the yellow streaks radiating from it. This is one of the nicest sunrises I've seen in a while."

Cat smiled at Billie. "This is nice, sharing the sunrise with you."

"This could be an everyday event if you'd only get your butt out of bed earlier, my love."

Cat stuck her tongue out at Billie.

"Tease."

"Go back to sleep. We have a few more hours before we get there."

"Have you made up with Maeve yet?" Billie asked. "I'd hate to have her lead you astray again while I'm asleep."

"Yes. I made her promise to lay off the whiskey until the campfire tonight." Cat drove on for several more minutes in silence.

"Thanks for talking to me again," Billie said. "I know I've been difficult to live with lately. I'm sorry."

Cat glanced at Billie and smiled. "Me, too. Now go back to sleep."

* * *

"Mama, I'm hungry," Tara said.

Skylar announced, "I gotta go potty, Mama."

"Will you two shut up so I can sleep?" Seth mumbled.

Cat reached over and nudged Billie. "Wake up, love." She glanced into the rearview mirror. "Can you guys wait for a bit longer? We're almost into town."

Both girls pouted, and Seth burrowed further into his pillow.

Cat looked at her watch and noticed that it was almost 10 a.m. "Damn," she said. "Half the morning is gone already."

"Mama, I gotta go potty," Skylar urgently reminded her mother.

Billie rubbed the sleep from her eyes. "Give me the GPS, Cat. I'll look for a service station."

Cat handed the electronic unit to Billie and grinned. "Unless Maeve's been sneaking sips on the sly, she should be sober enough to help us this morning."

"Well, after we found the gas station last night, she did a pretty good job getting us back on track."

Billie searched the points of interest and located a service station that would also fix their flat tire while they ate breakfast.

After receiving assurances that the tire would be ready in an hour, they set out to find a diner.

The group found a restaurant not too far from the service station that served a buffet brunch. The four adults and five children sat around the rectangular table and enjoyed a smorgasbord of breakfast and lunch foods.

Their waiter was a young, college-aged man, tall, and very good looking, with dark brown hair and blue eyes. Billie couldn't help noticing that he began to flirt with Cat as soon as they were seated. He smiled at her, flashing deep dimples and straight, white teeth. Cat smiled back, but Billie was sure she was totally unaware of the flirtation.

"Good morning," the waiter said to Cat. "What can I get for you this morning, pretty lady?"

Billie looked at Jen and raised an eyebrow. Jen placed a restraining hand on Billie's arm.

"You can get us some coffee, and juice for the kids," Billie replied for Cat.

"Right away," he said.

The waiter returned and poured coffee for the adults. "I assume you're having the buffet?" he asked.

"Yes," Cat replied.

The waiter held Cat's chair as she rose. "Help yourselves, and enjoy your meal. Oh, my name is Travis. Don't hesitate to flag me down if you need anything. Okay?"

"Thank you, Travis," Cat replied.

Billie followed Cat to the buffet table with Jen close behind. Jen flashed a warning glance at Billie. "You know he's just trying to be nice," Jen whispered.

"What he's trying to do is get a nice fat tip."

The group returned to their table with full plates and hungrily refueled after their long journey through the night. Billie nudged Jen's leg with her toe each time Travis passed the table and smiled at Cat.

Jen intentionally dropped her napkin on the floor between her and Billie. As she bent over to pick it up, she noticed that Billie didn't follow her down like she was supposed to, so she reached up and grabbed her arm and jerked her head down below the table level with her.

"If you keep that up, Cat's going to catch you. Jealousy doesn't become you," Jen said.

"I'm not jealous. Amused is more like it. I can't figure out why he doesn't see she's gay."

"You're the one who beeps, Big Guy. Cat—no so much."

"Beep?"

Yeah. You know, you send out gay vibes."

"Since when did you develop gaydar, Blondie?"

"What are you guys doing with your heads under the table?" Cat asked.

Billie began to rise and banged her head on the underside of the table. Everything on the table top rattled. "Ouch!" Billie rubbed her head as Jen suppressed a laugh.

"Billie, are you all right?" Cat asked as she rescued her coffee. "I'll ask again what are you doing with your head under the table?"

"I'm fine. Jen dropped her napkin, and I was picking it up for her." She shot a dirty look at Jen.

Cat looked back and forth between her wife and friend. "What are you two up to?"

Halfway through their meal, Travis returned to the table carrying a coffee pot. He placed his hand on Cat's shoulder. "How are things, folks. Is there anything I can get you? More coffee?"

Cat raised her cup to Travis. "Yes, please. How about you, love?" she said to Billie.

"I'd love more coffee, sweetheart," Billie replied. She slid her cup across the table toward Travis and locked gazes with him. Billie smiled to herself as she watched the realization dawn on the young man's face.

Travis was so flustered with the situation, that he overfilled Cat's coffee cup and poured coffee all over the table.

"Hey, hey, it's full!" Seth yelled.

"Oh my God. Uh... uh, sorry about that," Travis said, red faced. He grabbed a cloth and began to mop up the mess as Billie and Jen grinned at each other.

Cat squeezed Billie's leg under the table and waited patiently while Travis finished cleaning the spill and returned to the kitchen.

She turned to Billie and Jen. "What's the grin for?"

"He was flirting with you."

"So what if he was?"

"You knew he was flirting?"

"So what if I did?"

"I remember a certain redheaded spitfire stepping in between me and a certain female detective not too long ago. I had to hold you back to prevent you from scratching her eyes out," Billie reminded her. "And you said I have a temper!"

Cat had the good grace to blush while Jen and Fred looked at each other with raised eyebrows. "That was different," Cat said.

"Female detective?" Jen said. "Tell me more."

"How was it different? Flirting is flirting," Billie reasoned.

"Okay, all right. We're even." Cat put her napkin on the

table.

"Good." Billie looked around the table. "Bellies full?" She and Fred went to pay the bill while Jen and Cat organized the kids.

Cat met Billie at the register while Fred went to help Jen settle the kids, all of whom had run out of the restaurant ahead of the adults. Billie noticed their waiter preparing to seat another couple. She cast a mischievous look at the young man, winked, and led Cat out of the restaurant.

# Chapter 11

## She Has Many Skills

After a quick stop at the service station for their repaired tire, the troupe set off to find the Happy Trails Campground. Delayed by the flat tire and the joyride they nearly took into the cornfield the night before, they arrived about an hour and a half later than planned, so it was early afternoon when they pulled their vehicles into adjacent campsites. On one site, they planned to pitch the tents and set up a cooking and dining area. The other site was reserved for the cars, a fire ring, and a play area for the kids.

Billie pulled into the parking spot and turned off the ignition, followed closely by Fred in the space beside her. "We're here, finally," she declared as the back doors flew open and the kids spilled out of the cars. "Cat, let's survey the sites before we unpack, so we can decide how to lay things out."

"Okay." Cat followed the kids out of the car. "Don't venture far," she called out as the kids began to explore. "And hold Sky's hand. We don't need her getting lost."

Fred and Jen strolled over to their car. "Now, for the fun part—unpacking," Jen said.

"Let's take a look around first and decide where to set things up," Billie suggested. Fred readily agreed, and they began to plan the layout.

Cat draped her arm around Jen's neck. "What do you say you and I start unpacking the hamburger box? We'll put Billie and Fred in charge of setting up the tents."

Smiling, Jen snaked her arm around her friend's waist. "Good plan. We really can't unpack clothes and such until the tents are set up anyway."

Cat and Jen made several trips between the two campsites as they carried armloads of groceries and cookware to the area that would eventually become their dining room. They had unloaded most of the food related items by the time Billie and Fred completed their survey and agreed on a layout.

Billie approached Cat and Jen's work area and grinned at the growing mound on top of the picnic table. "It figures you'd work on the food first," she teased.

Cat pretended to be insulted. "Hey, I resent that remark," she replied as she swatted Billie's butt.

Billie captured Cat in her arms and nuzzled her neck. "Hmmm, I like spankings," she murmured.

Cat tried to wriggle out of Billie's embrace as the nuzzling tickled her neck. "Stop that. We have work to do, and you can start by setting up the screen tent so we can keep the bugs away from this food."

Billie stepped back and saluted. "Yes, Ma'am." She turned to Fred. "We have our marching orders. Do you remember which car we packed the screen tent in?"

A half hour later, the campsite was littered with tents, bikes, sleeping bags, toys, and clothing as Billie and Fred looked for the screen tent. Finally, when the cargo of both cars was nearly emptied onto the ground, Fred emerged from the back of his van carrying the sought-after item. "Here it is. Of course it was at the very bottom of the pile."

"Finally," Jen said. "If you would, please set it up near the picnic table so we don't have to move all this food again."

Billie and Fred laid out the poles, arranged them by size on the ground beside the table, then proceeded to unroll the tent.

"Okay, Fred, I think if we move the table and then stake the four corners down, we might be able to set up the frame around it."

"Sounds like a plan to me."

For the next ten minutes, they worked together to pull the corners of the screen tent tight and drive stakes into the ground to secure them, while Cat and Jen stood and watched. "Step one complete," Billie bragged. "Piece of cake. Now for the poles."

Cat crossed her arms and watched Billie and Fred attempt to assemble the poles. She nudged Jen. "Five bucks says they can't figure it out," she whispered.

"No way am I taking that bet," Jen replied. "I'm no fool."

"Uh, Billie, I think the bent poles have to fit together so the tent peaks," Fred suggested.

Billie picked up two bent poles and fitted them together. Once assembled, they formed a square rather than a peak. "Try again, Einstein," she replied.

"Billie, would you like the instructions?" Cat offered.

"This isn't rocket science, Cat. I think we're capable of putting a tent together."

"Suit yourself." Cat dropped the instructions on the table. "How about a cup of coffee, Jen. I think we're going to be waiting a while."

"Works for me."

"Billie, Fred, we're going to make a quick run to the office for coffee. Can we bring any back for you?" Cat asked.

"No need. As soon as we're finished setting up the tent site, I plan to break open a cold one," Billie said.

"I think you'll run out of daylight before that happens," Cat mumbled under her breath.

"What was that, Cat?" Billie asked.

"I said it's great that we have daylight to set up in."

"No kidding. Go get your coffee. Fred and I should have this just about finished by the time you return."

"Last pole. There, we did it. The frame is together," Billie said.

Billie and Fred stood back and admired their handiwork. "Now all we have to do is slide the completed frame into the opening and we'll be done," Fred said.

Billy preened. "Like I said, piece of cake." She reached for the folded portion of the tent that lay in accordion folds on top of the tent base. "Get the other side Fred."

"Sure, no problem."

Together they lifted the top of the tent as high as they could, which was about chest level. Billie looked at the assembled frame. It stood about six and a half feet at the peak.

"Houston, we have a problem."

"What the hell? The tent must have shrunk. The frame used to fit inside it," Fred said.

Just then, Cat and Jen returned. "How are you coming on the screen tent?" Jen asked.

"It shrunk," Fred replied.

"Shrunk? It's nylon. How could it possibly have shrunk?"

"Beats the hell out of me, Jen. All I know is the frame is taller than we can lift the tent."

"Try un-staking the corners," Cat called from the picnic table.

"The corners?" Billie echoed.

"Yes. It says here in the instructions, not to stake the corners until the frame is inside the tent. Otherwise, it will be too restrictive."

"We worked hard to stake down those corners," Billie whined.

"You'll work even harder trying to get that frame inside the tent if you don't."

"Damn it all to hell," Billie cursed as she grabbed the hammer and pulled up the stakes at the four corners of the tent. "There. Are you happy?"

Cat nodded. "Ecstatic."

"Okay, Fred, help me drag this frame over to the tent."

Billie and Fred positioned the frame directly in front of where the door was located on the screen tent. "Now help me slide it into the door opening."

"Maybe we should start by draping the top of the door opening over the peak," Fred suggested.

"Good idea, Fred. On the count of three, lift your side up. One, two, three."

Moments later, the peak of the frame was wedged inside the door opening, and the tent reached approximately halfway to the ground on either side.

"I'm telling you, it shrunk," Fred insisted.

"Ahem," Cat said from across the campsite, where she and Jen were reclining in camp chairs. Billie turned to see her waving the instructions. "Are you ready to read the instructions yet?"

"I don't need instructions, Cat."

"Stop being such a guy and admit you need help," Cat teased, while Jen struggled to hide a grin.

"Uh, that's kind of hard for me to do," Fred said drolly.

"Okay, smarty pants, why don't you and Jen put this damned thing together?" Billie challenged.

"And if we do?"

"If you do, Fred and I will clean up after dinner tonight."

"Hey, speak for yourself," Fred said.

Billie glanced at him. "Don't worry, Fred. I doubt they can do it."

Cat and Jen rose from their chairs and approached their spouses. "You're on," Cat said.

"Have at it. How about a beer, Fred?" Billie offered as they headed for the chairs Cat and Jen had vacated.

While Billie and Fred watched, Cat and Jen methodically disassembled the frame.

"Hey, we put a lot of work into that," Billie protested.

Cat glanced back over her shoulder. "Who's doing this, you or us?"

Next, they laid the tent base flat on the ground and, piece by piece, assembled one leg of the frame inside the tent by sliding each pole into its designated sleeve and connecting them end to end across the base. The process was then repeated across the other two corners. When they were together, the four stabilizer bars were inserted around the tops of each wall and connected to the crosspieces. Finally, the four bottom stabilizer bars were inserted, one on each side, and connected to the main poles at the corners. To finish, they hammered the stakes back into the corner pockets to secure the tent.

Cat dropped the hammer on the ground at Billie's feet. "Piece of cake," she said smugly.

Billie and Fred looked at each other in amazement. "Well, I'll be," Fred said.

"You wash, I'll dry," Billie replied.

With Cat and Jen's help, the children's tents were soon set

up. The children's tents were two three-man domes that went together relatively easy. They placed them so that their entrances faced each other in the center of the campsite. The sleeping arrangements had been decided by the kids, with Stevie and Seth in one tent, and Skylar, Karissa, and Tara in the other.

After securing a promise to ask for help if needed, Cat and Jen reluctantly allowed Billie and Fred to set up the adult tents while they organized the enclosed dining area.

"Fred, why don't you set up your tent, and I'll set up ours. It'll save a little time. The sooner we're finished, the sooner we can relax. I don't know about you, but I'm beat after that long drive last night."

"Sounds good to me."

"Call if you need help," Billie offered.

Billie and Cat's shelter was a larger version of the children's dome tents. Before long, Billie had it set up inside and out, positioned to one side of the smaller tents. They had enough extra space in their tent to store their family's suitcases and extra blankets.

Just as Billie finished, Cat poked her head inside. "Nice job."

"Food all put away?" Billie asked.

"Yes."

Billie sat down in the middle of their sleeping bags and pulled Cat down into her lap. She looked around at their cozy environment. "Maybe this won't be so bad."

Cat smiled and placed a feather-light kiss on Billie's lips. "I'm looking forward to making love to you in the wilderness," she whispered.

Billie lowered Cat to the pillows and lightly ran her hand over her breasts. "You are so beautiful, my love." She squeezed the supple flesh through the shirt and drew a soft coo from Cat. Her tongue demanded entry as she devoured Cat's mouth.

Sounds of bickering reached the ladies' ears just as Billie pulled Cat's shirt out of her waistband. Cat turned her face in the direction of the noise. "I guess we'd better go see."

Sighing in frustration, Billie rested her forehead on Cat's chest, then looked up into Cat's eyes. "Tonight."

"Sweetheart, I hate to burst your bubble, but you would've had to wait until tonight anyway. There's no way I'm doing the nasty with you in broad daylight, with the kids running around outside the tent."

"You've got a point there." Billie rose to her feet and helped Cat up, then took a moment to straighten her clothes before exiting the tent.

Jen and Fred were standing at the back of their van in the midst of the gear that was still strewn around on the ground. Jen gesticulated wildly as they argued back and forth. Cat and Billie walked over to them, hand in hand.

"Problems?" Billie asked.

"Ask Einstein here," Jen said.

"Tent poles," Fred said, looking chagrined.

"Tent poles," Billie repeated. When Fred remained silent, she looked around at the supplies that had been haphazardly thrown out of the van. Realization struck her. She looked back at Fred. "Don't tell me... you forgot them, right?"

"Right." He looked down at the ground and kicked the dirt around with his toe.

Billie raised her hand to her mouth to hide her grin.

At the look on Billie's face, Jen lost her cool. She stomped around. "Wonderful. This is just wonderful. We'll be sleeping with the mosquitoes tonight, and you think it's funny?"

"Jen, I understand how you're feeling, but there's no reason to be angry with Billie," Cat said. She wrapped her arm around Jen's shoulder. "Calm down. We'll think of something."

Hands on hips, Billie walked around the tent and found that the four corners were already staked to the ground. "Uh, Fred, didn't we already make that mistake?"

"Fred, I swear you have the memory of a goldfish," Jen said.

"Enough, already. How many times do I have to apologize?"

"Let's go to the office to see if they have any poles that were left behind by other campers," Billie suggested. "At the very least, the park ranger might have an idea how to jury-rig something for this."

A half hour later, Billie and Fred returned empty handed. "No luck," Fred said. "Apparently another set of campers had the same problem, and the only available poles have already been loaned out."

"Great, just great!" Jen said.

"Don't give up hope. I'm sure there's something we can do." Billie looked around the area and was dismayed to realize the campsite had been picked clean of fallen branches. *The last occupants probably used them for firewood. Now what do we do?* She looked up at the surrounding trees. Suddenly, she smiled. "Got some rope?"

An hour later, Billie and Fred had the four corners of the roof and the center peak of the tent tied to the trees by ropes. From a distance, the tent appeared to be as perfect as it would have been with the tent poles. Up close, it looked rather odd.

When the tent was secured, all four adults stood in front of it and looked up. Jen was the first to laugh. "Holy moly. Anyone walking by is going to think we're insane." Before long, all four of them were in varying degrees of incapacity from laughter.

The kids chose that moment to return from exploring the campground.

Seth tilted his head at the tent construction. "What the.. ?"

"Geez, that looks strange," Stevie added.

Jen tried to explain the situation but failed miserably as laughter rolled through her.

Seth turned to Stevie. "Are your parents as weird as mine?"

"Weirder."

The girls lost interest immediately, and they climbed into their tent to play dolls. Seth and Stevie just shook their heads and rummaged through the camping gear until they found their fishing poles.

"Where are you two going?" Fred asked.

"There's a great stream behind the campsite. We're gonna give it a shot," Seth said.

When the adults had composed themselves, Cat turned to Jen. "Okay, Jen, we need to grocery shop while Billie and Fred finish organizing the site. Are you ready to go?"

"Grocery shop?" Fred exclaimed. "We had to force the lid closed on the hamburger box, it was so stuffed with food. Why do we need more?"

Jen walked over to Fred and knocked on his forehead. "Hello! Is anyone in there?" she asked. "We need perishables. We have no meat, cheese, milk, butter, or eggs, and we need to get ice for the cooler. We'll be back soon."

"Oh, Billie," Cat said, "when we get back, be sure to look for your phone in the back of the car, okay?"

"Okay. Do you want Fred and me to take the kayaks off the roof before you go?" Billie asked.

Cat glanced toward the car, then back at Billie. "No. We can take them off when we get back. It's getting pretty close to dinner time, and I'd like to get back as soon as we can."

* * *

It was nearly 5 p.m. by the time the final piece of gear was stowed and the campsite fully organized. Upon returning from the store, Jen and Cat busied themselves with preparing the communal dinner while Billie and Fred took care of the kayaks and set up the campfire. Jen and Cat decided they would take care of cooking duties if Billie and Fred tended the campfire and kept the campsite clean. Considering that neither Billie nor Fred could cook anything edible, they all agreed it was a fine arrangement.

An hour later, with the kids gathered and hands washed, the two families sat contentedly around the picnic table enjoying a meal of hamburgers, chips, and corn on the cob.

"Great dinner, Ma," Seth said.

"Thanks, sweetie." Cat's attention was drawn toward Billie, who was yawning loudly. "Tired, love?"

"Beat is more like it."

"I, for one, am looking forward to my air mattress tonight," Fred offered.

Jen nodded. "Amen to that."

"Well, I think we accomplished quite a lot today," Billie

said. "We arrived in one piece, despite the flat tire and gas crisis."

"Don't forget Maeve sending us into a cornfield," Cat interrupted.

"And Maeve sending us into a cornfield."

"Do you realize we've been 36 hours without sleep?" Fred asked. "No wonder we're tired."

"I'm more tired from having to pick up the mess we made while emptying the cars than I am from driving here. I had to do it twice. Once to change the flat tire and another when we unpacked," Billie complained.

"Which reminds me—did you ever find your phone?" Cat asked.

"Nope. It appears to be AWOL."

# Chapter 12

# Help Me Make It Through the Night

Cat held the stick a few inches above the flame and carefully rotated the white fluffy marshmallow at the end of it for Skylar. The older children were all seated around the picnic table several yards away playing a board game.

"Don't let it burn, Mama," Skylar said.

"I'll try not to, sweetie."

"Hurry, Mama, the kids are playing the game without me."

"I'm going as fast as I can, sweetie."

Armed with a graham cracker and chocolate, Skylar waited patiently at Cat's side, ready to squish the marshmallow between the scrumptious layers as soon as it was toasted it to a golden brown color.

"Damn," Cat exclaimed as the marshmallow fell from her stick into the fire, where it immediately went up in flames.

"Aw, Mama."

"Here, let me do that." Billie took the stick from Cat and speared a fresh marshmallow. Within moments, it was perfectly toasted and sandwiched in Skylar's treat.

"Thanks, Mommy," Skylar said.

Cat glared at Billie. "How do you do that?" Billie opened her mouth to answer, but Cat interrupted her. "I know. You have many skills, right?"

Billie leaned forward and placed her hands on the arms of Cat's chair, then whispered in her ear, "I could toast your marshmallows, if you want me to."

Cat gave her a "not in front of the neighbors" look, then whispered back, "They're half melted already. Remember your promise."

"How could I forget?" Billie traced Cat's jaw line with her index finger and stopped under her chin, placing a delicate kiss on her lips before returning to her seat.

Cat watched as Jen leaned into Fred and took his hand. Fred lifted Jen's hand to his mouth and kissed it before he winked at her and turned his attention back to the fire. "I'm so glad we're here together. We need to do this more often," Cat said.

"Do you realize it's been, what, nearly five years that we've known each other, and this is the first time we've done something like this." Jen said.

"Has it been five years already?" Billie asked.

"Skylar was just a baby when you moved into the neighborhood, and she turned five this past May, right? I remember it like it was yesterday," Jen glanced at the children, then lowered her voice. "We were so naïve then. Who'd've thunk we'd be best friends with a couple of lezbos."

"If you want to speak lezbonics, get it right. The term is lezzie, lipstick, chapstick, carpet-muncher, gnome-stroker," Billie corrected.

"I've heard of lipstick, but what the hell is a chapstick?" Jen asked.

"A diesel dyke, boi, butch, stud. You know, a tomboy lesbian," Billie explained.

"I see."

Fred stretched his legs out in front of him and hooked his thumbs into his belt. "Yeah. In my wildest dreams, I never thought I'd be a fag-hag," he said.

"Fred!" Jen exclaimed, glancing once more at the kids.

"So you like to hang with gay men, do you, Fred?" Cat asked.

"I didn't say that," he replied quickly. "I meant I like hanging with you guys."

"I think the term you're looking for is lesbro, Fred," Billie offered.

"Yeah, that's exactly what I meant."

"Well, regardless of what you call it, we love you guys, and we're grateful you came into our lives," Jen said.

"Ditto, my friend, ditto," Billie replied.

"Hey, all this talk about lesbians reminds me of a joke," Fred said.

"Oh God, do you have to?" Jen objected.

"You'll like it. I promise."

"Go ahead, Fred. I'd like to hear it," Billie said.

"Okay. What's the difference between a lesbian and a Ritz cracker?" Fred looked back and forth between the women. No one replied. "Give up? One's a snack cracker and the other is a crack snacker."

Jen jumped to her feet. "Frederick Cornelius Swenson, I can't believe you said that in front of the kids!"

"Cornelius?" Billie repeated.

"What? They weren't even paying attention," Fred said defensively.

"I thought it was hysterical," Billie said as she wiped tears of laughter from her eyes.

"Speaking of the kids, it is getting pretty late," Cat said. She looked over at the picnic table. "It's nearly midnight guys. Time to hit the sheets."

"Aw, Ma!" Seth complained.

"Don't 'aw, Ma' me. It's been a long day. There'll be lots to do tomorrow that you'll need to be rested up for. Off to bed with you."

While Cat and Jen tucked the children securely inside their tents, Billie cleaned their campsite of chocolate bar wrappers and left over paper plates and napkins from their dinner and threw them into the fire. She then reached into the cooler and produced two beers, one of which she handed to Fred.

"I really want to thank you for your help with the tent today," Fred said. "I can't believe I left the poles at home. I can still see them leaning against the garage door."

Billie chuckled. "No problem. Hey, what's on the agenda for tomorrow?" she asked as Cat and Jen settled themselves back into their lawn chairs around the fire. Billie rose from her seat to get them each a beer and popped Cat's open for her before handing it over.

Cat smiled at her. "Thank you, love."

"Well, I read the brochure pretty thoroughly and from the sound of it, there's a lot to do right here, but we also might want to check out the attractions in the surrounding area. I understand there is a giant shopping mall not too far from here," Jen said.

"Shopping?" Cat perked up, her travel fatigue suddenly forgotten.

"Cat, if you do go shopping while you're here, you might want to check out the cell phone vendors. I'm going to assume my phone is lost forever," Billie said.

Cat frowned. "But I gave it back to you after you changed the tire. Don't you remember?"

Billie shrugged. "What I remember is having to pick up that huge mess on the ground behind the car and stuff it back inside. If you gave the phone back to me in the middle of all that, God knows what happened to it."

"Well, you shouldn't have thrown everything all over the place."

"So my temper gets the best of me sometimes," Billie said defensively.

"I remember your setting it on the bumper while we reloaded the car. Maybe you forgot it there?" Cat suggested.

Billie shook her head. "Anything is possible. My guess is it will be a miracle if we find it."

"Why don't you come shopping with us so you can pick out your own phone?" Cat suggested.

"Oh groan," Billie said.

"Ditto," echoed Fred.

Cat stuck her tongue out at the pair. Billie's eyes widened and, without thinking, she blurted out, "Don't stick your tongue out at me unless you plan to use it."

Jen spat out her mouthful of beer and started choking. Fred laughed as he rubbed her back. "Thanks a lot. I swear, Billie, you make it your mission in life to embarrass the hell out of me," Jen complained.

Cat covered her face with her hands, then sneaked a peek at Jen. "Don't worry, she does it to me too, all the time."

"Does what?" Billie asked. "Embarrass you, or put your tongue to good use?"

Cat smacked Billie's arm. Billie stuck her tongue out at Cat and wiggled it around as she raised her eyebrows up and down.

"Ahh!" Cat exclaimed. "What am I going to do with you?"

"Well..." Billie began.

"Never mind. Never mind. Forget I asked. Sheesh," Cat groaned.

Billie caught Fred's eye and winked.

"Well, time for bed," Fred said. He rose to his feet and grabbed the thick stick they were using as a poker and spread out the glowing embers inside the fire ring while Billie slowly poured half a bucket of water over them. Soon the fire was out, and the campers were on their way to bed.

As soon as they entered their tent, Cat turned on the lantern and then pounced on Billie, rolling her onto her back on the sleeping bags. She lay directly on top of her, nose-to-nose, and looked deep into Billie's eyes. "You, my love, are a big tease. You had Fred so hot, he couldn't wait to get Jen into their tent."

"He couldn't possibly be as hot as I am for you right now," Billie growled. She pulled Cat's mouth down to hers for a toe-curling kiss, which deepened as she rolled her over and pressed her firmly into the air mattress beneath them. Billie was so inflamed, she tore impatiently at Cat's clothes. "Cat, I want to feel you against me."

"Wait. Turn the lantern off. The entire campground can see our silhouette through the tent," Cat exclaimed.

Billie fumbled for the lantern and quickly turned it off, then returned to disrobing her wife. Between the two of them, they had Cat's clothes off and thrown into the corner of the tent in record time. Billie trapped Cat in place with her body as she kissed and nipped at her neck, causing her to writhe in agonizing desire.

Cat pulled roughly at Billie's clothing. "I need you, Billie. Please."

Just as Cat managed to drag Billie's T-shirt over her head, they heard a noise outside their tent. Both women froze.

"Mama?" the voice said. "Mama, I'm scared."

The sound of the zipper set both women into action. Billie

quickly pulled her T-shirt over her head, and then helped Cat locate her own shirt and panties. By the time the zipper was totally opened, Cat had her drawers in place and the two women were lying side by side, attempting to act casually. Had the intruder been anyone but a child, they would have noticed the flush on their faces and desire in their eyes.

Cat sat up. "Skylar, honey. What's wrong?"

"I'm scared. I can hear funny noises."

"Sky, they're just crickets. They won't hurt you. They can't even get into your tent," Billie explained. "Come on, I'll take you back and tuck you in."

"No." Skylar began to cry. "I wanna sleep with you. Please?" she begged.

Billie stared at her daughter. *Oh my God! Seriously?* She looked at Cat, who returned her pained expression. She took a deep breath and let it out slowly as she ran her hand through her hair.

"All right, all right, but only for tonight, okay?"

"Okay, Mommy," Skylar chirped happily as she crawled in between them and snuggled against Cat.

Billie couldn't resist a smile. Lucky kid, she thought. Out loud, she said, "I'm going to check on the other kids and make sure the girls' tent is zipped. Be right back."

After assuring herself that all was well, Billie went to the bucket of water they kept next to the fire ring and reached in with both hands. She pulled up a large double handful of water to splash over her heated face. Suddenly, she heard low moaning sounds coming from the direction of Jen and Fred's tent.

Great! This is going be a long night, Billie thought as she headed back to her tent.

# Chapter 13

# Your Sword In My Service

Cat woke the next morning to find Billie missing and Skylar sprawled out on top of her. Cat smiled at her daughter. *You are so sweet. It actually makes me want to forgive you for interrupting our fun last night.* Cat slowly dislodged herself from beneath the child without waking her and climbed out of the tent. Stretching, she enjoyed the feel of her vertebrae realigning after sleeping on the too-soft air mattress the night before. Jen was already in the process of setting up the camp stove to start breakfast.

"Good morning, Jen. How did you sleep?" Cat asked as she unzipped and entered the screen tent.

"Pretty well, once we went to sleep."

Cat noticed the pink tinge on her friend's cheeks. "Got lucky, huh? That makes one of us."

Jen raised her eyebrows. "You're kidding, right? The way Billie was talking last night, we expected you guys to easily drown us out."

"Yeah, well, Skylar put an end to any efforts in that arena. In fact, she's fast asleep in our tent as we speak."

"I see. Does she climb in with you often?"

"No, almost never. I think the unfamiliar sounds of the frogs and crickets scared her. We tried sending her back to bed, but she began to cry, and we didn't want her to wake Tara and Karissa, so we bit the bullet and let her stay. Needless to say, not a lot happened in the romance department last night, which is unfortunate since things have not been nearly so romantic of late."

"Are things okay with you and Billie?"

Cat ran her hand through her hair. "Yes… and no. A lot has changed since the surgery."

"I thought she was regaining her memory."

"She has, for the most part, but things aren't quite the same as they were before."

"How so?"

"Well, Billie isn't as patient as she used to be. She blows up pretty easily these days. Remember our discussion last night about the mess behind the car after she changed the tire?"

"Yes."

"Well, that's because she flew into a rage and literally ripped everything out of the car and threw it on the ground. That's not something she would have done before the surgery."

"I can see why you two are seeing a shrink."

"Doctor Connor has been a big help. She recommended this vacation. I just hope it doesn't backfire and make things worse. Sky crawling in with us last night didn't help."

Jen patted Cat's cheek. "Don't lose heart. There's always tonight."

"I sure hope so. I don't cherish the idea of two weeks with a five-year-old sleeping on my chest." Cat reached for one of the strawberries that Jen was slicing. "Speaking of Sky, would you mind keeping an eye on her while I run to the showers? I feel like a major grub after traveling for so long yesterday."

Jen frowned. "Where's Billie?"

Cat looked around. "I'm not sure. She was already gone when I woke up. My guess is that she's trying to work off some of her frustration from last night."

Jen chuckled. "I hear you. Sure, go shower. Take your time."

"Thanks, Jen."

Cat went back to her tent and collected her toiletries, a towel, and a change of clothes, then set off toward the showers. Before she got more than a few feet up the trail, she saw a familiar figure jogging toward her. Sweat stains darkened the neckline and armpits of her T-shirt, and a sheen of sweat glowed on her bare arms and legs.

Billie stopped in front of her and jogged in place. "Wait for me, I'll be right back."

"Good morning to you, too!" Cat called after Billie's retreating form.

Moments later, Billie met Cat on the trail with a clean towel and change of clothes of her own. She scooped Cat up into her arms and swung her around in a circle, then put her back on her feet.

"Hey, you're all sweaty!" Cat complained.

"So? You're on your way to the showers, aren't you?"

"Yes."

Billie backed Cat up against a tree and pinned her there with her own body. "Want some company?"

"And if I say no?" Mischief danced in Cat's eyes.

"Then I'll have to dishonor my family name by forcing myself upon you, My Lady."

"Is that a threat or a promise, fair knight?" Cat teased.

"What would you like it to be, My Lady?"

"Well, so far you haven't been very good about keeping your promises, brave knight. I desperately needed your sword in my service last night, and you failed me."

"Ah, great lady, but last night's folly was not my fault. The dragon child intervened. I had no choice but to yield to her power. Will you give me another chance, My Lady?" Billie took a step back and bowed.

"Give me a moment, and I will consider it." A split second later, Cat said, "Enough. I have made my decision. To the showers! And when we are through, dear knight, the shower stall had better not be the only wet thing in the room!"

A grin split Billie's face. "You have my word, My Lady. My sword will be in your service for as long as you need it. Total satisfaction, great lady, and wetness guaranteed."

"And if you fail me again, Sir Charland, you will receive the harshest of sentences."

"Pray tell, what might that be, My Queen?"

"Thirty days of hard labor, chained to my bed post and attending to my every need."

"My Lady, it is not only my duty to do your bidding, your punishment sounds delightful."

Cat took Billie's arm. "Then lead the way, brave knight!" They giggled all the way to the showers.

For the next full hour, the women in that area of the campground studiously avoided the showers. Several approached the building, including Jen, but quickly retreated at the sounds coming from within. Finally, two very satisfied women, one short and fair, the other tall and dark, walked hand in hand along the trail to their campsite.

Jen had set the percolator to brew on the propane grill not long after Cat and Billie left for their shower, so the coffee was ready when they returned. She motioned for them to sit down and brought three mugs and the coffeepot over to the table. She sat down opposite her friends and poured them each a mug of the rich, dark liquid.

Jen took a sip of her aromatic brew and said, "Sword in my service, huh? Which one of you is the screamer?"

Billie nearly choked on her coffee and both women turned several shades of red. "You heard that, huh?" Billie asked, while Cat found something very interesting to look at in her coffee cup.

"Big Guy, the whole campground heard it. It sounded like someone had a polecat cornered in there. So, which of you is the screamer?" she asked again.

Billie and Cat looked at each other and then back at Jen. "She is!" they both said.

# Chapter 14

## Out of the Mouths of Babes

The ladies were on their second cup of coffee when Fred meandered back to the campsite after his own shower. He wore a wide grin on his face. "You should have heard the racket up at the showers," he exclaimed. "Whoever it was, they were sure going at it hot and heavy!"

"Ahem." Jen cleared her throat to get Fred's attention as she ran her hand through her hair. Fred looked her way, and she tilted her head sideways and raised her eyebrows at their friends, who were contemplating the top of the picnic table.

"Get out!" His eyes wide were with disbelief. "No way! Really? Well, I'll be," he said. "Who's the screamer?"

"Oh, God." Cat dropped her forehead to the table; Billie looked up at the sky.

"Looks like rain," she said.

Cat and Billie were saved from further teasing by sounds of the kids in their tent. The adults' eyes were drawn to the two small tents in the center of the campsite as the zippers opened. Tara tore out of the tent, a look of panic on her face.

"Mama," Tara said, "Sky is gone."

"No, she isn't sweetie," Cat said. "She's in our tent. She crawled in with us not too long after you two fell asleep."

"Well, that explains a lot," Fred teased.

"Sure, blame it on the kid," Jen added.

Billie grabbed a handful of Jen's blonde hair, gently pulled her down onto the bench beside her, and whispered into her friend's ear, "Enough, Curly. Got it?" Then she unexpectedly kissed Jen soundly on the mouth before she released her.

Stunned, Jen looked back and forth between Cat and Billie.

"Wow!"

At that moment, Skylar emerged from Cat and Billie's tent. She ran directly into Billie's open arms, where she curled up in her lap and laid her head in the hollow between Billie's breasts.

Seconds later, she lifted her head and looked directly into Billie's eyes. "Your boobie pillows are softer than Mama's."

Cat, Fred, and Jen all spat their coffee at the pronouncement.

Billie looked at her daughter like she was an alien from outer space. "What did you say?" She cast a dirty look at the three laughing adults.

"Your boobie pillows are softer than Mama's," Skylar repeated. "Mama said you had soft boobies, and they make good pillows. She's right."

It was Cat's turn to blush. Billie realized that turnabout was fair play, so she prodded the child further. "What do you mean, mine are softer than Mama's?"

"I forgot my pillow when I went to your tent last night, so I used Mama's boobies, but they're not as soft as yours. Mama's boobies are smaller. Can I use your boobies tonight?" she asked innocently.

Fred and Jen doubled over. The red on Cat's face matched her hair color.

Billie tried to keep a straight face. "Sky, sweetie, you'll be sleeping in your own tent with Tara and Karissa tonight. My boobie pillows are off limits for the rest of this trip."

Skylar's bottom lip protruded. "But you let Mama use your boobie pillows. She sleeps on them a lot."

"That's different."

Skylar crossed her arms and lowered her chin to her chest, a scowl on her face. "That's no fair. Mama is a boobie hog."

"Fair or not, you're sleeping in your own tent tonight."

# Chapter 15

## It'll Hurt You in the End (Literally)...

Billie and Cat strolled hand-in-hand through the woods on their way to the stables. Fred and Jen walked close behind. Billie looked over her shoulder. "Have you ever been horseback riding, Jen?" "No, I haven't, but I've always wanted to. Hey, you kids don't

get too far ahead of us!" Jen called out after the four older children as they rode their bikes along the trails. Skylar rode her two-wheeled bike with training wheels on the trail directly in front of them.

"I've ridden before, but it's been a while," Fred offered. "I hope it's like riding a bike. You know, you never really forget how. How about you, Cat?"

"My grandparents own a plantation type home with lots of land, and my sisters and I spent a lot of time there in the summers. We learned to ride during those visits."

"A plantation home? Wow. That must be awesome," Jen said.

"More than awesome. It's huge. You walk into the entryway, and you feel like you're on the set of Gone With The Wind, complete with grand staircase. My sisters and I used to have races to see who could slide down the banisters the quickest. Turns out, Grandma Josie beat us all. She's a hoot, that one."

Jen caught up with Cat and put her arm around her waist. "She sounds like fun. I'll bet she drove your grandfather nuts."

"Correction. She drove my grandmother nuts, my other grandmother, that is."

Jen frowned. "Your grandparents are lesbians?"

"Oh, yeah. Josephine Wycliffe and Alexandra Spirakis. They're as different as night and day. Grammy Jo is a wildcat. She'd try anything on a bet, and Grammy Alex is regal and the epitome of a Southern belle. They're really cute together. They made me feel very loved growing up. In fact, one of the things that attracted me to Billie is that she resembles Grammy Alex—quite a bit, in fact. They're both tall, dark-haired, and very beautiful."

Billie squeezed Cat's hand. "You never told me that."

"It's true. You look so much like her, she could be your grandmother instead of mine. If you age as beautifully as she has, I'll be the luckiest geriatric in town!"

"Ha, ha, very funny. Oops, be careful not to trip over that branch," Billie pointed out as they maneuvered their way around the obstacle. "I can't wait to meet them. It's too bad they couldn't make our wedding."

"They would've come, but they were in Greece," Cat said. "They travel so often, they're almost never home."

"I know, but we've been married for what, almost three years, and I still haven't met them."

"With our jobs, school, and the kids' activities, all our lives are busy, Billie," Cat said. "We just need to set a specific date to visit that works for all of us."

"What were they doing in Greece?" Jen asked.

"Grammy Alex is a professor of history at The Citadel in South Carolina, and she's often invited to deliver keynote addresses and lectures around the world. Grammy Jo won't stay home without her, so they go together," Cat explained.

"I'm jealous. Maybe I should find a rich professor to travel the world with," Jen suggested.

"Hey!" Fred objected.

Cat and Billie's hand-holding drew curious looks from passersby as they walked down the path. Some smiled, others frowned, and a few even walked a wide berth around them. One such hiker was bolder than the rest; he intercepted them by stepping in front of them on the path. "You two need to get a room. Can't you see there are children around?"

Jen stepped between the stranger and her friends. "Take your prejudices elsewhere," she said.

"Mind your own business."

"These ladies are my business. You would be lucky to have a relationship like theirs."

"Not in a million years, lady."

Fred stepped in and put his hand on the man's shoulder. "Look, we don't want any trouble, just move on."

"This is a free country. I have a right to express my opinion."

"Yes you do," Fred said, "but not in front of our children." Fred squeezed his shoulder painfully tight. "You got my meaning?"

The man shook free of Fred's grasp and turned toward the path. "Yeah, yeah, whatever," he said as he walked away.

Fred grinned at his friends.

Billie placed a hand on Fred's shoulder. "Thanks, friend. Now, how 'bout we mosey on down the trail and find us some hosses to ride?"

"I reckon that's a good plan, pardner." He turned to Jen. "Whaddaya say, Ma?"

"Well, I reckon you might be right, Pa. What'cher wait'n fer?" she replied.

Cat hooked her thumbs into the belt loops on her jeans. "Lead the way, Billie-girl. I got a hankerin' for a trail ride. Let's git'er done."

All four adults broke into giggles as they continued on down the trail toward the stables.

* * *

"Here you go, young lady," the stable hand said as he handed the reins of a beautiful chocolate-colored Morgan mare to Jen.

Jen backed away as far as the length of rein would allow. She looked at Billie and pointed at the horse. "You expect me to ride that?"

Billie took the reins from her and approached the animal. She stroked the dark brown mane. "Don't be afraid. Animals can sense fear. She's a beautiful mount. All you need to do is relax, and you two will get along just fine."

Jen stood her ground. "That's easy for you to say. You're an experienced rider."

"Come here, I'll help you up," Billie offered.

Jen inched her way warily toward the horse until she stood beside it. She looked at the stirrup, which came about waist high on her. "I don't think I can lift my foot that high."

"Sure you can. Just grab the saddle horn like this, put your left foot in the stirrup, then hoist yourself up. When you're high enough, throw your right leg over her back." Billie demonstrated the mounting process, then patted the horse's neck. "Good girl."

Jen looked at Billie sitting easy in the saddle. "Easy for someone six inches taller than I am."

Billie dismounted and held her hand out to Jen. "Come on. I'll help you."

Jen stood on tiptoes and grabbed the saddle horn. The extension of her arms required her to press herself against the side of the horse with no clearance to lift her foot into the stirrup. The horse began to move. "Whoa!" Jen exclaimed as she ran alongside the horse, still grasping the saddle horn.

Billie came to her rescue by grabbing the reins. The horse immediately came to a halt. She handed the reins back to Jen. "Maybe this horse isn't right for you. Stay right here. I'm going to talk to the stable hand."

A few moments later, Billie returned. "We're flat out of luck. This is the last horse." She looked at the rest of her party and realized that her horse was even larger than Jen's, as were the ones being ridden by Fred and Cat. "Short of taking a smaller horse away from one of the kids, I'm afraid you're stuck with this one, Jen."

"Well, how the hell can I ride this beast when she won't even stand still long enough for me to get on her?"

"What's the holdup?" Cat said as she rode her horse toward them. "The kids are anxious to start riding, and oh, by the way, the most anxious kid is Fred."

Billie motioned her head toward Jen. "Pipsqueak can't get on her horse. Maybe you can give us a hand here."

"Sure." Cat dismounted and took the reins from Jen. "I'll hold her still while Billie helps you up."

"Okay, Jen, put your foot into the stirrup, and then I'll tush-push you up far enough for you to grab the saddle horn," Billie said.

Jen put her left foot into the stirrup, and Billie put her hands under Jen's bottom. "Nice ass," Billie said as she squeezed.

Jen's foot immediately came out of the stirrup. She turned around and slugged Billie in the shoulder.

"Ow!"

"Serves you right. You're supposed to be helping me, not feeling me up. In front of your wife, no less."

Billie rubbed her shoulder. The grin on her face belied the feigned pain. "Sorry. Couldn't help myself." She looked at Cat. "Forgive me?"

Cat smiled. "You're incorrigible. Now help her up. We need to get this show on the road."

"Okay, Jen, I promise to be good. Let's try this again."

Jen once again put her left foot into the stirrup as Billie pushed her bottom upward, high enough for her to grab the saddle horn. Before Jen could throw her leg over the animal's back, the horse sidestepped a full circle around the reins held fast in Cat's hands. Jen held on for dear life. "Stop! Help!" she screamed. Just as the horse came full circle, Jen lost her grip on the saddle horn and fell on her rump on the dusty ground.

Cat calmed the horse as Billie helped Jen up. "Sorry, Jen. She got away from me," Cat said, trying to hide her grin.

Jen rubbed her butt as Billie tried to brush the dust from her. "She hates me. That's it, that goddamned horse hates me. And you can wipe that smirk off your face, Red. It's not funny."

Billie picked Jen's cowboy hat up and put it back on her head. "She doesn't hate you, Jen, she just senses your nervousness. Now let's try this again."

Jen crossed her arms. "No fricking way."

Billie put her hands on her hips. "Curly, are you really going to let the kids show you up? Look at them over there."

Billie pointed to Seth, Tara, Stevie, and Karissa, all mounted and riding their horses around the stable yard while they waited for the adults. Skylar sat in the saddle in front of Fred.

"Sure, play the kid card," Jen said. "Okay. One more try. If I fall on my ass again, I'm done."

"This isn't so bad," Jen said as her horse obediently followed beside Billie's mount.

"Just relax, and it'll be fine," Billie assured her.

"It's almost as if the horse knows where we're going."

"It probably does. I'm sure they've traveled these same paths hundreds of times."

Some distance in front of the adults, the children were riding happily, with the exception of Skylar who transferred from Fred to Cat's saddle.

"Seth, Stevie, stay close," Billie warned as the boys guided their horses down the trails.

"Look at them," Jen said. "They act like they were born in the saddle."

"It amazes me sometimes how kids pick up new things so quickly. I think it's because they're fearless."

"Too fearless. I don't remember being that bold when I was their age," Jen admitted. Just then, her horse shook its head and sidestepped a few feet. "Whoa! What's she doing?"

Billie leaned over in her saddle toward Jen and stroked the mare's mane. "You're fine. You control the horse with pressure from your knees and reins. Squeeze her between your knees. That's it. Take it slow. You're doing great."

"Spoken by someone who is used to having something between her knees." Jen quipped.

"Jealous?" Billie asked.

"You're damned right, I am."

Billie laughed. "Difference is, it wouldn't be prudent to squeeze what's between my knees in those situations."

"TMI!"

"You brought it up, not me."

The ladies fell silent for a few moments as Billie watched Jen concentrate on the ride.

"I'm actually enjoying this," Jen said proudly as she moved

with the rhythm of the horse.

"Why don't you lead the pack, Jen? As the rookie, you need to set the pace for the rest of us," Billie said.

Jen looked insulted. "I'm not the only rookie here, you know. The kids haven't ridden before either."

"True, but look at them. They're already riding confidently. They think they're invincible at this age, remember?"

"Yeah, I remember. Okay, I'll take the lead, but I don't want to hear any whining if I'm moving too slow."

After about a half-hour on the trail, Jen's horse suddenly reared. "Holy shit! What's happening? Billie!" Jen screamed.

Billie urged her mount closer to Jen to see what had spooked the horse. There in front of them was a small snake making its way across the path.

"Don't panic, Jen. Calm down and hold on," Billie instructed.

"It's just a snake."

"Uh-oh," Fred breathed.

"A snake? Oh my God, I hate snakes. Get it away from me!" Jen screamed as she fidgeted in the saddle.

Jen's fear sparked the horse into a panic as it reared up on its hind legs and whinnied in fear. Jen held on to the saddle horn for dear life, shrieking loudly. The other three horses shied away.

As soon as the front hooves of Jen's horse hit the ground, it took off running across the meadow to escape the reptile. Jen bounced unmercifully as she clung to the saddle horn for dear life. As Cat and Fred collected the children, Billie skillfully directed her horse toward Jen and quickly pulled alongside the runaway horse. "Jen, try to get your feet back into the stirrups," Billie yelled.

"I... I can't," Jen cried, barely able to maintain her perch on the horse with the saddle horn grasped in one hand and a handful of mane clutched in the other.

"Reach for the reins, Jen."

"No! I'll fall off!"

Billie shifted her weight in the saddle and reached for the

trailing reins. As she pulled the frightened animal to a stop, Jen practically climbed up her arm and into her lap, her eyes wild with fear.

Billie wrapped her arms around her trembling friend. "You're shaking like a leaf, Jen."

Jen started to cry.

"It's okay. Calm down. I've got you."

"I've never been so scared in my life."

"You did well to hold on. Had you fallen off, you might have been trampled."

"Don't make me get on that beast again."

"No worries, I won't. We do need to get her back to the stables, though."

Billie helped Jen settle in front of her, then slowly approached the mare who was a few feet away, grazing on the grass. Billie reached for the reins, tied them to the saddle of her own horse, then started back toward where Cat and Fred waited with the children.

All the way back, Jen clung to Billie's arm wrapped around her midsection.

"I feel like such a fool," Jen said.

"Don't. It wasn't your fault the snake crossed our path."

"I know, but if I'd only kept my cool…"

"Don't stress about it, Jen. It's over, done. No sweat."

Reaching the others, Billie transferred her passenger to Fred, who wrapped strong arms around her. "Are you okay?" he asked.

Jen nodded, on the verge of tears.

# Chapter 16

## The Naked Truth

Jen was never so happy to have her feet on solid ground as she was when Fred lowered her from his horse at the stables. "I will never do this again, Fred."

Fred cradled her face between his hands and kissed her tenderly on the lips. "It's okay, Hon. Horseback riding isn't for everyone. I'm just happy you weren't hurt."

It was nearly lunchtime when they returned to the campsite. Billie and Fred took the van to the office to purchase more firewood as Cat put together a lunch of canned baked beans, hot dogs, and chips. Jen paced nervously around the campsite, hands on her hips. Every now and then, she stopped to run her hands up and down her butt.

Cat smiled at her friend. "Hurts, huh?"

"Oh, yeah. When are we going to the beach?"

"Right after lunch, if I have anything to say about it," Cat replied. "I'm looking forward to relaxing in the sun."

"I'm looking forward to lying down on my stomach. That's the only position I'm comfortable in at the moment."

"Then let's get this show on the road. Kids, come wash your hands. Lunch is ready," Cat called into the adjacent campsite.

"Aw, Mom, we were just starting a game," Seth whined.

"The sooner we eat lunch, the sooner we can go to the beach," Cat reasoned.

"The beach! Yay!" Within seconds, five children were gathered around the water spigot.

\* \* \*

"God, this feels so good," Cat purred as she lay on the blanket on her back beside Jen.

"The feeling is moo-chal, darlin,'" Jen replied in her best German accent.

"You're a nut," Cat said.

Jen turned her head sideway and placed her cheek on the blanket to look at her friend. "It's so beautiful and peaceful here."

"Peaceful is the operative word. I hope Billie is enjoying herself. She needs the break."

"So your doc prescribed a vacation, huh?" Jen asked.

"Yeah, although I'm not sure this is what Billie had in mind."

"Maybe not, but it'll do her some good to be out in the fresh air. It's much better than being stuck behind that desk of hers. I mean, look at this place. Beautiful beach, clean water, and not too many people around to crowd us out. It's our own little piece of heaven."

They had chosen a particularly quiet part of the beach, about a hundred yards from a very tall pile of rocks and boulders that separated the property of the campground from private land. Seth and Stevie explored the man-made boundary while Billie and Fred searched for seashells with the three girls.

"Yes it is. I'm surprised no one is at this end of the beach. I would think that rock wall over there would attract the kids, big time."

"You're right. It is kind of curious why it was so deserted. It's not like there're no kids here. Look at them all over there."

Cat looked down the length of beach to where there were several dozen kids playing in the sand and water while their parents sunbathed nearby. "Their loss, our gain. I'm glad we have this part of the beach to ourselves."

"Amen to that," Jen said.

Sometime later, Cat was awakened from a light doze by Billie's voice. "Cat, where's the sunscreen? Sky needs a fresh coat."

Cat located the sunscreen and handed it to Billie. As Billie slathered Skylar's back, Cat noticed Tara and Karissa, who were still searching for seashells at the water's edge with Fred. "Where are the boys?" she asked.

Billie continued to rub the lotion into her daughter's skin. "They're exploring the rocks."

Cat squinted at the ridge of rocks. "Where? I don't see them."

Billie raised her head and looked for herself. After a moment or two, she stood erect and shaded her eyes from the sun with her hand as she focused her gaze on the mountain of rocks. "You're right. I don't see them either. Fred, did you see where the boys went?"

Fred looked up from helping Tara and Karissa rinse the shells they had found. "They're right over there on the…" Fred stopped short as his gaze failed to locate Stevie and Seth. "Where did they go?"

"Sky, stay here with Mama, okay? I need to find your brother."

"Billie, wait. I'm going with you," Cat said.

"The boys are missing? You're not leaving me behind," Jen said as she struggled to her feet.

"All right then," Billie said as she picked Skylar up, "I guess we'll all look for them."

Tara and Karissa ran ahead of the adults as the group moved toward the mountain of rocks at the end of the beach. The girls reached the top before their parents made it half way up.

"Girls, wait for us before you go down the other side," Cat called. She watched to see if the girls would obey and saw Karissa stop short, covering her mouth with her hands. Tara stopped beside her. It was obvious to Cat, by Tara's expression, that what she saw on the other side shocked her.

Tara cupped her mouth with her hands. "Mama, they're naked!"

Billie looked at Cat, her eyes wide with dismay. "Oh, my God!"

Fueled by fear and panic that something unthinkable could have happened to the boys, Billie, Cat, and Fred made their way to the top of the ridge as fast as they could. Jen struggled upward at a much slower pace, as her horse riding injuries from earlier in the day greatly hindered her. What they saw when they reached the top made them stop in their tracks.

"Tara, Karissa, take Skylar and very carefully climb down the rocks and go back to the blanket on the beach. Do it now," Cat said sternly.

"But, Mama," Tara protested.

"Do as your mother says," Billie ordered.

"I agree," Fred added. "Karissa, go on, now."

On their way down the ridge, the girls passed Jen still moving upward. Moments later, Fred lent her a hand for the last few steps.

Finally, all four adults stood at the top and looked across the ridge.

"Holy Mother of God… a nudist colony!"

* * *

"I can't believe there's a nudist colony right next to a family campground," Cat railed at the park ranger.

"Ma'am, we have no say over how adjacent lands are being used," the ranger replied.

"Why are there no signs posted warning parents not to let their children climb the ridge? No wonder that end of the beach was deserted."

"We're in the process of replacing the signs. I'm afraid they haven't come back from the sign maker yet. Our sincere apologies."

"Yeah? Tell that to our sons. They've probably been traumatized for the rest of their lives," Jen added.

The ranger looked at the two eleven-year-olds. "You guys climbed the ridge?"

Seth and Stevie grinned; Billie and Fred exchanged amused gazes; Cat elbowed Billie in the side.

"Oh! Ahem, yes." Billie cleared her throat while she rubbed her side. She tried her best to don a serious attitude. "We found them sitting on the ridge halfway down the other side. They had quite an unobstructed observation point. Cat's right—

you need to post some kind of warnings or somehow block off access to the other side of the ridge, and you need to do it now."

"You're right, of course. I'll take care of it right away," the ranger promised.

"Thank you." Billie gestured to the group. "Okay, crew, back to camp."

Cat and Jen led the way out of the ranger's office, with Billie and Fred bringing up the rear. Before exiting the office, Fred placed his hand on Billie's arm, holding her back. "Billie, did you see that girl with the big—"

"Oh, yeah. I saw them... er... I mean, her."

She and Fred smiled all the way back to their campsites.

# Chapter 17

## Ghouls Just Wanna Have Fun

Billie watched as Jen walked painfully across the campsite.

"Jen, I'm really sorry for what happened this morning. The snake incident was unfortunate. I was probably wrong to have suggested you lead the way."

Jen settled herself into the camp chair as comfortably as she could. "Well, I would rather it was me than one of the kids. I'll get over it. You'll just have to listen to me cry and complain for a few days."

"That's nothing new," Fred observed. Jen slugged his arm.

Billie snapped her fingers. "You know, I might have something that will make your butt feel better." She ducked into her tent and returned a moment later carrying a jar of soothing salve. "This is really good stuff. I'd rub it on for you, but I don't think Cat or Fred would appreciate it."

"You got that right," Fred replied as he caught the jar Billie tossed to him.

"Okay, guys, drop the kindling right here," Cat directed as she led a train of children out of the surrounding woods, each carrying an armful of sticks that had fallen from the trees.

"Can we make s'mores again, Ma?" Seth asked.

"Sure. Why don't the four of you make a circle around the campfire with the chairs, while Sky comes with me to carry the marshmallows? Sound good?" The children nodded. "Billie, would you mind building up the campfire?"

"Can I give you a hand, Cat?" Jen offered.

"No. You just keep that sore butt of yours right where it is. We've got it covered."

"What can I do to help?" Fred asked.

"How about you come up with this evening's

entertainment? Besides making s'mores, that is. Use your imagination."

Fred grinned. "Okay. Give me a minute or two. I'll come up with something."

As night fell around them, the Charland/Swenson clan sat in a circle around the campfire.

"What are we going to do, Dad?" Stevie asked his father.

"Hmmm." Fred hesitated, then abruptly pulled a flashlight from his lap and held it under his chin. "How about a ghost story?"

"Yeah," the kids exclaimed.

Jen shook her head. "I don't know about this, Fred."

"Aw, come on, Mom," Stevie wheedled.

Jen looked at Cat and Billie, neither of whom objected. "Okay. You win. Go for it."

All of the children sat on the edges of their seats as Fred began his story.

"One rainy night, a man was walking home alone, down a dark, deserted street. Along the way, he had to walk right by a cemetery. Just as he walked by the gates, he heard a bump coming from behind a gravestone. Bump… bump… bump. He didn't dare to look back. Instead, he began to walk faster, but the bumping noise became came louder and faster. Bump, bump, bump.

"He stopped and turned to see what was causing the noise. What he saw terrified him. Coming down the road behind him was a coffin. It was standing on end and bumping from side to side— bump, bump, bump."

The kids' eyes widened as Fred provided the sound effects.

"It began to rain even harder as the man started to run. The faster he ran, the faster the coffin came after him. Bump, bump, bump. In the road ahead of him, he saw a branch that had fallen from a tree during the storm. He grabbed the branch as he ran by. He didn't dare to stop, so he turned around and threw the branch at the coffin. The branch splintered into a million pieces, and the coffin came after him even faster. Bumpity, bumpity, bumpity.

"The man turned the corner onto his street; he was almost home. When he reached his house, he ran through the front gate, the coffin right behind him. The axe he used to split wood rested against his woodpile. He grabbed it and turned to face the coffin. Using both hands, he threw it as hard as he could. Smash! The axe shattered on the unnaturally strong wood, and the coffin continued after him."

Skylar climbed into Cat's lap, and the two older girls were holding hands for moral support as Fred continued with his story.

"The man dashed into his house and slammed the door behind him. He slid all of the bolts closed, but the coffin crashed right through the door. He ran to the fireplace mantel and grabbed his shotgun off the wall. He blasted the coffin with both barrels, but the shots bounced harmlessly off the coffin. He began to panic; nothing seemed to stop it. With limited escape routes, he ran toward the stairs. The coffin followed him. Bump, clomp, bump, clomp.

"Scared to death, the man ran into the bathroom and locked the door behind him, but just like the front door, he knew it wouldn't do any good. The coffin banged against the door once, twice, and on the third time, the door exploded and the coffin came in. Desperate, the man reached out and grabbed a bottle of cough syrup from the medicine cabinet and threw it at the coffin. The bottle shattered, the cough syrup poured on the coffin, and the coffin stopped."

Fred shut off the flashlight, then sat back in his chair and looked at the children. Stevie and Seth looked at each other, their brows knit in confusion. The girls sat on the edges of their seats, waiting for Fred to finish the story. Cat, Billie, and Jen exchanged glances, suppressing their grins.

"Aren't you going to finish the story, Dad?" Stevie asked.

"I did."

"You did?"

"Yeah. The cough syrup stopped the coffin. Coffin... coughing. Get it?"

Stevie and Seth threw themselves back in their seats. "Aw, Dad, that was so lame," Stevie complained.

"Yeah, Dad. Lame, really lame." Jen threw a marshmallow

at Fred.

"Okay, troops, time to hit the hay. It's past midnight." Cat turned to Jen. "How does hot tea laced with honey sound?"

"Wonderful," Jen replied. "Give me a hand getting up, and I'll help you make it. Billie, Fred, any takers?"

"No," Billie said. "Got a cooler of beer right here with my name on it."

Fred rubbed his hands together in anticipation. "Ditto."

"Come on, Seth. Let's tell more ghost stories in our tent," Stevie said as he grabbed Fred's flashlight.

"Cool!" Seth followed his friend to their tent.

Billie tried to put Skylar down so she could go with her sister and Karissa to their tent, but the five-year-old clung to her. "I don't wanna go, Mommy."

"Why, lovebug?"

"I'm scared. What if the coffin comes?"

Billie hugged her daughter. "It was just a story, and a bad one at that. There is no coffin."

"But Uncle Fred said there was."

"Well, there isn't. It isn't real. Now give me a kiss and go with your sister. Bedtime."

Tara, waiting patiently for her sister, held out her hand. "Come on, Sky. Karissa and I will protect you. You can sleep with me in my sleeping bag, in case the coffin comes back."

Billie saw Tara grin at Karissa over Skylar's head.

Skylar ran back into Billie's arms. "Mommy!"

Billie frowned at her daughter. "Tara, did you have to do that?"

Tara laughed. "She's just so easy."

"Enough. Now take your sister and go to bed. And be nice to her, do you hear me?"

"Yeah, yeah, yeah," Tara said as she and Karissa escorted Skylar to their tent.

Billie turned to Fred. "You're a dork, you know that?"

Fred reached for a beer and handed one to Billie. "Yeah, but you love me anyway."

# Chapter 18

## Blazing Saddles

With the children securely tucked into their tents, the four adults sat around the fire ring enjoying their beverages and each other's company.

Jen shifted in her chair. "What a day we've had."

"You got that right," Billie said.

"Do you think the boys will be traumatized by having seen the nudists, Billie?" Cat asked.

"It isn't like they haven't see nakedness before, Cat."

"Karissa and Tara saw it too," Jen reminded them.

Fred nodded. "I'm more concerned about them than the boys."

"Why are the girls any different from the boys?" Cat asked.

"They're boys," Fred said. "Boys are expected to be curious about naked women. I had Playboy magazines under my mattress at their age."

"There were naked men there as well," Jen pointed out. "I don't like the idea that our nine-year-old daughters saw danglies."

"Neither do I," Fred said. "Maybe we should talk to them about it."

"Maybe we should just not make a big deal of it," Billie suggested. "Unless, of course, they ask us about it."

"Agreed," Cat said. Jen shifted in her seat. "How's your butt, Jen?"

"Sore. It's difficult to sit comfortably."

"I hope it doesn't keep you from trying horseback riding again."

"Don't hold your breath."

Fred smirked. "Maybe we should have gotten you a padded

saddle."

Billie crossed one leg over the other. "Well, use that salve I gave you tonight. It should help."

The friends fell silent as the flickering fire held them entranced.

… Until a few moments later.

"Ewww! What's that smell?" Cat pinched her nostrils shut.

Jen frowned. "Fred, you didn't!"

Fred donned his most innocent expression. "What?"

Pfffffft.

"Oh my fucking God! Fred, you are such a hog!"

"What?"

Pfffffft.

Cat looked at her wife. "Billie?"

Billie grinned.

Pfffffft.

Jen pulled her shirt up over her nose. "I'm going to puke."

"I'm right beside you, Jen," Cat said.

Pfffffft.

Jen struggled out of her chair and walked to the edge of the campsite. "You are so gross, Fred!"

"It's Cat's fault," Fred said.

"Why is it my fault?"

"Because you fed us beans for lunch."

Pfffffffffffffffffffffffft.

Cat jumped up from her chair. "Oh my God! Billie!"

"I'm with Fred. It's your fault," she said.

Cat ran over to join Jen. "How can the two of you just sit there in the middle of it?"

"Are you going to stand on the edge of the campsite all night?" Fred asked.

Jen glared at him. "Beats the hell out of the gas chamber you're sitting in."

"Yeah, the air hovering over you is green, for Christ's sake," Cat added.

Fred reached for the fire poker. "No!" Jen screamed. "You'll ignite the gas and blow us all to kingdom come!"

"Mom, what's that smell?" Seth called from his tent.

"Try to sleep, honey. It's just Mom and Fred digesting their lunch," Cat replied.

"It's gross!"

"I know. Just try to ignore it. Go back to sleep."

"Now look at what you've done. It woke the boys up," Jen said.

"They're guys, they'll understand," Fred replied.

"Again with the guy thing, Fred?" Jen complained. "You don't think girls can cut toxic wind? Hell, look at Billie."

Cat looked at Jen. "I don't know about you, but there's no way I'm sleeping with that tonight."

"My thoughts exactly." Jen looked at Billie and Fred. "You two can suffer together. I'm sleeping with Cat tonight."

# Chapter 19

## Once Bitten, Twice Shy

Cat was busy making coffee the next morning when Jen emerged from her tent. She couldn't help smiling as she watched her friend walk gingerly across the campsite. "You're walking like you have a load in your pants."

Jen grimaced. "Very funny. I've never hurt so much in my life. Walking is pure torture, and sitting is totally out of the question."

"You look tired."

"That's because I hardly slept a wink last night. I just couldn't get comfortable."

"Just think of how much worse it would have been if you had to sleep in the gas chamber."

"Amen to that. Last night it smelled like something crawled up inside them and died."

"I don't know what we were thinking when we put beans on the food list," Cat admitted.

Jen yawned. "Nudge me if I fall asleep today, okay?"

Cat handed her a cup of coffee. "Maybe this will help."

"Thank you. Maybe you should just pour it on my ass. The heat might do it some good."

Cat raised an eyebrow. "Now that's an idea."

"What?"

"Heat."

"Heat?"

"Heat. What do you say we ditch the kids and the fart machines, and spend the day at the hot spring?" Cat suggested.

Jen grinned. "Now that's an offer I can't refuse."

The two families sat around the picnic table and enjoyed a hearty breakfast of scrambled eggs, sausage, and toast, all except for Jen, who ate her breakfast standing up.

"I'll take another cup of that." Billie raised her cup to Cat.

Cat filled Billie's cup, then topped off her own. "Anyone else want some before I put it back on the burner?" She returned to the picnic table and sat down beside Billie. "Have I told you yet today how much I appreciate you?"

Billie frowned. "Uh-oh. What do you want?"

"What do you mean? Can't a girl tell her wife how much she loves her?"

Billie reached for Cat's hand. "I love you, too, but I can tell when there's a motive behind your sweetness."

"Am I that transparent?" Cat asked.

"Like glass."

"Then I guess there's no sense in beating around the bush. Why don't you and Fred take the kids exploring in the caves today?"

"Caves?" Seth and Stevie said together.

"Yes. I read about them in the brochure. They're in the rock face on the far end of the campground. A few of them are supposed to be really deep."

"Are there bats in the caves?" Karissa asked. "I hate bats."

"Don't be such a girl," Stevie teased his sister.

"Hey, I was born this way," she replied.

"You're afraid of bats?" Tara asked. "Bats are cool."

"So, what are you and Jen going to do while we're in the caves?" Billie asked.

"We're going to relax in the hot spring. The heat will do wonders for Jen's sore butt."

"I can warm your butt up for you," Fred said to Jen.

"Dad, you are so gross," Stevie said.

"I second that," Jen replied. "Remember you're in mixed company, sweetheart."

"What do you say, Fred? Are you up to a little spelunking?" Billie asked.

"Spelunk away," Fred replied.

"So, does that mean we're going?" Seth asked.

"Only if we can get Mom to pack us a lunch to take along."

"It's a deal," Cat said.

"I'll help you," Jen offered.

Cat and Jen put on their bathing suits and set off toward the hot spring, towels thrown over their shoulders.

"I'm so looking forward to this," Jen said. "No kids, no husbands—"

"Or wives," Cat interjected.

"Or wives. No dishes to do, laundry to fold, rugs to vacuum. Just hot water, peace, and tranquility. It's a dream come true."

"I'm with you on that one, sister."

They sat on the underwater ledge that skirted the manmade pool fed by the sulfur hot spring. Steam rose around them as they relaxed in the hot water. As luck would have it, they were alone.

"It kind of smells like last night," Jen said.

"Last night?"

"Yeah. The smell of the sulfur reminds me of the green air we had hanging over the campsite after Billie and Fred graced us with their gastric emissions."

Cat laughed. "That was pretty gross."

"No kidding. I could hear Fred letting loose all night long, even from your tent. I wonder how Billie slept through it. I hope she sleeps with her mouth closed. I'm willing to bet someone could die from inhaling that shit."

"Billie was just as bad. Until last night, I never knew a woman could emit such disgusting odors."

"This sulfur smells like roses compared to those two hogs."

"Swine! They're swine, I tell you!" Cat agreed. She tilted her head back and sighed. "This feels wonderful. Don't you think?"

It took Jen a few minutes to seat herself somewhat comfortably in the pool, shifting from cheek to cheek periodically to relieve her residual discomfort. She leaned her head back, closed her eyes, and sighed as the heat from the spring permeated her sore butt.

"Cat, you're a lifesaver. Thank you for suggesting this. It feels great."

"I didn't need to twist your arm very hard."

"No, you didn't. I'm a ho for hot water."

Cat looked at Jen out of the corner of her eye and grinned. "I'll keep that in mind."

Jen fell silent, contemplating the water for long moments. "A penny for your thoughts," Cat said.

"I… I was just wondering what it's like to be gay. I mean, I look at your relationship with Billie, and I think how wonderful it would be to be with someone who actually gets you on an emotional level. I love Fred very much, but sometimes he just doesn't understand how I'm feeling."

"For me, that's probably one of the biggest benefits. I mean, men and women are conditioned differently—by society, by their parents, by their peers. Men are conditioned to be defenders and breadwinners, while women are conditioned to be nurturers and caretakers. I know the saying is that opposites attract, but when it comes to lesbian relationships, having two people whose first instinct is to nurture is a huge bonus. Don't get me wrong, Billie and I aren't always on the same wavelength, especially since her surgery, but when we hurt one another, I think there's a greater understanding of how the other feels."

"That makes sense." Jen fell silent.

Cat reached out to touch Jen's arm. "Are you okay? You seem preoccupied."

"See? That's just what I mean. If it were Fred sitting beside me right now, he'd have no idea there was something on my mind. He's oblivious."

"He loves you very much."

Jen smiled. "I know he does, and I love him, too. I just wish sometimes he was more intuitive about how I feel."

"Don't be afraid to tell him that. My guess is he'd be willing to try. Fred's a good man."

"Yes, he is, and I'm lucky to have him."

"You're lucky to have each other. Like Billie and me, you're like two old souls that have been together through time."

"He's a keeper, that's for sure. Thanks for listening."

"No problem."

"So, why do you think Billie's been behaving badly since the surgery? It was almost two years ago that she was shot. She seemed okay after her recovery, didn't she?"

"She hasn't really been behaving poorly, just different. She's a little needier than she used to be, and, like I said before, her fuse appears to be shorter than normal."

"Could the surgery have caused it?"

"That's possible, but not probable. The bullet entered her frontal lobe, which, as you might know, contains synapses that control the personality. I hate to put it this way, but the bullet kind of gave her a minor frontal lobotomy. Personality changes are pretty much expected when that happens. But like you said, she was fine for the first two years after the shooting. The surgery was to remove the scar tissue that formed along the path of the bullet and was suffocating her brain. I guess, in a way, the surgery may have caused the change, but if she hadn't been shot in the first place..."

"Forgive me for asking, but she isn't being violent, is she?"

"Not with me and not with the kids, but I have to admit that her temper has become quite unpredictable of late."

"Well, I hope this vacation helps." Jen yawned loudly. "Damn, I'm tired!"

"Well, lay your head back and relax. Doctor's orders," Cat said.

Jen promptly fell asleep with her head and arms resting on the edge of the pool. Cat looked at her friend and smiled, then leaned her head back and closed her own eyes. Soon, she too was fast asleep.

For a short while.

"Yikes!" Cat screamed as a searing pain shot through her thigh, jolting her out of a most pleasant dream. She grabbed her leg and screamed again as she scrambled out of the spring.

Jen was startled awake by Cat's screams. "What the hell! Cat, what is it?"

"Get out of the water, Jen. Quickly, get out," Cat yelled.

"Why?"

"Water snake!"

Jen reacted instantly. Despite her sore bottom, she was out of the water like a shot, quickly scooting behind Cat and peering over her shoulder into the water in time to see a long, shiny black snake slither away. "Oh, my God. Oh, my God," Jen said. "I hate snakes."

"It bit me!" Cat squealed. "The bastard bit me!"

"Let me see."

There on Cat's thigh were two small holes about half an inch apart, with a milky, bloody substance oozing from them.

"Are you okay? How do you feel?" Jen asked.

Cat took a moment to take stock of how she felt. "I'm a little lightheaded, but I don't know if it's from the snakebite or adrenaline. My leg feels kind of weird, though. I hope the snake wasn't poisonous."

"Poisonous? Are you serious?"

"Very. If that was a cottonmouth moccasin, I'm in big trouble. Venomous snakebites can be deadly if not treated quickly."

Jen grabbed Cat's towel and draped it over her shoulders. "We need to get you some help."

"Jen, I can't imagine the campground would allow anyone in the hot springs if there were venomous snakes around. It was probably just an ordinary water snake."

Jen put her hands on her hips. "And if it wasn't? What then?"

Just then, Cat's leg gave out, and she fell into Jen's arms. "Shit, my leg is numb. Maybe getting help is a good idea."

It didn't take long for Jen to find a park attendant at the hot spring. In no time, a Jeep was arranged to transport Cat to the campground infirmary.

The campground physician poked around the bite, which was rapidly swelling. "What did the snake look like?" he asked.

"It was long and black with a white belly," Cat said.

"How long?"

"I don't know, maybe five or six feet. Jen, you saw it. How long would you say it was?"

"At lease five or six feet, maybe longer. Is it poisonous?" Jen asked anxiously.

"Was it thick bodied, or thin?" the doctor asked.

"Thin. Definitely thin," Cat said.

"Well, your blood pressure and pulse are good. Are you having any trouble breathing? Any nausea or vomiting?"

"None," Cat replied. "So is it poisonous?"

"Poison is ingested or inhaled, venom is injected. Snakes are not poisonous, they're venomous," the doctor explained.

"Thank you for the biology lesson, Doctor. Now please answer the question. Is Cat going to die?" Jen demanded.

"Do you feel any weakness or tiredness?"

"Do you not understand English?" Jen shouted.

"Jen, calm down," Cat said. She turned her attention back to the doctor. "There is numbness and tingling at the site of the bite. No shock and no apparent invasive tissue damage. Obvious swelling. And before you ask, no pain at the site, but that could be explained by the numbness. There are no sign of ptosis, dysphagia, or diplopia, nor do I seem to be suffering from hemotoxic or neurotoxic effects. Now, we would appreciate a diagnosis, Doctor. Does this case warrant a trip to the emergency room, or should I assume your laissez faire attitude is because you know the snakes in this area are not venomous?"

"You go, Cat!" Jen said.

The doctor sat back and raised an eyebrow. "Ah, yes. From your description of the snake and from your apparent expert diagnosis, Doctor...?"

Cat offered her hand in a firm shake. "Charland. Doctor Caitlain Charland. Nice to meet you."

"Yes, Doctor Charland. As I was saying, from the description of the snake and your symptoms, it appears you were bitten by a rat snake."

"Rat snake? How much more disgusting can you get?" Jen said.

"Rat snakes resemble cottonmouth moccasins, which are venomous, except they are much slimmer. Two weeks ago, another camper was also bitten by a rat snake. They're quite harmless, however, the site of the bite will swell. After the initial numbness and temporary loss of coordination wear off in a couple of days, it might be painful to the touch for an additional day or two. I prescribe immobility until the feeling and strength return to your leg. That should happen in the next day or two. Unless you have any questions, you can get dressed. I'll speak to the park attendant and arrange for a ride back to your camp site."

Jen helped Cat to dress after the doctor left the room.

"Great, just great," Cat said. "Billie's going to have a fit. What else can go wrong on this trip?"

"What do you mean?" asked Jen.

"Billie wasn't too crazy about this camping trip to begin with. So far, I'm inclined to agree with her. I mean, look at us: a flat tire on the interstate, that flirt at the restaurant, the tent poles left at home, the shower incident, that homophobic guy on the trail, the nudist colony at the beach, your ride on 'Trigger, Horse from Hell', noxious gas around the campfire, and now this snakebite. What else can go wrong?" she exclaimed. "This was supposed to be a nice, relaxing vacation. 'Rest, take it easy,' Doctor Connor told us. The last thing Billie needs is more to worry about "

# Chapter 20

## Laughter is the Best Medicine

"Bugs! I hate bugs!" Billie ranted as Cat applied anti-inflammatory cream to Billie's body. Her face was so swollen, she was barely recognizable.

"Billie, are you allergic to stings?" Cat asked. "You're awfully swollen."

"Not that I know of. I've been stung before without having a reaction."

Cat counted the hornet stings on Billie's face. "Eight, nine, ten. Maybe the swelling is due to the sheer quantity of stings. Whatever possessed you to walk into a hornet's nest?"

"Whatever possessed you to go swimming with snakes?" Billie retorted. "Do you think I did it on purpose?"

"Okay, I deserved that." Cat slapped Billie's hand away for the umpteenth time. "Stop scratching at yourself."

"This itching is driving me crazy!" Her voice rose an octave with each word.

"Itching is an allergic reaction. It's a good thing they gave you a shot of adrenaline at the infirmary." Cat squeezed another dab of cream onto her finger. "Billie, hold still. Your squirming is making this difficult. Don't forget, I have limited mobility here. I can't go chasing you around the tent to spread this cream on you."

Billie tried to remain still, lying on her stomach in the tent while Cat applied the cream to her shoulders. Neither woman spoke for long moments. Finally, Billie turned her head and said to Cat, "Does it hurt?"

While running her hands over her wife's lean, muscular shoulders, Cat had allowed her mind to drift back to the dream she was having in the hot springs. Billie's voice startled her back to reality. "Huh?"

Billie's brow knit in irritation. "I asked if it hurt."

"Does what hurt?"

"The snakebite, Cat. Hey, are you all right?"

"Oh, that." Cat smiled. "Sorry, I was a little distracted. No, it doesn't hurt. It's quite numb, as a matter of fact. It hurt like hell when it happened, though."

"Want me to kiss it and make it better?" Billie offered, wiggling her eyebrows.

Billie's eyes wandered to the place high up on Cat's thigh where the snake bit her, and Cat was aroused. "Cream's starting to work, huh?" She leaned down and placed a light kiss on Billie's lips. Suddenly, Cat burst out laughing and threw herself backward onto the pillows.

"What the hell is so funny?" Billie demanded.

Cat wrapped her hands around her midsection while she laughed and rolled around on the sleeping bag. "I'm... I'm sorry, love. It's just that—" Cat burst out laughing and couldn't continue.

"Damn it, Cat, you're pissing me off."

"I'm sorry, Billie. It's just that your face, it looks so funny all swollen up like that," she managed to say. She could see Billie was not amused.

"Stop it, Cat," Billie demanded, an injured expression on her swollen face.

"I'm sorry, really I am." Cat tried not to look at her wife. She hazarded a glance to see whether Billie accepted her apology, and then again burst out laughing uncontrollably.

Billie grabbed her T-shirt, threw it on over her head, and stormed out of the tent, ignoring Cat's apologies and pleas that she return.

Billie stomped back and forth in front of the campfire, kicking up dirt along the way.

Jen reclined in a nearby lounge chair, reading a book. She lowered the book into her lap. "Want to talk about it?"

Billie stopped pacing. "Jen, where are the kids?"

"Fred took them to the playground. Stop avoiding the

question. Sit," Jen ordered.

Billie looked like she was going to object, but gave in and sat on the edge of the lounge chair. She lowered her face into her hands.

"Are you okay?" Jen asked.

"Fucking peachy."

"You sound angry."

"Angry is putting it mildly. I'd like to punch something right now."

"Talk."

Billie pouted. "She laughed at me."

"Cat laughed at you? Why?"

"She seems to find my appearance amusing."

"Well, you do look kind of funny right now, Big Guy," Jen said seriously.

Billie raised her eyebrows and looked at Jen. "You, too?" she asked angrily. "I should have known you'd side with her. I didn't laugh at you when you were hurt."

Jen grabbed Billie's shoulders. "Now you just wait one minute, girlfriend."

Billie waited for the explosion that didn't come.

"No, no, wait. There's a better way to do this. Wait right here. Don't move." Jen rose from her chair and went into her tent. Moments later she returned and sat down next to Billie. "Close your eyes, Billie."

Billie looked at her as if she were insane.

"Come on, humor me."

Billie finally gave in and closed her eyes. A moment later, Jen said, "Okay, now open them."

She opened her eyes and looked directly into her own reflection in the mirror Jen held in front of her face. Her first reaction was shock. Her second reaction was to break out in hysterical laughter, bending over and clutching her stomach. When she finally regained control, she looked at Jen and wiped the tears from her eyes. "Oh, God," she gasped, "I've never laughed so hard in my life."

Jen nodded. "Now do you blame her?"

Billie had the decency to look embarrassed. "No, I guess not," she admitted. "I guess I should do some damage control, huh?"

Jen rose to her feet. "I think I'll go find Fred and the kids. We should be back in, say... two hours? Yeah, two hours sounds good."

Billie stood and hugged her friend. "Thanks for making me see what a horse's ass I've been."

"Don't you ever mention the words horse and ass in the same sentence in front of me again. Got that?" Jen said as she started for the trail toward the playground.

"Got it." Billie went back to her tent.

# Chapter 21

## Sunshine on My Shoulder Makes Me Happy?

The next morning, Cat poured five glasses of orange juice and handed them out to the children sitting around the picnic table.

"Here you go, kiddoes. There's cereal as well, if you want some."

"Thanks, Mom."

"Good morning." Jen unzipped the dining tent and hugged Cat. "Coffee smells good."

"Have a seat, and I'll pour you a cup. Is Fred still sleeping?"

"Actually, he's getting his shower gear together. I'll head that way myself after breakfast."

"That's where Billie is right now."

"How's she feeling this morning?"

"Pretty good. No ill effects from the bee stings, other than that she looks like she has chicken pox."

"You were right about her temper. She was fit to be tied when you laughed at her yesterday."

"I couldn't help myself. She looked so funny all swollen like that. The old Billie would have taken my reaction more lightly."

"You know, you might just have to get used to the way she is now. This may be the new Billie."

"Yeah, I've thought about that. It will take some getting used to."

"Well, don't give up on her. She loves you very much, despite how quick she is to anger."

"I know she does. I'm trying, really I am, but some days I

just want to give it right back to her."

"I hear you, but just like the advice you gave me about Fred, let her know how her reaction makes you feel. Maybe she doesn't even realize it."

Cat hugged Jen. "Thanks."

"Speaking of how you feel, how's the leg?"

"A little tender where the snake bit me, otherwise, full mobility has returned."

"That's good. That snake scared the bejesus out of me."

"Yeah! At the risk of sounding like a health clinic, how's your backside this morning?"

"Better. As long as I take it easy, I'll be as good as new in a couple of days."

"When I suggested this camping trip, I didn't anticipate all the health hazards. Geez, we've had more medical emergencies in three days than we normally have in a year," Cat said.

"We're out of our element," Jen replied. "There's bound to be more screwups when you're in unfamiliar surroundings."

"You have a point."

"Hey, ladies," Billie said, entering the screen tent.

"How was your shower, love?" Cat asked. She grabbed another cup and poured coffee for Billie.

Billie rezipped the tent behind her. "The shower was great. Thanks for the coffee. Morning, Jen."

"Hey, Billie. You look much better this morning. Swelling's gone."

"Thank God for that. Where's Fred?"

"He should be back from the showers any minute. In fact, there he is," Jen said as Fred walked across the campsite toward the dining tent.

"Is there any coffee left?" he asked.

"Come in and have a seat. I'll pour you a cup," Cat said.

The two families sat around the picnic table, enjoying their breakfast and chatting about possible plans for the day.

"What are we going to do today?" Seth asked.

Cat raised her hand. "I vote we do something non-involved. After the past two days, I just want to relax."

"Amen to that," Jen added. "How about shopping?"

Tara, Karissa, and Skylar eagerly agreed.

"Shopping? You've got to be kidding." Billie was afraid that Cat would force her to go along for the ride. She hated shopping. "How's that relaxing?"

"Count me out," Fred said. "Shopping is definitely not for me. I opt for a day of fishing. What do you say, boys?" he asked Stevie and Seth, who nodded their heads vigorously.

Billie shot him a pathetic look that begged him to invite her along. When he didn't, she began whimpering. When he still didn't tumble, she kicked him under the table.

"Ow! What did you do that for?"

Billie frowned at him and tilted her head slightly in Cat's direction.

"Oh! Uh, Billie, how about joining me and the boys?"

Billie broke into a relieved smile. "I'd love to go fishing," she said, as nonchalantly as she could.

Cat reached across the table and tilted Billie's chin. "You're so transparent, my love. Go. Have a good time, and catch us some dinner. 'Kay?"

Billie kissed Cat tenderly. "Thanks." She grabbed her fishing pole to follow Fred and the boys down the trail to the lake, but stopped part way down the trail. "Cat, why don't you get me a new cell phone while you're out?"

"Billie, I'd really rather you were there to pick it out."

"My last phone was just like yours. Just get me another one similar to that. I'll be happy with whatever you pick out."

"Okay, but don't complain if you don't like it."

"Deal. Love you!" Billie scurried down the path after Fred and the boys.

Cat watched her go, then turned and looked at Jen. Jen raised her hand and accepted the high five from Cat.

"Way to go, O Wise One," Jen said. "Now we can shop till we drop without listening to them whining."

"Never doubt there's a method to my madness. Now go take your shower so we can hit the road."

While the ladies enjoyed a day at the mall, Billie, Fred, and the boys basked in the sunlight in a boat in the middle of the lake, happily trying to catch dinner.

"I got a bite!" Stevie whipped his pole back, and the line went slack.

"You probably ripped the hook right out of his mouth," Fred said. "Pull back more gently next time. Reel in your line, so I can see if you have any worm left."

"What a beautiful day," Billie said. "The sunshine feels great. This is definitely better than dragging my butt through the stores behind Cat."

"You got that right," Fred said as he handed another worm to Stevie. "I hate shopping. It's got to be the most boring thing on Earth, except for maybe visiting the in-laws." Fred pointed his finger at Stevie. "Don't tell your mother I said that."

"That's where I'm lucky. I like my in-laws. Doc and Ida are great, and Cat's sisters are a hoot, especially when they're all together."

"She has three sisters, right?"

"Yes. She's third in line. There's Amy, Bridget, Cat, and Drew. Get it? A, B, C, and D."

"Well, that's inventive."

"Mom, I got a big one. Help!" Seth's pole was nearly bent in half.

"Keep the tension on it, son," Fred said. "That's it, hold your pole back and reel it in steady-like, and don't stop or it'll give him slack and let him spit the hook." Fred looked at Billie and Stevie. "Reel your lines in so Seth's fish doesn't get caught up in them."

Fred reeled his own line in and set his pole inside the boat. Seth struggled to hold on to his pole and reel at the same time, as the fish took a beeline under the boat.

"Keep the tension on it, Seth. You're doing fine." Fred grabbed the net just as the fish cleared the surface of the water.

"Argh! He's gonna to get off!" Seth yelled.

The fish dove back into the water and once more headed under the boat, nearly taking Seth's pole with him. Stevie leaned way over the side to see the fish. The top rim of the boat came precariously close to the water. Billie grabbed his shirt and pulled him back. "Whoa, get back here. It won't do us, or Seth's fish any good if we capsize the boat," she said.

The fish headed toward clear water. Seth's reel squealed as the fish pulled out more line.

"Mom, help me," Seth yelled.

Billie maneuvered herself onto the seat behind her son and wrapped her arms around him. She grasped the fishing pole and pulled back. "Reel!" she yelled.

Seth reeled as Billie kept tension on the pole. For the next five minutes, they struggled to gain ground as the fish continually pulled line out of the reel.

"Hold steady," Fred said. "It should begin to tire soon."

True to his words, the squealing stopped and Seth was finally able to make progress against the fish as he reeled with all his might. "How much line is on this reel?" he complained.

"Just be patient. We're almost there," Fred said.

All four occupants of the boat stared intently at the point where Seth's line disappeared into the water. Suddenly, a gray object appeared near the surface.

"There it is," Fred said as he gently lowered the net into the water and positioned it just behind Seth's line. "That's it. Keep reeling." Fred suddenly scooped the net upward. "Got it," he exclaimed as he lifted the net out of the water and into the boat.

"Wow!" Seth said. "It's a monster."

"That it is. Ya done good," Fred said as he accepted a high five from Seth.

They all watched as the lake bass flopped around on the bottom of the boat, tangling itself in the net. Seth beamed at his mother. "Thanks for helping, Mom. I would've lost him if you didn't help."

"Looks like we'll be bringing back dinner after all," she replied. "Nice job."

Fred untangled the large fish from the net and hooked the scale in the corner of its mouth. He lifted it high into the air and studied the digital read out. "Looks like a ten-pounder. Cool!"

Stevie rebaited his hook and cast his line into the water. "My turn," he said.

\* \* \*

Cat, Jen, and the girls stood in line to be seated at a busy restaurant in the mall.

"Do you really think she'll like it, Jen?" Cat asked.

"Of course, what's not to like? She said to get a phone like yours."

"I know, but sometimes she's just so picky."

"Well, beggars can't be choosers. She could have come with us to pick it out herself, but she chose to go fishing instead. God only knows why. I can't imagine ever choosing fishing over shopping."

"I'm with you on that one, sistah. Billie took me fishing once, and I fell asleep sitting on the lawn chair. A fish bit on my line and pulled the pole right out of my hands. It startled me awake, but not in time for me to grab it before the fish swam away, pulling my pole behind it. I never laughed so hard in my life. Needless to say, Billie was not amused."

"When we were dating, Fred took me fishing. He was quite exasperated because I wouldn't bait the hook. There was no way in hell I was touching that slimy worm, much less sticking a hook through it. It looked way too much like a small snake. I watched him do it once, and some type of liquid, I could only imagine was worm piss, flew out and hit him on the cheek. I told him he had to be crazy to voluntarily subject himself to a worm pissing on him. And when I actually caught a fish, I refused to take it off myself. He said he could have accomplished the same result if he had gone fishing by himself and used two poles."

"Mom, the buzzer just went off," Karissa said. She held the flashing pager toward her mother.

"Great. That means our table is ready. Here comes the hostess to seat us."

\* \* \*

Fred rowed the rented boat quickly toward land and ran it aground on the sandy shore. Billie hopped out and pulled the nose further onto the sand to stabilize it as they all climbed out. Fred turned his back to Billie to retrieve their gear from the boat.

"Holy shit, Fred! Look at your back! I knew taking your shirt off was a mistake."

Fred glanced over his shoulder. "Ah, that's nothing. Don't worry about it."

Billie looked at him doubtfully as she grabbed the stringer of fish and the tackle box. The boys took the poles and other tackle and headed back to the campsite, with Fred walking ahead of them. "I don't know, Fred. It looks really bad from back here." She pushed her baseball cap further back on her head.

Fred flexed his shoulders. "It does sting a little. Maybe you're right."

"I suspect it will sting a lot, very soon," Billie said. "I'll rub some aloe on it when we get back to camp," she offered.

"Okay. Thanks."

\* \* \*

"I'll get this one," Cat said as she grabbed the bill in Jen's hand. They played tug-of-war with the piece of paper for a moment or two.

"Only if you let me buy next time."

"Deal."

"We'll meet you outside," Jen said as she gathered their children and their purchases while Cat paid the bill. Cat's phone rang just as she rejoined Jen in the mall. "Fred?" Cat answered.

"Nope. It's Billie."

"Why are you calling me on Fred's phone?"

"Because mine's missing in action, remember?"

"Duh, of course. Is everything okay? The kids—"

"The kids are fine. Fred, however, is another story. I need you to stop at an herbal medicine store and pick up some more aloe salve, lots of it."

"Aloe salve?" Cat asked. Then suddenly remembering that they used the salve for burns, she said, "God, Billie, he didn't!"

Cat glanced at Jen, who was standing at her elbow, a

questioning look on her face.

"He did. Red as a lobster," Billie replied.

"And what about you and the kids?"

"No problem. We all had our shirts and hats on. Fred's the only cooked goose here."

"Okay. Aloe salve, lots of it. I think there's an herbal store right here in the mall. We'll be on our way soon. We should be there in half an hour."

"Okay. See you in a bit. Love you."

"Love you too. Bye." Cat closed her cell phone and slipped it into her purse.

Jen looked at Cat. "Well?"

"Did you bring sunscreen?" Cat asked Jen.

Jen looked at her blankly for a moment, then realization hit. "Oh God, tell me he didn't. Damn! Sometimes I swear that man has shit for brains," she exclaimed.

"Aloe salve... herbal store," Cat directed as the two women gathered up the girls. Ten minutes later, they were headed toward the car and on their way back to a badly sunburned Fred.

* * *

"Kill me, Jen, please." Fred sat bent over at the picnic table, his head lying on his crossed arms while Jen rubbed the soothing salve across his shoulders.

"All right, I'm finished," she announced. "Here, put this back on." She handed him his shirt.

Fred refused. "I really don't want to put anything on it."

Jen glared at him impatiently.

Billie stood near the campfire, stoking it to life for the burgers they planned to grill for lunch. The area surrounding the fire ring was bathed in bright sunlight. "Fred, c'mere a minute, will you?" she said.

Fred slowly rose to his feet. He moaned. "Damn. It feels like every little movement is stretching the burnt skin on my back. My nerve endings are protesting pretty loudly right now."

When he reached Billie, she handed him the poker. "Here, stoke this up for me while I line the grill with foil. Okay?"

Fred took the poker and started moving the coals around as

Billie walked toward Jen with a grin.

"What are you smiling about?" Jen asked.

"Just wait, and learn."

The two women watched as the heat from the growing fire combined with the sun beating down on Fred's back made him squirm.

"I think he's had enough. Give me his shirt," Billie said. She winked at Jen, then walked back to Fred. Fred looked up as she neared, and she could clearly see the pain on his face. She handed the shirt to him. "Ready to put this on now?"

He growled at her, grabbing for the shirt. "Women!" he muttered. "Always have to prove a point."

Jen quickly went to Fred and helped him pull the T-shirt down over his shoulders with as little discomfort as possible, while Billie walked over to Cat, who was making hamburger patties.

"You're so mean," Cat said, a half smile curling her lips. "I saw what you did to Fred."

Billie's attention was on Cat's hands, which were squeezing and shaping the ground beef into a circle. She was clearly mesmerized by the sight.

"Billie?" Cat asked, drawing Billie's attention away from the meat in her hands.

"What? Oh, I'm sorry, I wasn't paying attention. What did you say?"

Cat leaned into Billie's neck and left a light kiss there before pulling away to look into her eyes. "Just what were you distracted by, my tall lover?" she asked seductively.

Billie's body jolted at the kiss. She gulped audibly and looked back into pools of emerald green.

Cat never broke eye contact as she lowered the burger to the foil covered grill, then wiped her hands on the towel lying on the table.

Billie ran her tongue across suddenly parched lips as she held Cat's gaze.

Cat reached across the table for a bowl of strawberries and chose an especially succulent one. She parted her lips ever so slightly to allow the ripe berry into her own mouth, following the berry with her tongue, licking the sweet juice from the fingertips, snaking it out moments later to lap up the juice that had run down her chin.

Billie's eyes opened wide. "God, Cat!" she whispered hoarsely.

Cat reached for another berry and lifted it towards Billie's mouth. Billie's lips closed around Cat's fingers as the smaller woman pushed the berry past her teeth. Cat threw her head back and closed her eyes. Intense desire jolted her to her very core as Billie sucked her fingers clean. "Billie," she whispered.

"Okay, you two, any more of that and those burgers will be cooked by just your body heat," Jen teased as she approached.

Cat and Billie looked embarrassed as their eyes roamed around the campsite, skillfully avoiding Jen's smirking face.

"Besides, you're making me jealous," Jen added. "With Fred in that condition," she gestured at Fred sitting in the shade away from the fire, "it's going to be a lonely night."

Billie grinned as she looked down at Jen. "With Fred in that condition, plan on several lonely nights."

"Ahhh! I hate you!" Jen slapped Billie's arm and stomped away.

Billie looked at Cat and smiled. "Now, what was it you were saying about being mean?" she asked as she drew Cat's fingers towards her mouth.

# Chapter 22

## A Face Only a Mother Could Love

Billie, Cat, and Jen sat around the campfire that evening in silence. It was nearly midnight, and the children were fast asleep in their tents, worn out from a busy day. Billie was busily setting up the preferences on her new cell phone.

"Dinner was great, Cat," Jen said.

"We have Billie, Fred, and the boys to thank for it," she replied.

Billie looked up from her phone. "I don't know how you do it. Everything you cook turns out so tasty."

Cat grinned. "That's because you have only your own cooking to compare it to, love."

"Ouch!" Billie grasped her chest.

"Am I right?"

"Busted."

"You can thank Jen for the suggestion of cooking it in the coals."

"That's the way my mom used to do it when we camped. Wrap the fish in aluminum foil and throw them on the coals. In fact, she cooked a lot of our camping meals that way: fish, chicken, corn on the cob."

Cat nodded. "Well, it was a great idea."

"You can bet it'll be the only fish meal we eat on this trip," Billie said. "I don't think Fred will be in any condition to go fishing for a while."

"He has second-degree burns on his shoulders. I can only imagine how much pain he's in right now. He'll surely blister," Cat added.

"I swear that man is dumber than a box of rocks sometimes.

He knows better than to stay in the sun too long without sunscreen. He's paler than a ghost and burns so easily. That's why he's such an old mother hen about the kids wearing it. What was he thinking?" Jen griped.

Billie chuckled. "He was thinking that he needed to make his escape before you dragged all of us shopping with you."

"I'd venture a guess that he wishes he'd gone shopping with us now."

"You're probably right. I hope he's getting some rest," Billie said.

"He's actually in the tent instead of out here because he's worried about the heat from the campfire making him uncomfortable. I suspect he won't sleep very well tonight."

"Slather him down with the aloe before you go to bed," Cat suggested. "It won't do that much for the pain, but it's important to keep the skin as moist as possible while it heals. It's going to itch like a bastard if it dries out too much."

"Thanks for the advice. I think I'll head that way right now. I'll see you in the morning."

Jen hugged both ladies before heading toward her tent.

"G'night," Cat and Billie called.

"Thanks for picking up my new phone."

"You're welcome. I hope you like it. Apparently, it's the latest in Smart Phone technology," Cat said.

"Very cool."

"Don't lose this one. It was really expensive."

"I'll guard it with my life." Billie slipped the phone into her pocket and picked up a long stick beside her chair to poke at the fire. "I feel sorry for Fred."

"I do, too. He's in for a few very uncomfortable days."

Billie sat back in her chair, lifted Cat's hand to her lips, and kissed her knuckles.

Cat smiled. "Are you having fun, Billie?"

Billie chuckled. "I'm not sure I'd exactly call it fun, but moments like this—spending time with you, alone, with the crickets chirping and the frogs singing, and the smell of a campfire burning, and most of all, with the moonlight reflecting off your hair—well, it gives me a feeling of warmth and gratitude for everything we have together. I love you, Cat."

"I love you, too. Thank you for coming on this trip. I know everything hasn't been perfect, but we're here together, as a family. We'll never be able to get this time back."

"I know. It hasn't been as bad as I expected, and quite frankly, my heart has only had an irregular beat a couple of times since we've been here. For a while there, it was jumping all around in my chest for most of the day."

Cat frowned. "You never told me it was that bad. That's a sign of severe anxiety. It can be dangerous if it goes on too long."

"That's what I'm worried about."

Cat squeezed Billie's hand. "Billie, are you happy? I mean, are you truly happy with me... with our lives?"

"I think it's impossible for someone to be happy all the time, but honestly, I love my life. I love you, and I love the kids. I feel a sense of completeness that I've never felt before, even when things were good between me and Brian."

"I'm glad. I want you to be happy we're together, Billie. No regrets."

"Do you have regrets? Are you happy, Cat?"

"The truth?"

"Absolutely. I insist."

"I love being married to you. I love being the mother of your children."

"But?"

"But I'm concerned about the changes in you since the surgery."

Billie fell silent for a few moments before responding. "I'm sorry, Cat. I feel it too. It's like some unknown force, some unknown fear clenches my stomach and then I find myself becoming angry. Unfortunately, more often than not, you end up on the receiving end. I'm sorry."

"Better me than the kids."

Billie's eyes opened wide. "I would never hurt the kids, Cat."

"I know you wouldn't, love. Not intentionally. Look, I love you. I love you with all my heart, and if you hear anything I am saying, hear this. I am not going anywhere. Whatever is causing this problem, I'm here for you. I will stand by you, no matter what. We'll see this through together. Understand?"

"Thank you." Billie's finger traced Cat's cheek. "You are so beautiful. Do you have any idea what you do to me?"

"I most certainly do. I don't know what's hotter right now, the heat coming from you, or the heat coming from the campfire."

"I'll make you a deal: I'll take care of the campfire's heat, if you'll take care of mine."

"That's an offer I can't refuse. I'll fetch the water for you."

Billie watched Cat pick up the bucket and saunter across the campsite to the faucet, fill it, and return to the campfire. Each step Cat took served to fan the inferno that was raging within her. Cat placed the bucket at Billie's feet. "Here you go, lover. I'll meet you in the tent."

Billie made short work of the campfire as she poured water on the coals and spread them out. When she was satisfied it was safe to leave them unattended, she hurried to their tent. Cat was inside, lying naked on top of the sleeping bags. Billie sank to her knees and inhaled the aroma of Cat's desire that perfumed the air. As quickly as possible, she disposed of her clothing and lay beside her lover. Billie's breath sputtered as she fought for self-control. She wanted to savor every second and every inch of skin for as long as possible. Until this very moment, finding time alone to make love to her wife had been nearly impossible.

Billie began by caressing Cat's breasts. She ran her tongue around each nipple and slowly took each tender bud into her mouth. Cat responded by arching her chest and throwing her head back. Her rapturous moans heightened Billie's desire as she placed a trail of kisses from Cat's breasts to her collarbone, then gently nipped her way towards Cat's shoulder. It wasn't long before Billie felt Cat pushing her head southward.

"Billie, I need you."

"Patience, my love," Billie said as she wound a torturously slow path from Cat's shoulder downward. By the time she reached her destination, Cat was writhing with desire. Billie looked upward into Cat's face and felt a rush of love and need for this woman she had committed her life to.

"I love you, Cat," Billie said just before she gave Cat what she was aching for.

"Oh my God, Billie, harder," Cat demanded.

Billie held Cat as she fell over the edge, then collapsed into her arms. Several moments later, Billie was convinced Cat had fallen asleep. "Cat?"

Cat opened her eyes. "Damn, that was good," she said, a wide grin gracing her features. "My turn," she added as she rose to her knees and straddled Billie's thighs.

Billie gripped the sleeping bag as she surrendered herself to Cat's probing tongue. It was a struggle to control her own desire as Cat suckled her breasts and ran her tongue down her abdomen and into her navel. She pushed back her disappointment as Cat reversed direction and headed back up toward her breasts, and then to her neck. Soon Cat was hovering over her, their noses mere inches apart. Not a word passed between them as Billie was unable to look away from her lover's eyes, when quite unexpectedly, she felt Cat's fingers plunge deep into her. She arched forward, and her face scrunched into a mask of concentration and desire.

"God, Cat. Don't stop."

"Not a chance," Cat replied. Within moments, Cat felt Billie's body spasm and close around her fingers. "That's it, my love. Let it go. I love you, Billie."

Billie clung to Cat as waves of release passed through her, then subsided into sweet euphoria.

Cat kissed her tenderly, then snuggled down into Billie's shoulder. Moments later, Billie realized Cat was giggling. She turned her head to look at Cat. "Care to share what's so funny?"

"You are?"

"Excuse me?"

"I'm sorry, Billie. I can't help it." More laughter. "While we were making love, you… you were making fuck faces."

"I was making what?"

Cat rolled onto her side and laughed even harder. "Oh, my God. My stomach hurts."

Billie grabbed her shoulders. "I was making what? Cat, talk

to me."

Cat wiped the tears from her face. "You were making fuck faces. I can't help it. It was funny."

"Fuck faces? What the hell is fuck faces?"

"You know, your face gets all wrinkled up, your mouth opens, your eyes roll into your head."

Billie burst out laughing. "That's funny!" she said. "And oh, by the way, you were making fuck faces too!"

"I know. That's why I'm laughing. I was just wondering if I looked as funny to you as you looked to me."

"Hell yeah. Thank God you didn't laugh in the middle of the action—that would not have been pleasant."

"Talk about putting a damper on the libido!" Cat exclaimed. Cat snuggled down again into Billie's shoulder.

"Hey Cat," Billie said.

"Yes?"

"Look at me."

Cat raised her head and immediately burst out laughing as Billie displayed her most dramatic fuck face. "Oh my god, stop it! My stomach hurts from laughing!"

Before long, they were face to face and making each other laugh even harder by posing with various fuck faces they had seen the other make during their lovemaking.

Never again would lovemaking be the same.

# Chapter 23

# The Seven Rear Itch

Billie knelt on one knee beside the fire ring and arranged kindling in a teepee shape, then held the propane lighter at the base until the flame took hold and began to spread. She gently blew on the small fire until it consumed the wood. The sound of a zipper drew her attention toward Fred and Jen's tent. Billie smiled as Fred emerged, bare-chested and wearing Bermuda shorts and flip-flops. He carried the tube of aloe gel in his hand.

"Good morning, Fred. How'd you sleep?"

"Sleep? What's that?"

"I was afraid of that. Give me a moment to get the fire going, then I'll set up the coffee pot."

Satisfied that the kindling was burning strong, Billie placed two larger pieces of wood on the fire and watched as the flame encircled them. She rose to her feet and brushed off her knee, then looked at Fred, who was now sitting at the picnic table. "You look like hell, my friend."

"Well, I look better than I feel. This sunburn is killing me."

"Here, give me the aloe. I'll put it on for you." Billie took the tube from Fred and squirted a long line of it down his back.

Fred flinched. "Holy shit, that's cold!"

"Better cold than hot. I'll try to be gentle," she said as she spread the soothing ointment across Fred's shoulders. Try as she might to apply the lightest of touches, she felt Fred quiver as her fingers ran over his skin. "Sorry, dude. I'm being as gentle as I can."

"It's okay. I'm a big boy. I can handle it."

"I'll try to be as quick as I can. Here, you do the front while I do the back," Billie said as she squeezed a generous amount of aloe into his hand. Moments later, she snapped the cap closed on the tube of gel. "Finished. I hope it helps."

"Thanks. It feels a little better already."

"We'll do this periodically throughout the day. Cat says we need keep the skin moist, or it will itch like a bastard when it dries out."

Fred wiped the remnants of the gel on the exposed areas of his receding hairline. "I guess I should have worn a hat, as well."

"Ya think?"

"That's the problem. I didn't think." Fred rose from the table. "I'll be right back, gotta get a shirt."

"I'll get the coffee started."

Billie put a few smaller pieces of wood in the embers, then placed the cooking grate across the fire ring. By the time Fred returned to the fire, she had the percolator set up. She pulled a couple of camp chairs closer to the fire. "Have a seat. The coffee should be ready soon."

"Thanks."

"Any idea what's on the agenda for today?" Billie asked.

"Beats the hell out of me. I'm going to be somewhat limited. I think I should stay out of the direct sunlight for a few days."

"I hear you. I guess we'll have to see what Cat and Jen have planned."

"Did I hear my name?"

Billie swung around and looked toward her tent. "Cat. I'm sorry, did we wake you?"

"Actually, the coffee did. That, and Mother Nature. I'll be right back." Cat made a beeline toward the bathhouse.

"Miss Walnut Bladder. I swear that woman can't walk past a bathroom without having to use it."

"Jen's the same way. And for some reason, there's always a line at the women's room but never in the men's room. Why is that?" Fred mused.

Billie shrugged. "Maybe it's because men don't have to partially disrobe to pee. That really sucks, by the way. Maybe it's because along with using the potty, women tend to primp in front of the mirror. Maybe there're more urinals in the men's room than toilets in the women's room. Lots of reasons."

"Coffee," came a voice from behind them.

Fred looked at Billie. "That would be Jen."

"It's just about finished perking, Jen. Come have a seat," Billie said. "Oh, and I must say, your cavewoman hair-do is quite fetching."

"Up yours," Jen replied as she attempted to tame her wild, bedhead curls.

Jen kissed Fred on top of the head. "Hey, love. How'd you sleep?"

"Not very well."

"Give me the aloe and I'll spread it on your back for you," Jen offered.

"Billie already took care of that."

"Okay." Jen looked around. "Is Cat still sleeping?"

"No. She's gone to the bathhouse," Billie said.

"That sounds like a good idea. I'll be right back."

"That's another thing I don't understand," Fred said as he watched Jen walk down the path to the bathhouse."

"What's that?" Billie asked.

"Why is it that when women are out with friends, all of them have to go to the bathroom together?"

Billie poked at the fire. "Fred, you have way too much time on your hands."

\* \* \*

"Mom, can you pass the catsup?" Stevie asked.

"Sure, sweetie." Jen handed the bottle to her son.

"For the life of me, I can't imagine how catsup makes eggs taste better," Cat said.

"I think it's a guy thing," Jen replied. "Karissa, use your napkin, not your hand to wipe your mouth."

"What are we doing today, Ma?" Seth asked.

"We're going hiking," Tara said. "I heard Mama and Aunt Jen talking about it last night."

"Cool," Seth replied.

"I'm not sure I should be out in the sun, Jen," Fred said.

Jen gave her husband an appraising stare. "You're probably right."

"I'll stay with him," Billie offered.

"You don't have to do that," he said.

"No, it's okay. I brought a book with me that I've been wanting to read. Really, I don't mind."

Jen clapped her hands together. "All right, that's settled. Let's get breakfast cleaned up and hit the trail."

A short time later, Cat took Billie aside. "Are you sure? You're going to miss a good walk," she whispered.

"I hate to leave him here alone. You and Jen go ahead and have fun with the kids."

Soon Cat and Jen were on their way up the path, using the trail map they had picked up at the office.

It was a long while later and well out on the trail when Skylar said, "Mama, I gotta pee!"

"Sky, honey, can you hold it until we get back to camp?"

"No. I gotta pee real bad," she whined, crossing her legs.

"Okay, okay. Come on." Cat took the child's hand and led her into the bushes. She looked back over her shoulder at the rest of the group. "You might want to take advantage of the pit stop, as well. It's a long hike back to the campsite."

Moments later, after a trip to the bushes for everyone, the little entourage was on its way back to camp.

"How was your hike?" Billie asked as Skylar climbed into her arms and rested her head on her shoulder. "Don't go to sleep, little one. It will be time for dinner soon."

"The hike was great," Cat replied. "The kids should sleep well tonight. It was a bit strenuous in places."

"Never mind the kids, I can't wait for bedtime," Jen said. "I'm beat."

Cat kissed Billie's head and then Skylar's. "How was your afternoon? And where's Fred?"

"Fred is napping. The poor guy didn't sleep at all last night. I've been reading for the past couple of hours. It's been relaxing."

"Just what the doctor ordered," Cat said.

"Karissa, Stevie, try to keep the noise down, your dad is sleeping. Okay?" Jen asked.

"Okay, Mom. Me and Tara are going to play dolls in our tent," Karissa said.

"Tara and I," Jen corrected.

"Seth, wanna play catch?" Stevie asked.

"Sure."

Jen stood in the middle of the campsite with her hands on her hips. "Well then, I guess I'll start dinner."

Later that evening, after a satisfying supper, they all sat around the campfire and roasted marshmallows. Before long, the children started to nod off and were sent to bed. In consideration of Fred's condition, the Swenson tent was pretty quiet that night. The same was not true for the Charland tent. After tucking the children in, Billie led Cat back to their tent and gently laid her down on the sleeping bags. Covering the smaller woman's body with her own, she placed her elbows on either side of Cat's head and supported her weight on them.

Billie looked into Cat's face. "Cat, I have never known anyone as beautiful as you. I love you with all my heart. I feel honored that you have chosen to love me."

"You are so corny."

Billie raised an eyebrow. "Give me a break here. I'm trying to be romantic."

"Then kiss me."

Billie lowered her mouth to Cat's neck and gently brushed her lips across the tender skin. She ran her fingers through Cat's hair and tilted her head back, teasing Cat with several light, butterfly kisses.

Cat's breath caught in her throat. "God, Billie, you have no idea what you do to me," Cat exclaimed breathlessly as Billie nibbled on her neck.

Billie pulled back and looked at her. "If it's the same as what you do to me, then yes, I do know." She kissed her again then drew back to look into Cat's face.

Cat reached up with one hand and pushed a lock of hair

behind Billie's ear. "Your hair is getting long," she said. "Your bangs will need a trim soon."

"Yeah, it's getting there," Billie observed. "It killed me when they shaved all my hair off for the brain surgery."

Cat caught Billie's face between her palms. "Billie, you are, and will always be, the most beautiful creature on this earth. Dark or gray, young or old—nothing can mar your beauty in my eyes."

Billie smiled mischievously. "Are you trying to tell me that I'm getting old and gray, Mrs. Charland?"

Cat tried to look insulted. "Me?" she asked. "No, never."

"Because if you think for one moment that I can't keep up with you, you are sadly mistaken," Billie said, an evil glint in her eyes.

"Really? Care to prove it?"

Billie smiled wickedly. "I was hoping you'd ask, if you think we can make it through without fuck faces."

"Is that a challenge, my love? If so, you're on."

Hours later, Cat melted into the arms of the woman she loved and fell fast asleep.


The next morning, Cat was awakened by a nagging itching on her butt. When she reached back to scratch it, she encountered Billie, who was spooned up close to her. Cat wedged her hand down between their naked bodies and tended to the itch, only to be nagged by another one on the other cheek. "Damn." She rolled over onto her stomach and tried unsuccessfully to look over her shoulder at her butt.

Billie was awakened by Cat's fidgeting. She raised herself onto one elbow and looked at Cat. "Honey, what's wrong?"

"My butt itches."

Billie rubbed the sleep out of her eyes. "Run that by me again?"

"My butt itches, and I can't see why." Cat craned her neck.

"Roll over. Let me take a look."

Cat rolled onto her stomach, exposing her naked hind end.

"Holy shit!"

"What? Billie, what is it?"

"Cat, you have poison ivy."

Cat bolted up onto her knees and strained to see her buttocks. "How could I get pois—Oh, my God! I know how. Billie, get up, quickly. We need to check on Jen and the kids." Billie threw the blanket off and started to rise. "Ahhh! You're covered too. Even your chin!"

Billie looked down at herself. Dozens of red marks spotted her abdomen. "Damn! How are we going to explain this one?"

Cat quickly dove into their first-aid kit and retrieved the bottle of calamine lotion and a few cotton balls. "Hold still," she said, then proceeded to paint Billie's chin, abdomen, and thighs a pretty shade of fleshy pink before handing the bottle over to her. "Here, do my butt."

"Doing your butt got me into this mess," Billie joked.

"Ha ha, very funny, now dab, the itching is driving me crazy."

As soon as they were dressed, they climbed out of the tent, armed with the lotion. No sooner had they cleared their tent than they heard Jen's voice, loud and clear, coming in their direction.

"Thank you very much, Cat," she ranted. "The rest of you might want to take advantage of the pit stop, she says. It's a long hike back to the campsite, she says. Damn you, Cat. You can play connect the dots on my ass."

Cat approached Jen with her hands up, trying to calm the distraught woman. "Okay, Jen. I know. I have it too, and so does Billie."

"Billie? How did Billie get it? She wasn't even with us yester– Oh, I get it. You two rolled around like a couple of crazed weasels last night, and she caught it from you. Well, serves you right," Jen raged into their faces.

"Jen," Billie said in her best intimidating voice, "Cat had no way of knowing there was poison ivy in the bushes, so back off. Okay?"

Jen threw up her hands. "Okay, okay, you're right. I'm sorry. Question is, what do we do now?"

Cat held up the calamine lotion. "How do you feel about the color pink?"

Before long, each member of the camping party, save Fred, was doused in pink.

Throughout the day, other campers passing their campsite cast curious glances at the menagerie of gropers, each grabbing at various body parts, trying to get relief from the itching. After one particularly interested viewer passed by, Jen turned to Billie and said, "They probably think we have body lice or something."

Billie just chuckled and reached for the bottle of calamine.

# Chapter 24

# True Grit

Within a day or two, the Charland/Swenson clan recovered enough from the poison ivy to resume normal camping activities. Early on the second day after the poison ivy incident, they packed the cooler with sandwiches, soda, and chips and headed to the beach. The kids went straight for the water as the adults set up the blankets, beach chairs and umbrellas, near one of the picnic tables.

"Stay where we can see you," Cat called to the kids. "And stay away from the rock mountain."

"And before anyone goes into the water—sunscreen!" Fred added.

Soon the area was arranged, and everyone was settled in peacefully. Fred, healing but still sensitive from his sunburn, sat in the shade of the umbrella wearing a T-shirt, while the women rubbed oil on each other's backs before laying out on the blanket, all in a row on their stomachs with Cat bookended by Billie and Jen. They made an impressive sight – one tall and two of medium build; one dark, one gold, and one light; all slim and scantily clad in skimpy bikinis. Fred sat among them, proud as a peacock and laughing as one gawker tripped over his feet because he was too busy watching the ladies to look where he was going. Halfway through the morning, the ladies rolled over to sun their fronts after liberally spreading more oil over their lean bodies. Billie reached out and covered Cat's hand with her own, entwining their fingers.

After a time, the kids moved from the water to the beach and began building a large sand castle. The boys worked on the main structure, while the girls built castle walls and a moat surrounding the entire display. Skylar busied herself by filling the moat with water she repeatedly transported to the structure in a small red bucket.

Soon, Billie became bored with just lying in the sun. She opened her eyes and peered at Cat and Jen. Their eyes were closed, apparently asleep. A spark of mischief ignited in her belly as she grabbed a handful of sand. Grinning from ear to ear, she rolled onto her side and held her hand over Cat's chest. Very slowly, she allowed the grains of sand to trickle from her fist as she moved her hand slowly downward, across Cat's breasts and abdomen. Cat absently brushed them away in her sleep. Grabbing another handful of sand, Billie continued her path down one of Cat's legs and then up the other.

All the while Billie was engaging in her mischief, Fred watched, chuckling under his breath. "She's going to kill you when she wakes up," he warned.

"If she can catch me," Billie said, smiling at Fred.

When Billie was finished, she leaned back and observed her handiwork. Cat was covered with a fine layer of sand. "Not bad, if I do say so myself." She looked at Jen and glanced at Fred.

A smile broke out across his face. "Go for it!" he said.

Billie giggled with glee as she grabbed another handful of sand and proceeded to coat Jen with a fine layer, finishing just as Cat began to stir.

Cat felt an itchy sensation on her chest, just at the base of her throat. She reached up sleepily and began to scratch. Suddenly, she realized that something was wrong. She sat up quickly and felt a considerable amount of sand slide inside her bathing suit as her hand came away from her chest, covered in suntan oil and sand.

Billie moved quickly to her feet, ready to make her getaway.

"What the hell?" she exclaimed, coming instantly awake. She looked at Billie, who was standing beside the blanket. Cat could see she was trying to hold back her laughter. "Billllllllie!" she growled.

Cat looked at Jen and saw that she, too, was covered in

sand. "Jen. Jen!" Cat said, shaking her friend awake. "Jen, wake up."

Jen brushed Cat's hand away. "Leave me alone, I'm on vacation, for crying out loud!"

"You're also covered with sand!" Cat said.

"What?" Jen sat up abruptly. She, too, felt her bathing suit fill with sand. "Son of a b—Who did this?"

Hearing Fred chuckle, Cat and Jen quickly looked at him. He tried to keep a straight face. Assuming that Fred and Billie were probably in on the prank together, the two ladies jumped to their feet, scattering sand in all directions, except for the sand that was stuck to the lotion covering their bodies.

Fred and Billie looked at each other and said in one voice, "Uh-Oh!" then took off running toward the water with Cat and Jen right on their heels. When Billie reached the water's edge, her long legs allowed her to take huge leaps through the water until it reached mid-thigh, dramatically slowing her down and allowing Cat to catch up with her.

Working together, the two smaller women managed to grab Billie and Fred and pull them under the water. Fred and Billie promptly returned the treatment. Soon they were frolicking in the water like children, splashing and dunking one another, screeching and laughing hysterically.

In one particularly enthusiastic tackle, Cat pulled Billie down into the water by the straps of her bikini top. When Billie came up for air, her top didn't come up with her, but instead floated away from the splashing adults. Billie stood there in all her glorious bare- breastedness, water running in sheets from her hair, onto her breasts and back into the lake. At that very moment, Fred surfaced from a dunking of his own, coming up directly in front of Billie's erect nipples. All he could do was stare open-mouthed at Billie.

Cat pushed Fred backwards into the water and pulled Billie down. Turning around, she stood with her back to the taller woman in an effort to hide her wife's nudity from their friends. Fred resurfaced, spitting and sputtering. Jen clamped her hand over Fred's eyes and pulled him back under the water.

"Damn it, Jen!" he said. "You ruined my view!"

"Fred Swenson, you pervert!" Jen shot back, splashing a wave of water into her husband's face.

"Why, you little..." Fred growled as he took off after Jen, who was running as fast as she could through the water. He caught her almost immediately, picked her up and headed toward the shore. As he approached the beach, he stumbled over the bucket Skylar was using to fill the moat, lost his footing, and landed on top of Jen,right in the middle of the sand castle the children just finished building.

There was dead silence as the kids stood there, slack jawed, eyes bulging at the mess that was once the fruit of their labors. Stevie and Seth looked at each other incredulously, then yelled together, "Get 'em!" before charging the two adults who were lying in the middle of the sand pile. Soon the girls joined in and, between the five of them, they managed to bury Fred and Jen with sand and mud. All the while, Fred complained about the abrasive sand on his tender, sunburned skin, even through his T-shirt.

In the meantime, Cat retrieved Billie's bikini top and tied up the strings enough to make it back to the beach to get Billie's T-shirt. As they passed their neighbors lying in the mud, Jen looked up at the pair and cursed.

"Damn! I have sand in places that have never seen the light of day! I'll get you for this, Billie!"

Billie threw her hands up. "What did I do?"

"You and those killer breasts of yours! You should register them as lethal weapons!" Jen exclaimed, flashing them a brilliant smile.

"Yeah, you can hold me hostage with them anytime, Billie," Fred piped in, earning himself an angry glare from Jen.

"Well, you can just forget it, Fred," Cat said. "They're my lethal weapons, and I don't share!"

"Selfish bitch," Fred said under his breath.

Billie narrowed her eyes and took a step toward Fred. "What was that?"

"Shell... fish. I said shellfish. See, a clam, right over there. See?" Fred said nervously, pointing to a spot down the beach.

"I thought that's what you said," she replied. She turned to

Cat, smiled, and winked at her before taking her hand and walking back to the picnic table to prepare lunch, leaving Fred and Jen heading for the water to rinse off the gritty sand.

# Chapter 25

## War and Peace

The day at the beach turned out to be wonderfully relaxing, despite the striptease show and subsequent mud wrestling that resulted from Billie losing her bikini top in the water.

Considering that the adults' antics had totally destroyed the sand castle the children built, they committed themselves to assisting in the reconstruction and spent the rest of the day crawling around the sand like a bunch of ants, shaping and molding it into an elaborate labyrinth of buildings, roads, and walls.

The adults worked diligently, long after the children lost interest and retreated to the playground to pursue other activities. They made quite an I interesting sight – three women and one man, on their hands and knees, covered in mud from their knees to their toes, and from fingertips to elbows, scurrying around their creation like sand crabs. Finally they were finished and stood back to look at their work of art.

Jen placed her hands on her hips and cocked her head. What lay before them was essentially a small kingdom made of sand. "Kind of went overboard, didn't we?"

"Well, maybe the gallows outside the jailhouse was a bit much," Fred remarked.

Billie stood behind Cat, her sand-covered hands resting on Cat's shoulders. She too cocked her head. "Well, maybe, but where else would you put the gallows? I mean, if you're going to have a jailhouse, you need a gallows, right?" she reasoned. "We are talking about a medieval castle here, after all."

"I don't understand why we needed a jailhouse in the first place," Jen said.

"Where else would you put the bad guys?" Cat asked.

Jen walked over to Cat and took her chin in her hand. "Look, sweetheart, I know you're a history freak and really enjoy this medieval stuff, but for crying out loud, you didn't have to make stick men for the sand castle," she said in a raised voice as she motioned to the small stick figures standing by the gallows in the courtyard of their sand castle.

"What's wrong with them? They're cute," Cat said defensively.

"Cute? Cat, they're sticks. And that horse..." Jen stared.

"What's wrong with the horse? They didn't have cars then. They've got to have some sort of transportation," Billie commented over Cat's shoulder, a slight grin on her face.

"Well, I happen to have something against horses at the moment," Jen said. "Anyway, the people are just sticks with seaweed hair. The horse is a piece of rotting driftwood, with toothpicks for legs," she said.

Billie could tell Cat was becoming irritated with her friend's teasing. She thought about stepping in, but decided to let Cat handle it, hoping that she'd teach Jen when to back off. Fred started to reach for Jen's shoulder to stop her, but Billie caught his eye and gave him a look that said, "No, let them duke it out."

Billie placed a quick kiss on Cat's head, then stepped back and motioned for Fred to join her in a game of Frisbee while the other two ladies settled their dispute. Fred and Billie tossed the disc back and forth along the water's edge as they listened to phrases like "stifle what creative talents?" and "medieval mumbo-jumbo," not to mention "they're only stickmen, Cat!" while they watched the two women face each other, nose to nose, arms gesticulating wildly. After what seemed like an eternity, Fred and Billie stopped throwing the Frisbee and stood side by side, watching their wives argue. Billie elbowed Fred's ribs to draw his attention away from their wives to where she was pointing out over the water.

"Uh, girls?" Fred said.

Jen and Cat continued to argue. Billie covered her mouth with her hand to stifle a laugh.

"Uh, girls?" Fred said again, a little louder this time. "Girls!"

Cat and Jen turned together, hands on their hips, and yelled at Fred, "What!"

Fred pointed out across the water, getting their attention just in time for them to see a large wave sweep up over the shoreline, totally destroying the sand castle and soaking the two women clear to their knees.

"Ahhh!" Cat screamed. She threw her hands into the air and stomped off to the picnic table where she started packing up their belongings. Billie followed to lend a hand.

Jen stared in disbelief at the pile of sand that had been their castle. She looked at Cat's retreating form and pointed to the heap. "Creative talents, my butt! It's nothing but a pile of wet sand! And your stick men can't swim!"

Cat turned and her eyes shot daggers at Jen. Billie stopped her with an arm around her waist as she took a step toward Jen. Jen was just as ready and willing to go at it again as Cat was, but for Fred's restraining arm around her waist.

"That's enough, Jen," Fred said. "It was just a sand castle, for crying out loud."

Billie cringed at Fred's words and held onto Cat more tightly, knowing that the redhead would object to their friend's dismissive comment.

"Just a sand castle, Fred? Just a sand castle? I think not!" Cat fought to break free from Billie's grasp.

"Cat, honey, calm down. Look, we're all tired. It's been a long day. Let's just pack up and head back to camp, okay?" Billie successfully turned Cat back to their chores.

Fred grabbed Jen by the hand and propelled her toward the picnic table, where they all finished packing the gear, Jen and Cat throwing hateful looks at each other the whole time.

Back at the campsite, Cat vigorously shook the sand out of the blanket the adults had used at the beach and threw it over the clothesline to air out, while Jen stomped around, lighting the grill and making general preparations for their evening meal. A cold silence descended between the two ladies. The only sounds were from the children, who played amicably nearby, and a low murmur between Fred and Billie.

"What are we going to do about them?" Fred asked, inclining his head in the direction of their stubborn wives.

"I don't know," Billie replied as she added wood to the campfire. "You know, if Jen had only backed off about Cat's creative side, this could have been avoided."

Fred looked at Billie indignantly. "Billie, this is about a sand castle, a sand castle, not some award winning piece of art!"

Billie stood to her full height and stared at Fred, lifting an eyebrow into her hairline. "This is not just about a sand castle, Fred. This is about respecting someone's talent." She tried to be patient, but the tone of her voice belied the undercurrent of anger raging through her at his ignorance.

"Talent? Billie, it doesn't take a lot of talent to make a horse out of a rotting piece of driftwood, some seaweed, and toothpicks," Fred observed dryly.

Billie grabbed the front of Fred's T-Shirt and was pulling him closer when they were distracted by the sounds of the children yelling.

"You broke it!" Seth yelled.

"I did not," answered Stevie in a defensive tone.

"You did too. See, you broke the wheels off it," Seth exclaimed, holding out his toy car.

"Did not."

"Did too!"

"Did not!" Stevie repeated as he pushed Seth backwards.

Tara, who was playing off to the side with Karissa and Skylar, launched herself onto Stevie's back, dragging him to the ground and sitting on top of him. Cat was the first to arrive on the scene, and she managed to grab her daughter and drag her off Stevie before she could throw the punch she had cocked her fist for.

"All right, that's enough. Want to tell me what's going on here?" Cat demanded as the other three adults joined the group. Jen helped Stevie to his feet and brushed the dirt off his backside. Fred stood off to the side, his arms crossed in front of him.

"Stevie broke the wheels off my car, Ma," Seth explained angrily.

"I did not," Steve denied. "They were already like that."

"Enough!" Cat yelled, restraining Tara from lunging at Stevie again.

Billie reached out and scooped Tara up into her arms. "Okay, rug rat, calm down and tell me what happened," she said to her daughter.

"Mom, I saw Stevie push Seth. Let me go. I'm gonna pound him," Tara demanded, squirming to get out of her mother's arms.

Billie took Tara's chin in her hand and looked her straight in the eyes. "You'll do nothing of the sort, young lady. Do you hear me?" she scolded.

"But Mom!" Tara protested.

"I said no. Do you understand?"

Tara crossed her arms in front of her and stuck her bottom lip out in a pout. Billie set her back down on the ground and kept a restraining hand on her shoulder as she addressed the group. "All right, then," Billie said. "Seth, what happened here?"

"The wheels are broken off my car. Stevie was playing with it," Seth accused.

"Did you see him break the car, Seth?" Billie asked. Seth set his jaw firmly in place before shaking his head. "Well, then, you don't really know that he did it, right?"

Seth's forehead creased into a deep scowl. Kicking the dirt with the toe of his shoe, he said grudgingly, "I guess not "

"Okay, then, I think it would do us all some good if we split up for a while and cooled off," Billie suggested. "Okay?"

"That's a very good idea," Jen said. "Stevie, Karissa, I want the two of you to come over here for a while."

"And you three..." Cat said, beckoning to her own children "...can play together over here." She motioned to the opposite side of the campsite.

Cat watched as Fred led Stevie and Karissa to the picnic table and dug out the coloring books and crayons. Not realizing that Jen was still within hearing range, Cat muttered, "Spoiled brat" under her breath, indicating exactly what she thought of

Stevie's behavior.

Jen was on Cat in an instant, grabbing her shoulder and spinning her around.

"What was that?" she demanded, her nose within an inch of Cat's face.

Billie immediately grabbed Jen around the waist and pulled her away from Cat, depositing her on her butt in the bushes next to their own tent before returning to Cat. Billie glanced over at Fred and sent a silent message to him to keep his family on his side of the campsite for the time being. Fred nodded slightly as he helped a very angry Jen out of the bushes.

Not a half hour after the skirmish, the children were playing again, totally oblivious to what had caused their earlier spat. Promising to look after their sisters, Stevie and Seth escorted the girls to the playground just a short distance from the campsite, while their parents contemplated how they were going to fix dinner from their community food stores without talking to each other.

Billie watched her wife and their friend pace back and forth along the imaginary line dividing the campsite in half, each one sending furtive looks at the other as though sizing up an enemy for battle. Fred sat on the other side of the campsite, his head following them back and forth as if he was watching a tennis match. When Billie couldn't stand it anymore, she stood and raised her arms into the air.

"Okay, children, at this rate, we're all going to starve. Time to kiss and make up," she announced.

Jen and Cat stopped and looked at each other, then looked at Billie as though she was crazy.

Billie tried again. "The kids had a spat. It happens. They're already playing together again," she pointed out. "Get over it."

Jen and Cat turned their backs on each other and crossed their arms, each holding her ground, neither wanting to be the first to give in.

Billie stood with her hands on her hips, looking at the two women in disbelief. "I can't believe this," she said, exasperated. "You two are acting like babies."

Cat was the first to object. "She started it, Billie."

"Bullshit!" Jen exclaimed. "Your son started it."

Billie's feathers ruffled at the accusation, and she clenched her fists and jaw. She was tempted to show Jen just what happened to people who attacked her family, but instead, she took a deep breath and refused to be baited. Cat had no such reservations; she scooted around Billie and got into Jen's face, once again rehashing the argument about sandcastles and undisciplined children.

Billie held Fred back as he stepped forward to break them up. Beckoning him to follow her, she grabbed the bucket and dishpan and led him to the spigot. Seconds later, Cat and Jen found themselves doused with cold water, gasping for breath as they wiped the water out of their faces. Their eyes shot back and forth between Billie and Fred, who stood there grinning, empty containers in hand.

"Had enough?" Billie asked.

Cat was furious. She faced her attackers, hands on her hips, feet shoulder width apart. "You've got two minutes to explain why that was necessary, Billie," she demanded angrily.

Billie walked over to Cat and leaned down into her face. "It was necessary because the two of you..." she pointed to Jen without looking at her "...were acting like spoiled children who needed cooling off. That's why."

Cat looked at Jen, taking in the wet hair and dirt smudges on their faces and clothes. Cat grinned and covered her mouth with her hand to prevent a laugh from escaping. Jen looked shyly at the ground, then back at her friend, and broke into a full-fledged grin.

Billie stepped aside to let Cat pass as she walked over to Jen and extended her hand. Soon the two friends were laughing and hugging, apologizing for their behavior. After Cat and Jen cleaned up, they prepared burgers for the grill while Fred and Billie took care of stoking up the campfire and setting the picnic table for their evening meal. When they were finished, Billie fished two beers out of the cooler and handed one to Fred. They sat down side by side in front of the campfire while their wives completed preparations for dinner. Billie lifted her beer in toast to Fred, very proud of herself for resolving the feud between the two ladies. All of a sudden, they found themselves sluiced with sheets of cold water.

"What the hell!" she and Fred exclaimed together as they jumped out of their chairs and swung around to face their attackers.

Empty containers in hand, Cat and Jen smiled. "Paybacks are a bitch, love." Cat stood on tiptoe and kissed Billie lightly on the lips, then walked away, swinging the bucket.

# Chapter 26

## Bear With Me

Later that evening, after the children were asleep, the adults sat around the campfire contemplating their day. The atmosphere was infinitely more congenial than earlier that afternoon, but a hint of uneasiness remained. With their chairs in a semicircle around the campfire, Jen and Cat bookended by Billie and Fred, the friends sat quietly, staring into the flames. When the silence became unbearable, Cat reached toward Jen and placed her hand, palm up, on the armrest of Jen's lawn chair. Jen looked over at her and smiled, placing her hand in Cat's and lacing their fingers together in a bond of friendship.

"I'm sorry, Jen," Cat said softly, capturing Jen's gaze.

"Me, too," Jen replied, squeezing her fingers a little tighter around Cat's.

A more comfortable silence descended over the group like a blanket. After a time, Jen broke the silence. "Why do you think it happened, Cat?"

"I assume you're talking about our little disagreement today?"

Jen flashed Cat a crooked smile. "Yeah."

Cat took a deep breath and let it out slowly. "I don't know. It could be that we're not used to living in such proximity, and we're getting on each other's nerves," she reasoned.

"You may be right," Jen said. "In any case, I'm afraid we haven't set a very good example for the kids."

"Don't worry about the kids," Billie interjected. "They know better than anyone that it's okay to let off steam and then get on with the fun. Heck, they were playing again just minutes after they started fighting. We're the ones who couldn't let go of the anger. If anything, they set an example for us."

"Maybe you're right, Billie. Maybe you're right." Jen yawned.

"Looks like someone is tired." Fred clasped Jen's chin. "Ready to turn in, love?"

Jen smiled and nodded. She showered both of her friends with hugs and kisses before wishing them pleasant dreams, then following Fred into their tent.

Once Fred and Jen were gone, Billie doused the campfire, then reached her hand toward Cat, helping her out of her chair. Billie kissed each knuckle of Cat's hand in turn, all the while keeping her eyes on the fire.

Cat's heart began to pound wildly in her chest. She tilted her head to one side and closed her eyes as Billie's lips roamed over the sensitive skin on the back of her hand.

"Hmmm. I'll give you two hours to stop that," Cat whispered.

Billie responded by turning Cat's hand over and kissing her palm, then slowly working her way toward Cat's wrist to the tender skin on the inside of her forearm.

Cat gasped with pleasure as Billie's tongue flitted around the crook of her elbow and worked its way upwards across her bicep before finding the hollow on her neck carved out by her collarbone. Cat tilted her head back to allow Billie greater access to her neck.

Billie cupped the side of Cat's face and righted her head so that she was looking deeply into her eyes. Billie's gaze roamed over Cat's face, watching the firelight dance patterns across her lover's brow and set her hair ablaze with autumn colors.

"Cat, you have the power to stop my heart with one look." Billie's breath came in rapid pants.

Cat looked deeply into the depth of Billie's azure eyes, then leaned forward and touched her forehead to Billie's. She closed her eyes and whispered words meant only for Billie's ears. "Make love to me, Billie. I need to feel you. Make me yours."

Billie cradled Cat's face between her palms and kissed her with wild abandon, her tongue seeking and gaining access to the sweetness within. For long moments, the women tasted each other, tongues memorizing every hidden curve and crevice, faces canted to maximize their pleasure.

Soon Billie abandoned Cat's mouth and placed a string of kisses along her jaw line and down her neck. Cat clung to Billie's head by two handfuls of dark hair, holding her captive, begging for the nips and bites that were flooding her with spasms of desire.

"Billie... please." Cat grabbed at Billie's tank top, trying to push it down over her shoulder. "Please..."

Billie captured Cat's bottom lip between her teeth, before invading once more with her tongue. In one smooth motion, she reached under Cat's legs and easily lifted her up without breaking the contact between their mouths, and then walked toward their tent. Dropping to one knee, she rested Cat there as she reached over and unzipped their tent. Moments later, they were lying side by side on the sleeping bags, hands roaming over one another with an urgency born of heated sexual need.

Cat made short work of Billie's clothing, throwing each piece into the corner of the tent as she removed it from Billie's body.

"God, Cat, I want you so much," Billie growled as she pushed Cat's T-shirt over her head.

Cat arched her back to raise her chest closer to Billie. Billie accepted the blatant invitation as she leaned down to take Cat's sweet offering into her mouth, nipping and sucking, capturing the swollen nubs between her teeth until tiny cries escaped Cat's lips and tremors of desire radiated through her lover's body.

"Billie, you're driving me mad."

Just as Billie reached down to unbutton Cat's shorts, a loud shuffling noise sounded outside their tent. Billie's head snapped up, ears perked and listening for further sounds.

Cat's desire dulled her senses, and confusion set in at her lover's sudden retreat. "Billie, don't tease me like this, please," Cat begged, trying to pull Billie's mouth back toward her breasts.

Billie placed her index finger across her own lips. "Shhhh," she hissed, then she strained to hear.

"What is it?" Cat asked, finally realizing that something

else had caught Billie's attention.

"I don't know. Stay here, I'll be right back." Billie pulled on her shorts and T-shirt, then grabbed the flashlight and clicked it on. Holding the light out in front of her, she unzipped the tent and slowly made her way outside. She scanned the entire campsite with the bright yellow beam, allowing it to fall on each of the other tents, assuring herself that all was safe and secure.

During her walk around the perimeter of the camp, she came across a set of animal prints near the refuse barrel. Billie smiled to herself as she said under her breath, "Critters. Harmless enough. I must have scared them off." She scanned the site one last time. Satisfied they were safe, she turned back toward their tent, looking forward to an evening that promised to bring out her own animalistic nature.

Had anyone else been awake, they would have been convinced that there were indeed wild critters around, at least two of them, critters that growled and groaned, and occasionally giggled before shrieking out in near ear-piercing tones, and then quieting down for the night.

The early hours of the next morning found Cat and Billie entwined in a lover's embrace, to the point where it was not obvious where one naked body started and the other left off. It was in this position that they greeted the dawn. It was from this position that Cat struggled to free herself in order to answer the call of nature. Finally escaping the circle of Billie's arms, she quickly located and donned her T-Shirt and shorts before making her way out of the tent and up the trail to the bathhouse.

Cat was still half asleep as she walked to the bathroom and back, her eyes barely open. Her intention was to return to bed, to the arms of her wife. It was with these thoughts that Cat approached their campsite. It was with these thoughts that she blindly walked toward their tent and nearly into the arms of an intruder—a tall, hairy, black, 300 pound intruder, with big teeth and sharp claws. Cat stopped dead, a mere twenty feet separating her from their visitor. Paralyzed with fear, she did the only thing she could think of, she screamed.

Within seconds, the entire campsite erupted, as did a few neighboring sites. The bear reared up onto its hind legs, teeth exposed, guttural growls emanating from its throat. Fred, Jen, and Billie hurried from their tents. All five of the kids were still inside their tents, but peering out through the unzipped windows. Shrieks were coming from the girls' tent, while exclamations of "Wow!" and "Cool!" came from the boys.

"Everybody freeze," Billie shouted. "And don't make any threatening moves," she commanded.

Cat stood her ground, frozen to the spot, terrified as the face-off began. The bear dropped to all fours and slowly moved toward Cat.

"Cat, please don't move," Billie urged.

Cat stood ramrod straight, not moving a muscle as the bear circled and sniffed her. "Oh, God! Oh, God!" Cat muttered under her breath.

When the bear apparently decided that Cat was just a weird looking tree, he walked away from her and pursued his original goal – raiding the food stores. Within minutes, the food locker was torn open and the rest of the supplies eaten or scattered about by the carnivore. All the while, the two families were rooted where they stood, motionless and terrified.

The bear made short work of their food supplies, then turned and sauntered back toward the forest, but fell short of his goal, victim of a tranquilizer dart from the park ranger's gun. One of the neighboring sites had apparently summoned the ranger, and he had arrived in time to stop the perpetrator from fleeing the scene of the crime. Fortunately for the campers, the only victim had been their food supply.

As soon as it became obvious the bear was down for the count, Cat ran to Billie and wrapped her arms around her waist. She was shaking and in a state of shock. Billie wrapped her arms around Cat and held her close, as she silently asked Fred and Jen to check on the kids.

When Cat calmed enough to take in her surroundings, she leaned back in Billie's embrace and looked into her face. "Do you always have to take things so literally, love?"

Billie was confused and raised an eyebrow in query. "Bare

essentials. Bare necessities. Barefoot In the Park. Or, in this case, in the campground," Cat prompted as she ran her eyes up and down Billie's body.

All of a sudden, Billie realized that she was standing there stark naked, surrounded by her friends, family, the park ranger and neighboring campers, not to mention one comatose black bear. "Holy shit!" She dove for the cover of their tent.

Cat threw her head back and laughed. "I can barely take all this excitement," she exclaimed.

"Caaaatttt!" came the warning voice from inside their tent.

Cat continued to pick. "Bear with us, Billie. We'll only tease you about this for say... a week."

"Caitlain Maureen O'Grady Charland, stop that right now!"

"Uh-oh. She's using my full name," Cat said to the audience of friends and family. "I'm shaking in my boots out here, Billie. I can't possibly bear up under this burden of fear," she teased.

Without warning, Billie shot out of the tent, fully dressed.

"Holy Zeus," Cat exclaimed as she turned and ran as fast as she could down the trail, a grinning Billie close on her heels.

# Chapter 27

## You Can Lead a Horse to Water, But You Can't Make It Cook

Billie and Cat returned to the campsite to find the park ranger talking to Fred and Jen, while another ranger stood over the unconscious bear with a second tranquilizer dart at the ready. The children huddled nearby, anxious to get a good look at the bear.

"Ma'am, I'll have to ask you all to vacate your campsites until arrangements can be made for the zoo to collect this animal," the park ranger said.

Billie looked around. "Okay. I guess we can go into town for breakfast."

"Sounds good. Let's take two cars so Jen and I can hit the grocery store on the way back. I'm afraid the bear demolished our supplies," Cat said.

Fred looked at Billie. "I guess that means we're on babysitting duty."

"Yep, that's what it means," she replied.

Jen headed for their tent. "Okay, then, let's get this show on the road."

They had only a couple of days left before their camping trip was over, so shopping didn't take nearly as long or fill as much space in the car as when they set out almost two weeks earlier. The ladies arrived back at the campsite and stowed away their food. This time they were sure to store it well out of the reach of critters, in plastic bags hung high in the trees.

Cat looked around the abandoned campsite. "I wonder where everyone is?" she said.

"Probably at the park or the beach," Jen guessed.

"Maybe we should go find them."

"Are you nuts? We actually have free time to ourselves for a change. Let's enjoy it, girlfriend."

Cat placed her hands on her hips, a look of wonder on her face. "You're right! What was I thinking? Okay, what do you want to do?"

Jen walked over to the ice chest and extracted two Wild Berry wine coolers. She handed one to Cat, then unscrewed the cap on hers and sat down in one of the reclining lawn chairs. "I, for one, am planning to relax, read, sleep, and enjoy a refreshing cooler on a hot summer day, not necessarily in that order."

Cat took the hint and quickly retrieved a book from her tent, then pulled her own lawn chair beside Jen. "Cheers," she said as they clinked bottles.

The next several hours were spent as Jen predicted— drinking wine coolers, reading, drinking wine coolers, talking, drinking wine coolers, singing, drinking wine coolers, giggling... all in that order. By the time the rest of the family returned to the campsite, there were eight empty wine cooler bottles on the ground under the lawn chairs, and two very relaxed, giggly ladies sprawled on the chairs.

The boys were the first ones to arrive at the site just before sunset. "I won!" Seth said as he tagged the picnic table before Stevie.

"No fair. You had a head start," Stevie whined.

"You're both whiners... I mean winners," Jen said as she saluted them with a wine cooler.

The boys turned to look at her. "Mom?" Stevie said. "Are you drunk?"

Cat leaned forward and squeezed her thumb and forefinger together. "Maybe a tiny bit."

The boys took one look at each other and ran back in the direction they had come. Cat and Jen burst out laughing.

Within minutes, Billie and Fred arrived. Billie stood at the foot of the lawn chairs, hands on her hips, and looked down at the two women. "Just what do you two think you're up to?" she asked.

Cat looked up at Billie. "What're we up to? Well, I'm about five foot-four. What about you, Jen?" she asked, a shit-eating grin on her face.

Jen looked up, as though trying to see the top of her own head. "I don't know, probably five-six. What about you, Oh Incredibly Sexy Tall One? What're you up to?"

Jen and Cat broke into peals of laughter at Jen's remark.

Billie tried to hide the grin threatening to break out on her own face. Shaking her head, she walked away from the ladies and back to Fred.

"They're shit-faced! Looks like you and I get to cook supper tonight."

A chorus of groans rose from the children at the mention of Billie and Fred cooking.

"Mom, is that a good idea?" Seth asked. "The last time you cooked, I was able to use the hamburgers for hockey pucks."

"Your cooking tastes like doodoo," Skylar whined.

Billie's eyes narrowed at her daughter's choice of words. "Thanks so much for the compliments, kids," she answered. "Well, Fred, how are you at cooking?"

"No," Stevie and Karissa chorused in panicked voices.

"Guess that answers that question." Billie ran her hand through her dark locks. "Okay, boys," she said to Seth and Stevie, "rummage through the food supplies and find something I can't possibly screw up, okay?"

While the boys sorted through the groceries Cat and Jen had picked up that day, Billie pulled Fred closer to the campfire where she could see the bandage on his face more clearly. She pulled the bandage from Fred's nose. "You took a nasty hit." After replacing the bandage, Billie turned to re-pack the medical supplies, and noticed that their spouses had full bottles of wine cooler in their hands. "Now where the hell did you get those?" she said, exasperated.

Cat and Jen grinned at Billie and tried very hard to look innocent while they swayed back and forth in their chairs, just barely able to keep their balance. "From the cooler, while you were making out with my husband," Jen answered, raising her bottle in Fred's general direction.

"Making out? Jen, I wasn't... Oh hell, Fred, come here."
She beckoned to him. When he didn't move fast enough, she
grabbed his arm and pulled him over to put him on display in
front of Jen and Cat.

Jen shrieked when she saw the bandage on her husband's
nose. She sat up quickly and nearly fell off her chair. "Oh my
God, Fred! What happened?"

"Croquet," he said.

"Crow kit?" Cat repeated. "What the hell is that?" She
belched loudly. "Ooops! Sorry." She covered her mouth, cheeks
glowing red in drunken embarrassment before she and Jen fell
into a fit of laughter.

"No, croquet. We were playing croquet, and the big guy
here hit me right in the nose with her ball," Fred explained,
pointing to Billie, who was standing nearby looking guilty.

It was Cat's turn to sit up quickly, only she wasn't as
graceful as Jen, and succeeded in falling flat on her face on the
ground next to the lawn chair. Miraculously, she managed to
keep the wine cooler from spilling when she fell.

Billie shook her head and helped Cat back into the chair. "I
think you've had enough wine, Cat," she said, reaching for the
cooler in Cat's hand.

"Nooooo!" Cat pulled her drink in close and held on to it
tightly. "Mine!" she insisted.

"Okay," Billie said. "It's your head."

"Speaking of heads, what did you do to my husband?" Jen
asked, and then took another long drink from her wine cooler.
Billie sat Cat more securely on the lawn chair, then turned to
Jen. "Like he said, we were playing croquet. I hit his ball, so I
had the right to send it flying. It's not my fault that he was
standing in the line of fire," Billie protested. "We rushed him to
the clinic for treatment. He has a broken nose, and will sport
very attractive raccoon eyes for a couple of weeks," she added.

"And I'm having trouble breathing," Fred wheezed.

Further discussion on Fred's mishap was interrupted by
Stevie and Seth, who proudly dropped their selected food onto
the picnic table.

Billie turned to the boys. "Did you find something edible?"

They stepped aside and revealed their idea of a good supper. There on the table were cookies, chips, pretzels, cold cereal, cold hot dogs, and several cans of soda.

The commotion at the picnic table drew the girls away from their dolls. They approached the table and saw the snack food lying there. "Is this for supper?" Tara asked hopefully.

"Yep," Seth said with pride. The three girls cheered and jumped up and down, Skylar clapping her hands gleefully.

"Whoa, wait a minute. I didn't say this was for supper," Billie interrupted.

The cheers immediately died down, followed by exclamations of "Aw, Mom!"

Billie looked at Fred, and then back at the snack food on the table. Suddenly realizing she didn't have to cook any of it, she said, "Aw, what the heck, eat up."

All five children jumped for joy as they dove into the goody pile and quickly devoured everything on the table.

# Chapter 28

## Come On, Baby, Light My Fire

"What are we going to do with them?" Fred asked.

Billie looked over her shoulder at Cat and Jen, who had each just opened another wine cooler. "I say, let 'em go. Their hangovers tomorrow morning will pretty much prevent this from happening again. Besides, they're kind of funny."

"You're right, but I could do without the singing."

Billie turned from tending the campfire to look at Jen and Cat, who were gyrating wildly on their lounge chairs.

"'I feel the earth move under my feet,'" they sang in melodious disharmony while chair dancing.

"We'll have to shut them off soon, you know. Otherwise, we'll get kicked out of here for violating the late-night noise ordinance,"

Fred said.

Billie looked at her watch. "It's only 8:30 pm. If we're lucky, they'll either pass out or run out of coolers soon," Billie replied.

"It would have been nice to at least get some dinner into them to soak up the alcohol."

Billie chuckled and placed her hand on Fred's shoulder. "Fred, if you had a choice between wine coolers and our cooking, which would you choose?"

"You've got a point there. I'm just worried they'll be sick."

"They probably will. Serves them right if they are." Billie turned her attention back to the campfire. "This looks like it's just about ready for s'mores."

Moments later, the kids were all holding long sticks with fluffy marshmallows over the fire, while Fred and Billie helped

Cat and Jen move their chairs closer. No sooner had their butts hit the seats than they began singing again.

"'Come on, baby, light my fire,'" Cat sang badly.

"'Try to set the night on fire!'" Jen screamed, holding her wine cooler and her right leg high in the air.

The kids looked at them and rolled their eyes.

Cat straddled the lounge chair, her feet on the ground on either side. She held her wine cooler high and leaned forward. "Oh, I got one for you."

"Sing it, girlfriend," Jen squealed.

"You hafta use yer 'magination. Pretend I'm Elmer… ah, Elmer… Damn, I forgot his name."

"Who you talking about?" Jen asked.

Cat swayed side to side. "You know, the guy on Bugs Bunny."

"Oh, I know who you mean. The wascally wabbit guy," Jen said.

"That's him." Cat thrust her wine cooler in Jen's direction, spilling some of the contents. "What's his name?"

Jen thought for a moment. "Elmer Fox."

"It's Elmer Fudd, Mama," Skylar said.

"Thank you, baby girl. Isn't she smart?" Cat said with pride.

Jen nodded. "Very smart."

"So where was I? Oh yeah – you have to use yer 'magination an' pretend I'm Elmer Fudd."

Billie looked at Fred. "Brace yourself, Fred. I've seen her do this sober, and it isn't pretty."

Cat sat up tall on her lounger and held her wine cooler out in front of her. "I dwivin' in my caa, I tuhn on the wadio," she sang, her voice slurred. "You move a wittle cwooooooseh, I just say no."

All eyes at the campsite were on Cat. The kids began to giggle.

"You say you don't wiiiiiike it. I say you'weh a wiiiiiar. When we kiss… oooooo, fiiiiweh."

Jen threw herself back in her lounger in a fit of laughter, which caused the foot of the chair to rise in super slow motion until she was flat on her back with the foot section of the lounger folded on top of her.

Cat, Billie, and the kids roared with laughter while Fred ran to Jen's aid. "Jen, are you all right?" he asked.

"I'm fine, just don't spill my wine," Jen said. "Hey, that rhymes."

"Mom, can we do the sparklers?" Seth asked.

"Yay, sparklers!" Tara chimed in. "Can we, Mom?"

"Sure. I'll get them." Billie returned moments later and handed out sparklers to the kids. "Now be sure to hold them away from yourself so you don't get burned," she said as she and Fred lit each one.

Seth and Stevie immediately pretended they were swords and began fencing with them.

"Hey, you two, be careful not to hit each other with those, they're hot," Fred warned.

"I wanna do it too," Cat said

Jen nodded vigorously, her head bobbing. "Me too."

Billie and Fred simultaneously turned and said, "No!"

For the next hour, the adults watched the kids make circles and draw their names in the air with the sparklers.

"Okay, rug rats, time to hit the sheets," Billie said when the last sparkler had burned out.

Billie put the girls to bed, while the boys quickly retreated to their own tent. While Fred cleaned the campsite of spent sparklers, Cat and Jen each opened another wine cooler. He stopped in front of them. "Haven't you two had enough?"

"Chill, Freddie-boy. We're on vacation," Jen said.

Fred shook his head and settled into his chair by the fire. Moments later, Billie joined him. "Are the girls all tucked in?" he asked.

"Yes. Of course, they'll talk for the next hour or so before falling asleep."

"Of course. The boys beat feet awfully quickly to bed."

Billie glanced at the boy's tent, its interior lit by a flashlight. "They'll settle down soon."

Fred glanced at Cat and Jen, sitting side by side in lawn chairs by the fire, leaning against each other and holding half empty bottles of wine coolers in their hands. They were giggling almost uncontrollably between sips of wine. "They'll sleep well tonight," he said.

"Well, they'd better, because they'll be in a lot of pain tomorrow when the hangovers set in." Billie threw another log in the fire ring before settling down comfortably in her chair.

Fred stared at the fire for several minutes in a lengthening silence, until at last Billie said,

"You okay?"

"Yeah. I'm fine."

"You don't look fine. You look like you've lost your best friend." When Fred shrugged, she persisted. "Okay, spill it. What's going through your mind?"

"I'm worried about Jen."

Billie glanced at their wives. "Like I said, they'll be sorry in the morning."

"No. I mean, I'm worried about Jen and me," Fred said.

Billie frowned. "Really? Things seem fine between you two, at least in front of Cat and me."

"It's not something I can put my finger on. I... Hell, I sometimes wonder if she'd rather be with a woman."

Billie sat back in her chair. "Really? What makes you think that?"

"Well, look at her and Cat. There are no inhibitions between them."

"That's because they're drunk off their asses," Billie said.

"That's not it. She really loves Cat. She loves both of you. I've never seen her behave this way with anyone else."

"Well, we love her too, Fred. And she may love Cat and me, but she is in love with you."

"I want to believe that."

"Has she said anything to you?"

"Well, after she and Cat came back from the spa, she asked me if I would try to be a little more sensitive with her. I'm not sure what she meant by that."

"I think I might know." Billie leaned forward and put her hand on Fred's arm. "What she needs is for you to be more in touch with how she's feeling. You know – ask her how her day went when you come home from work, ask her opinion about things, pay her compliments. That's one of the benefits of being in a same-sex relationship. We connect on the same level emotionally."

"So I've got to be less like a guy and grow some ovaries?"

Billie smiled. "Something like that."

"Well, I'd appreciate a nudge now and then, if you don't mind."

"Gladly." Billie picked up a long stick and poked at the fire. "So, can I ask you a question?"

"Ask me anything."

"Do I seem different to you?"

"What do you mean?"

"Cat says I'm different than I was before the surgery."

"Do you feel any different?"

"Kind of. I don't feel as confident as I used to. In fact, sometimes I get this anxious feeling in the pit of my stomach, like something catastrophic is about to happen."

"Well, you've been through a lot in the past year."

"She also says I seem angrier."

"I can honestly say I haven't seen that side of you."

"Well, I have. I've caught myself being impatient with her for no reason at all. I don't understand it, but sometimes I almost feel like I'm baiting her on purpose, maybe to see what she'll do."

"Do you feel like you need to test her? Cat is as loyal as the day is long."

"That's just it. I don't know why I do it. It would kill me to lose her, so I totally don't get why I try to push her away sometimes. Hell, when I thought she was having an affair with Jen, I wanted to die."

"You thought she was having an affair with Jen! When did that happen?"

"When I was still in the hospital and my memory hadn't returned yet. Cat was my lifeline, and every day Jen would come in, and they would hug and hold hands. I have to admit I was really jealous."

"Jen is that way with both of you all the time. Like I said

earlier, she loves you both very much."

"I know that now, but at the time, it really bothered me. My point is, I know what it feels like to be jealous and to worry about losing Cat, so I don't understand why I sometimes intentionally needle her."

"Maybe you should discuss it with your doc when you get home."

Billie nodded. "That's just what I plan to do. Thanks for listening. I feel better about it already. At least something good will come out of this trip."

Fred stared at the fire. "You know," he said, "this really hasn't been such a bad vacation."

Billie looked at him like he had grown another head. "Well, I guess that depends on what you call bad," she commented dryly.

"What do you mean?"

"Where do I begin? Let's see…" Billie ticked the negative events off on her fingers. "Flat tire on the highway, lecherous waiter, missing tent poles, water snake." She rose to her feet and began to pace. "Trigger, Horse from Hell, poison ivy, sunburn, killer hornets, bear attack, broken nose, drunken wives, lost cell phones. Am I forgetting anything? Oh yeah, how could I forget? Dueling neighbors, a regular Hatfield and McCoy feud between Cat and Jen." Billie stopped in front of Fred. "Christ, Fred, the only thing that hasn't tried to ruin this vacation is a rainstorm."

No sooner were the words out of Billie's mouth than a large clap of thunder resounded and lightning tore across the sky.

"You just had to go and say it, didn't you?" Fred admonished.

Billie looked up at the sky and shook a fist in defiance. As she looked back at Fred, her attention was suddenly drawn toward a rapid flickering of light in the boy's tent. "Fred," she started.

"Mom! Help!"

Smoke began to billow from the screens as the nylon material melted before their eyes.

"Oh my God! Seth, Stevie!" Billie and Fred ran to the tent

and ripped it open, allowing the boys to escape.

"I'll get water," Fred said as Billie checked out the boys.

After Billie was sure the boys were okay, she grabbed each of them by a shoulder. "What the hell happened?"

Seth began to cry. "We lit sparklers in the tent, and the tent caught on fire."

Fred dumped a bucket of water on the burning tent and went back for more.

"You did what? What were you thinking!" she barked

"I'm sorry, Mom."

"Me, too," cried Stevie.

Billie hugged both boys as Fred dumped a third bucket of water on their tent. "Thank God you're not hurt. You scared the life out of me. Do you realize what could have happened?"

Both boys nodded.

"That should just about do it," Fred said. "Want to tell me how this happened?"

"Sparklers," Billie answered.

"Holy Jesus!" Fred replied. "You two could have been killed. It could have spread to your sisters' tent as well."

The boys struggled with their tears.

Fred hugged his son. "Don't ever do anything like this again, do you hear me? If we ever lost you to something foolish like this, it would kill your mother and me."

"I won't, Dad," Stevie said.

"All right. Since your tent is ruined, I guess you'll have to sleep with us tonight. Go on and crawl in. Your mom and I will join you soon," Fred said.

"You too, Seth," Billie said. "You'll have to sleep with Mama and me. Go on."

Billie watched the boys retreat to their parents' tents. "How the hell did they get the sparklers?" she asked.

"They must have stashed a couple while all the kids were playing with them." Fred shook his head. "I hope they've learned something from this."

"No doubt. I guess we'd better spread the sleeping bags out and douse them again to be sure they won't flare up," Billie suggested.

Before Billie and Fred could move, large drops of water began

to fall from the sky.

"Strike that. I think Mother Nature will take care of it for us," she said.

# Chapter 29

# Texas Chainsaw Massacre

"Fred, quick, get Jen into your tent. After the girls are inside, I'll take care of the campfire," Billie said.

Billie took Cat's arm. "Come on, Cat, into the tent with you."

"Hey, I'm having a drink with my best girlfriend. I don't want to go to bed," Cat protested.

"No choice. It's starting to rain."

"You too, Jen," Fred said. "Let's go."

"I know I'm as sweet as sugar, Fred, but I promise I won't melt," Jen replied.

Cat gave Jen a high five. "That's a good one, Jen. I'll have to remember that one."

"Sugar or not, you're going to bed." Fred hoisted Jen into his arms. "I'll be back in a minute to help with the fire, Billie."

"Come on, Cat, party's over," Billie said.

"You're no fun," Cat protested as she allowed Billie to lead her to the tent.

Back at the fire, Fred and Billie worked together to douse the flames. "I can't believe those two were totally oblivious to the boys' tent catching fire," Fred said as he spread the coals.

"I suspect they'll be sorry for their night of fun come sunrise," Billie said. "Once they experience the hangover and memory loss, they'll think again about doing this." Just then, the heavens broke open and the deluge began. "See you in the morning, Fred," Billie shouted as she ran to her tent.

"Ditto."

Billie, Cat, and Seth sat in their tent for long moments,

listening to the torrential rains cascading around them. "You realize everything we have is getting soaked out there right now," Billie said. "The chairs, the beach towels."

"I left a bag of chips on the picnic table," Seth said.

"Well, it'll be mashed potatoes by morning," Cat joked.

"Did you and Steve hoist the food bags back into the trees, Seth?" Billie asked.

"Yes."

"At least those will be safe from the bears. I just hope the bags don't fill up with rain."

"Billie, did you grab the wine coolers?" Cat asked.

"You've had enough wine coolers, Cat."

"What's that noise?" Seth asked.

"Noise?" Billie said.

"Yeah. It sounds like yelling."

"I don't hear anything."

"Billie, I want another wine cooler."

"Cat, you don't need another wine cooler. Now please be quiet so I can hear."

"There it is again," Seth said.

Billie frowned. "Sounds like Fred and Jen arguing. Maybe I should check it out." She reached forward to unzip the tent and came face to face with a saturated Fred, Jen, and Stevie. Fred was holding Jen up, who was still too intoxicated to stand on her own.

"Our tent collapsed. The ropes let loose from the trees. Can we come in?" Fred asked.

"Of course, of course." Billie made room for her soaking wet guests.

Jen immediately crawled over and snuggled up against Cat, who was totally oblivious to the woman's wet state. They immediately fell into spasms of giggles over their predicament. Billie shot a look in their direction and just shook her head.

"Jen, come over here beside me. That's Billie's spot," Fred said.

"No. I'm sleeping next to my best friend."

"Let them be, Fred. Better they breathe booze breath on each other than on us," Billie said.

Stevie and Seth moved as close to the side of the tent as

they could to make room for the adults. "This is cool," Seth said.

Fred was very apologetic. "I'm really sorry about this."

Billie placed a hand on his shoulder. "Relax. Why don't you get out of those wet things and scoot over here under the covers?

You too, Jen."

"But we'll be in our underwear," Fred said.

"Fred, I love you dearly, but trust me. You have nothing I'm interested in."

Soon all four adults were lying side by side in the small tent, with Billie and Cat wedged between Fred and Jen. Seth and Stevie squeezed into the space between Jen and the side of the tent. Just as everyone settled in, a loud clap of thunder ruptured the silence. Within seconds, the zipper opened and all three girls piled in.

"What the… You girls need to go back to your tent," Billie said.

"We're scared," they whined, almost in unison.

"Great. Just great," Billie mumbled.

"Why is everyone in this tent?" Tara asked.

"Our tent burned down," Stevie said. "It was awesome!"

Billie looked at Fred. "Your son has a warped sense of humor."

"He gets it from his mother."

"Mom, can we sleep with you?" Tara wheedled. "The thunder really scares us."

Billie looked at the pitiful expressions on the girls' faces. "All right, all right. You'll have to squeeze in where you can find room."

Within moments, Fred was sleeping and Billie was drifting in that world between sleep and wakefulness, listening to Cat and Jen giggle well into the night.

Billie was dreaming she was strolling through the woods, the birds chirping in the background, the sound of dry leaves crunching underfoot. She marveled at the beauty of the trees, breathing the smells of the forest deeply into her lungs. In the distance, she could hear a sound—a rumbling, low and growly. A motorcycle? she thought. The sound grew louder and closer. She stood in the midst of the trees, trying to locate the origins of the sound. Suddenly a tree fell beside her, then another, and another. The forest quickly thinned around her until there was one tree left. As the last tree fell, she saw the chainsaw, and it was coming directly for her, growing louder and louder as it approached, the teeth on the chain threatening to tear her from limb to limb. As it closed in on her, she stumbled and fell.

"Noooo!" Billie sat bolt upright in the tent and looked around wildly. On one side of her were Cat and Jen, still giggling in a state of alcohol-induced silliness, and on the other was Fred, snoring like there was no tomorrow.

"Chainsaw," she said, her heart moving from her throat and back down into her chest. She lay back on the sleeping bag and looked up at the ceiling of the domed tent. Giggles to the left, Texas chainsaw massacre to the right. What did I ever do to deserve this? She covered her face with her hands and released a long sigh. "This is going to be a long night!"

# Chapter 30

# Barfing in the Briar

On the verge of wakefulness the next morning, Billie felt a heaviness on her chest. It was so intense, she had trouble breathing. She also had a headache, and her body felt stiff and sore, so much so, she found it difficult to move her arms and legs. In her half wakened, half sleeping state, she imagined herself gravely ill. After much struggle, she was able to turn her head sideways and open her eyes in search of Cat. It was then she realized that she wasn't ill at all. In fact, she was trapped in her own bed. Skylar was sleeping on her chest, hence the weight, and Billie was wedged tight between Fred and Cat, to such an extent that she couldn't move a muscle. To top it all off, the humidity inside the tent, made worse by the early morning sun beating down on them, was suffocating, which enhanced the smell of smoke, alcohol, and body odor. Billie lay immobilized. *Why did I agree to this camping trip? Oh yeah, Cat played on my vulnerabilities, that's it. "Sweetheart, don't be such a baby," she says. "You'll have fun," she says. Some fun. This has been the worst vacation of my life. It's almost over, Billie. Just hang in there... for Cat.*

Billie really needed to use the bathroom. The question was how to dislodge herself from the sardine can without waking the other fishies. Little by little, she worked one arm free, and then the other. Next, her legs. With her arms free, she was able to gently push Cat's leg off her thigh, but her other side, she was literally stuck to Fred's bare leg. Ewww! *Remind me again why I don't sleep with men!* Slowly, painfully, she peeled her skin away from Fred's hairy leg, bringing back memories of the vinyl seats in her parents' car in the summertime. She bit her tongue to stifle her groan, but her leg was free, albeit minus a layer of skin. The final segment was to shimmy out from under Skylar. Billie thanked the heavens above that her youngest daughter was a sound sleeper.

Billie sat up and looked around the tent. There were bodies packed shoulder to shoulder, from one end of the tent to the other, making it impossible for her to retrieve clean clothes and shower gear, so she unzipped the tent, extricated herself from the tangled mass, then stepped out into the fresh morning air.

The campsite was a total disaster zone. Fred and Jen's tent was leveled, Seth and Stevie's tent was a pile of melted nylon, and the girls had left their tent unzipped when they left it in the middle of the night, so everything inside was undoubtedly soaked. There were wine cooler bottles scattered on the ground; the potato chip bag left on the table the previous evening had been picked up by the wind and its contents were scatted all over the site; the beach towels that were hung on the line to dry the night before were now sitting in the mud below the line; and critters had apparently invaded the trash can and strewn its contents everywhere. "Holy shit! This site looks like a bunch of cavemen live here," Billie said. "But the cleanup will have to wait until I get back from the bathroom."

When Billie returned from the bathroom, Fred was up and busy cleaning the campsite. "Looks like a tornado came through here last night," he said when he saw her.

Billie put her hands on her hips. "Fred, answer me honestly. Are you having fun?"

Fred grinned. "Actually, yes. Stuff like this is all a part of camping. I have to admit, we've had a little more bad luck than normal on this trip, but I can honestly say I've enjoyed it."

"Bad luck? Is that what you call it? I, for one, think it's the Furies."

"Furies?"

"They're characters from Greco-Roman mythology, three sisters named Alecto, Tisiphone, and Megaera. They were the goddesses of vengeance and known to torment their victims psychologically."

"You might be onto something there, but regardless, it

wouldn't be a real camping trip without a few mishaps," Fred said.

"I guess I just wasn't cut out for roughing it."

"You'll look back on this someday and laugh," Fred said. "At least you'll have some stories to tell."

"You got that right!" Billie retrieved a trash bag from the screen tent and began picking up the debris around the campsite.

Fred took the bag from her. "I'll make you a deal. I'll pick up the trash if you set up the coffee pot. I think our wives are going to need a good strong cup when they finally roll out of bed."

"Are you sure?"

"Positive. Besides, I kind of need a cup myself."

"Deal."

Signs of life emanated from the tent by the time the coffee finished brewing. All five of the kids apparently woke at the same time, as they appeared one by one and made their way to the bathhouse, ultimately returning to the picnic table where Billie served them cereal and juice for breakfast.

"That was fun with all of us sleeping in one tent last night," Skylar said.

"Speak for yourself, little one. I hardly had any room to sleep," Billie said.

Tara said matter-of-factly, "Uncle Fred, you snore really loud."

"Sorry about that."

"Mom and Aunt Cat were really funny last night," Stevie said.

"I've never seen my mom drunk before," Seth observed. "It was kind of weird."

Stevie nodded. "I know. My mom was just as bad."

Billie and Fred exchanged glances over the kids' heads. "I suspect neither of them will feel very good this morning, so it might be a good idea if you guys keep the noise down until they feel better," Billie suggested.

"Maybe we can go to the park," Tara said. "Karissa and I will take Sky with us."

Seth shook his head. "I'd rather go fishing."

"Me, too," Stevie agreed.

"That sounds good. Boys, I'd rather you fish in the stream instead of the lake. Maybe you can bring home some trout for dinner," Billie said. "Girls, you can go to the park without an adult if you go to the one just across the road there, so we can keep an eye on you from here."

"Aw, Mom. We're not babies, you know," Tara complained.

"I agree. It's not about you being babies, it's about making me feel better. Okay?"

"Okay." Tara put out a hand to her sister. "Come on, Sky."

A short time later, Fred and Billie were cleaning up the last of the storm damage on the campsite. They were just beginning to disassemble the boys' tent when Cat and Jen emerged.

Cat climbed out of the tent holding her head. "Kill me, please," she whimpered.

"Me first," Jen said from behind her.

Both women stopped short when they realized what their spouses were doing. "What happened to the boys' tent?" Cat asked. "Was it struck by lightning?"

Billie took Cat's and Jen's hands and led them to the picnic table inside the screen tent. Fred ran ahead of them and poured two cups of coffee. "Sit," Billie said.

Cat sat, propped her elbows on the table, then cradled her head in her hands. Jen sat, crossed her arms on the table, and laid her forehead on them. Neither one touched her coffee.

"What do you remember from last night?" Billie asked.

"What part of last night?" Jen moaned.

"Any part of it."

"Umm." Cat couldn't come up with anything on such short notice.

"Do you remember singing?" Fred asked.

"Singing?"

"Yeah, Elmer Fudd," Billie supplied.

Cat crossed her arms and lowered her head onto them. "Oh

my God. Please tell me I didn't do that."

"You did it, all right."

"How much did we drink?" Jen asked.

Fred pointed to the line of bottles artfully arranged on the picnic table near the fire ring. "You can count them yourself, but there's at least sixteen bottles there."

"Holy Mother of God! No wonder I feel like shit," Cat said.

Jen sighed. "Did we do anything to embarrass ourselves, other than the singing, that is?"

"Well, you accused me of making out with Fred," Billie said.

"I what?" Jen looked up at her husband. "Oh my God, Fred. How did you get the black eyes?"

"Billie punched me for making out with her." Jen's mouth dropped open, and he quickly said, "Just kidding. Billie and I took the kids to the park while you were shopping for groceries. I was injured in a lively game of croquet."

"I woke up in Cat and Billie's tent this morning. How did that happen?" Jen asked.

"Take a look at our tent, Jen." Fred pointed to the heap on the ground. "Don't you remember? It fell down in the middle of the storm last night, and you and Stevie and I had to bunk in with Billie and Cat and Seth."

Cat raised her head. "We all slept in the same tent?"

"That's right," Billie said. "Seth and Stevie burned their tent down last night, so it was all six of us, until the girls got scared by thunder and climbed in with us as well. Trust me when I say it was not a great night for sleeping."

"The boys burned their tent down! Are they hurt?" Cat asked.

"No. Luckily we were still up when it happened," Billie said. "The little shits lit sparklers inside their tent, and it went up in a matter of seconds. Fred and I reached them in time to get them out before they were hurt, but the tent was destroyed, along with their sleeping bags."

Cat gaped at Jen. "I... I don't remember any of it. Do you?"

Jen shook her head.

"That's the last time I touch wine coolers!" Cat proclaimed.

"At least in that quantity," Billie qualified.

Jen suddenly stood up. "Oh my God. I gotta go." She covered her mouth with her hand.

"Oh no, you don't, not in the food tent." Fred grabbed her arm and led her to the bushes.

Billie looked at Cat. "Cat?" Cat covered her mouth and nodded. Billie took her arm. "Let's go."

Jen and Cat were bent over the bushes, with Billie and Fred hovering nearby. "Are you guys okay?" Fred called. When the sounds of vomiting came in reply, he backed away. "Okay. We'll just be over here cleaning up the boys' tent."

# Chapter 31

# Whipped Pussy

Billie and Fred spent the morning roping the Swensons' tent back to the trees, so it could dry out after the previous night's rain, and so they could sleep in their own quarters that night. While they worked, Cat and Jen laid on the loungers, nursing headaches and upset stomachs. Around noon, the kids returned to the campsite for lunch.

"What's for lunch?" Tara called as she and the other girls returned to the campsite.

Cat rose from her lounger and went over to her daughter. She tucked an errant lock of hair behind Tara's ear. "What would you like for lunch, sweetie?"

Tara shrugged. "I don't know. A sandwich, maybe?"

"Sounds good to me," Karissa said.

"I think I can manage that. Why don't you three go wash your hands." Cat turned to Jen. "Are you up for a bite to eat?"

Jen joined her at the picnic table. "Not especially, but I'll give you a hand making lunch. Billie, Fred, are you hungry?"

"Be right there," Fred replied. "We've got just one rope left to secure." He and Billie stood back and admired their handiwork.

"What do you think?"

"I think it looks like the Persistence of Memory," Billie replied.

Fred frowned. "The what?"

"Persistence of Memory. You know—that painting of the melting clocks by Salvador Dali."

Fred placed a hand on Billie's shoulder. "You, my friend, are weird."

"What do you mean?"

"I mean you're weird. Who on earth would ever think that looks like melting clocks?"

Billie shook her head. "Fred, I didn't say it looked like melting clocks. What I was implying is that the way the tent sags at the bottom suggests it's melting, like the clocks in Dali's painting."

Fred crossed his arms and stared at the tent. "I still don't see it."

Cat approached the pair as they contemplated the tent. "Are you two going to eat? Hey, that looks like Persistence of Memory," Cat said.

Billie turned to Fred. "I rest my case." She put her arm around Cat and escorted her toward the picnic table. "I'd love some lunch."

Fred looked again at the tent, then at the retreating backs of his friends. "You're both weird!" he called after them.


Stevie and Seth returned to the campsite just in time to join their families for lunch. They carried with them a stringer of medium sized trout.

"Nice catch," Billie said. "I'll help you dress them right after lunch."

"Count me in. I'll help as well," Fred added.

Seth proudly held up the stringer. "I think there's enough here for dinner."

"I hope I'm feeling better by then," Jen said. "I'd hate to miss out on fresh trout."

"Still not feeling good, huh?" Billie asked.

"I'm better than I was this morning, so maybe by dinner I'll be back to normal."

Billie nodded at Cat. "How about you?"

"I'm okay. A slight, lingering headache, but otherwise I'm good."

"That's great, 'cause Fred and I plan to take the kayaks out after we help the boys dress the fish." Billie smiled.

"We are? I mean yes, we are."

"What are we gonna do?" Tara asked.

Billie picked up the Happy Trails Campground booklet on

the picnic table and leafed through it. "Says here there's a miniature golf course and roller skating rink on the premises."

"Cool! Can we go, Mama?" Tara asked.

"I wanna go, too," Skylar said.

Fred paddled his kayak alongside Billie's. "I hope we're not in too much trouble when we get back."

"Why would we be in trouble?"

"Well, we kind of stuck the girls with the kids. I'm not sure that was such a good idea, what with their hangovers and all."

"I think it's good for them. Maybe they'll think twice about getting shit-faced again." Billie grinned at Fred. "You're not pussy-whipped, are you, Fred?"

"So what if I am? Hell, I only win about five percent of our arguments, so I tend to choose my battles. Most of the time it's easier to give in and let Jen have her way."

"That can't be very satisfying for you."

"Well, if you want to know the truth, she's usually right. How about you? I mean, who wears the pants in your family?"

"We both do."

'Yeah, right."

"No, really. I'm not saying I don't give in and let Cat have her way occasionally, but when I feel strongly about an issue, I stand my ground."

"Occasionally, huh?"

"Yes, occasionally."

"You mean, like this camping trip?" Fred teased.

"That's not fair. Cat was so excited about this trip I just didn't have the heart to say no."

"I'm willing to bet she used the libido card on you and you caved, just like my tent in the storm last night."

Billie grinned. "Busted." Suddenly distracted by an unusual noise, she scanned their surroundings. "What's that?"

"Beats the hell out of me."

Billie rested her paddle across the bow of her kayak. "Stop paddling, Fred. I want to isolate where the sound is coming from."

Billie listened intently as they glided silently through the water. "Hey! It's my new cell phone. I didn't recognize the ring tone."

Billie dug the phone out of her pocket. "Hello? … Yes, this is Billie Charland. Yes, my wife purchased it for me. Yes, I said 'my wife.' So far, so good. I haven't really used it much yet. No, I don't think I have any questions at this point. Okay. Thank you for calling."

Billie tapped the touchscreen to end the call.

"That was a pretty cryptic call. Who was it?"

"It was the cell phone company asking how I like my new phone and wondering if I had any questions."

"How do you like it?"

"So far, so good. Look. I can get on the Internet, and it has a GPS." Billie leaned over to show Fred the phone. "Whoa!" she screamed as the cockpit of her kayak began to fill with water. "Lean the other way," Fred shouted.

"Too late." The kayak rolled, dumping Billie, and her new cell phone, into the lake.

"Billie!" Fred yelled at the hull of Billie's kayak.

Billie surfaced a few feet away, as her lifejacket buoyed her above the water. "My phone!" She thrust her hand out of the water in an attempt to keep her brand new cell phone from the depths of the lake.

While Billie bobbed, holding her phone above her head, Fred paddled over to recover her kayak, which was drifting downstream. He managed to snag the handle on the bow and pull it over to him, then rolled it upright. "There's no way you're getting back into this thing without being on dry land," he said. "Give me your phone, and then swim to shore. I'll tow your kayak to you."

"Good idea," Billie said.

Fred set Billie's phone on the floor of his own kayak and paddled toward shore while Billie swam. Along the way, Billie's kayak worked loose from the bungee cord Fred had used to secure it to his own boat, and it was heading toward the rapids. Billie stopped to rest, looking back at Fred to see how he was progressing. "Ahhh! Fred, my kayak is loose!"

Fred snapped around quickly and lunged for Billie's kayak.

Billie watched in dismay as his kayak was upended.

\* \* \*

Billie and Fred walked along the path toward their campsite, each carrying a lifejacket and wearing soaking wet clothing. Billie's hair hung in tufts around her shoulders.

"Cat's going to kill me," Billie said.

"Relax. She'll be happy you're okay." Fred didn't sound as if he had even convinced himself.

"No, she's going to kill me." They walked in silence for the next few moments. "She's going to kill me," Billie said with a sigh.

"Billie, will you stop saying that? She's not going to kill you."

"You don't know what she's like when she's pissed, Fred."

"Cat's a reasonable person. She'll understand."

"First, we leave them with the kids, and now this. It won't be pretty."

Fred stopped. "I thought you weren't worried about leaving them with the kids."

"I lied." Billie looked around. "Maybe we can find the road and hitchhike home," Billie suggested.

"Now who's pussy whipped?"

# Chapter 32

# Hello Kitty

When Billie and Fred strolled back into the campsite, Cat looked up from setting the picnic table for dinner. "Well, it's about time you got—What the f—You're wet!" Cat said.

"Soaked is more like it," Billie replied.

Jen brought a plate of hamburgers to the table. "Where're the kayaks?"

"Uh…" Fred stammered.

"Actually, Fred and I have to go find them," Billie said.

"Find them? What do you mean, 'find them?' And why didn't you answer your phone when I called you?" Cat asked.

Billie looked at Fred and grimaced. "Well—"

"Don't tell me," Cat said. She paced back and forth while Billie looked on nervously. Finally, she stopped in front of her. "Where's your phone, Billie?"

"Um… at the bottom of the lake."

"Really? Really, Billie? It was brand new! How could you drop your phone into the lake?"

"And why are you wet, Fred?" Jen asked.

"I was towing Billie's kayak to shore, and it got away from me. When I reached for it, my kayak rolled. That's kind of when Billie's phone drowned."

"So here you are, your brand new, expensive phone sitting at the bottom of the lake and no kayaks," Cat repeated.

"That about sums it up," Billie agreed.

"Great, just great!"

"I'll ask again," Jen said. "Where are the kayaks?"

"They floated downstream into the rapids," Fred replied.

"God knows where they are now!" Cat said.

"That's exactly why Fred and I need to go look for them

while we still have daylight. Come on, Fred," Billie said.

Billie and Fred climb into Billie's car and sat there for a few moments. Finally, Billie got out and approached Cat. "Car keys?" she said.

"We're lucky it's dark," Billie said.

'Yeah. Maybe they won't notice the damage so much,' Fred replied.

"I'm surprised we found them at all."

"It was probably a good thing they went over the rapids without us. As much damage as they sustained, we might have been looking at something much worse than a drowned cell phone," Fred said.

"You got that right. We're here," Billie said as she pulled the car into the campsite. They could see their wives and children sitting around the campfire, toasting marshmallows.

"We're back," Billie announced.

"Yeah," Cat said dryly.

Jen waved her marshmallow stick at them. "Did you find the kayaks?"

"Yes, but not the paddles," Fred answered.

"There are a few burgers left, but they're cold," Cat said.

"Cold is good," Billie said in as cheerful a voice as she could muster. "How 'bout you, Fred?"

"I'm fine with cold. I'm so hungry I'd eat dog poop right now."

"Ewww!" the kids said in unison.

Billie and Fred retreated to the screen tent to devour a quick dinner of cold hamburgers and chips.

"Shit!" Billie whispered. "We're in big trouble."

"I'll say," Fred replied. "It's colder than a witch's tit around that campfire."

"Well, prepare for another Ice Age when they see the kayaks tomorrow morning."

"I don't think I'll sleep a wink tonight, just worrying about it," Fred said.

Billie shook her head. "You're right, Fred. We're

whipped."

"Who wants another s'more?" Billie asked.

"I do, Mommy."

"Okay, Sky. Why don't you run over to the screen tent and grab another pack of graham crackers for me."

"Mom, can you sing that funny song you do when we have a fire in the backyard?" Seth asked.

Billie glanced at Cat. "I'm not sure Mama is in the mood for that song."

"Aw, come on," Seth begged.

"All right."

Billie cleared her throat and began to sing. "'Put another log on the fire. Cook me up some bacon and some beans. Go out to the car and change the tire. Wash my socks and sew my old blue jeans. You can fill my pipe, and fetch my slippers, then boil me up another pot of tea. And put another log on the fire, babe, and then come tell me why you're leaving me.'"

Billie spared a glance for Cat, who was not smiling.

Seth grinned. "Sing some more, Mom."

"'Now don't I let you wash the car on Sunday? Don't I warn you when you're gettin' fat? Ain't I gonna take you fishin'? Well, a girl can't love a woman more than that. Ain't I always nice to your kid sister? Don't I take her driving every night? So, sit here at my feet 'cos I like you when you're sweet, and you know it ain't feminine to fight.'"

Fred cringed.

"'So, put another log on the fire. Cook me up some bacon and some beans. Go out to the car, pick it up and change the tire. Wash my socks and sew my old blue jeans. You can fill my pipe and fetch my slippers, and boil me up another pot of tea. Then put another log on the fire, babe, and then come tell me why you're leaving me.'"

Seth clapped. "Yay!"

Billie took a deep breath, hoping she hadn't just dug her grave deeper. Suddenly she realized Skylar hadn't yet returned with the graham crackers. She turned toward the screen tent. "Sky–"

"Hi, pretty kitty," Skylar said.

Billie froze. "Sky, honey, don't touch the kitty. Walk away slowly," she said in an even tone, which got the attention of everyone else around the campfire.

"Mom! It's a skunk!" Seth yelled.

"Skunks aren't white, idiot," Tara said to her brother. "They're black with white stripes."

"Well that one is white," Seth said. "And you're an idiot, not me."

"That's enough," Cat warned.

Everyone sat on the edge of their seats.

"It's not a skunk, Mommy," Skylar said. "It's a white kitty."

"Sweetie, it's a skunk," Billie confirmed.

"But, Mommy…"

"Cat, Jen, Fred, slowly get the other kids away from the campsite. I'll grab Skylar," Billie said evenly.

Very slowly, the seven occupants around the campfire rose to their feet and tiptoed toward the adjacent site where the cars were parked. Once the rest of the campsite was evacuated, Billie gingerly took a step toward Skylar. "Don't move, honey."

"But, Mommy–"

"Shh. Please don't move, Sky."

The skunk paced nervously within feet of Skylar as Billie slowly tiptoed closer. Finally Billie was close enough to reach her daughter. The skunk turned around the moment Billie lifted Skylar into her arms. All Billie could do was turn her back on the animal to protect Skylar from the spray, then it ran off into the bushes.

Cat tore across the campsite and took Skylar from Billie's arms, then ran back to the other campsite.

"Oh, gross, Mom!" Tara yelled.

Seth held his nose. "That's an understatement."

"Oh my God, I'm going to puke," Jen said.

Billie took a step toward her family. A chorus of "no" rang out, stopping her in her tracks.

"Billie, go wash it off," Cat said.

Billie obeyed, rinsing her bare legs under the faucet at the edge of their campsite while the rest of her party stayed as far away from her as possible. Try as she might, the intense odor lingered.

The kids all pulled the necklines of their T-shirts over their noses. "Mama, this is gross," Tara whined.

"How do you think I feel?" Billie said.

"It'll take hours for this smell to dissipate. How are we going to sleep tonight?" Jen asked.

Fred raised his hand. "I vote we get a hotel room in town."

"I second the vote," Jen added.

"Fred, you're supposed to be on my side!" Billie said.

"All bets were off as soon as the skunk entered the picture," he said. "Sorry."

"Cat?" Billie said.

"I... I don't know what to say, Billie. Jen's right. There's no way any of us will sleep with this smell."

"Fine. Just fine. Desert me then. I'll just say right here with the stench. Some family you are."

"Bye, Mom," Seth, Tara, and Skylar said as they ran to the car.

# Chapter 33

## Woof—Woof Woof—Who Let the Dogs Out?

"Billie. Billie, wake up."

Billie opened her eyes and squinted against the brightness of the sun. "What?"

"We're back," Fred said.

"What time is it?"

"A little after eight. Did you spend the whole night out here?"

Billie sat up and rubbed her eyes. "Yes. I didn't want to contaminate the tent or bedding. Where is everyone?"

"They've all run to the bathhouse. Look, you were right about the kayaks. The girls were pretty upset this morning when they saw the condition they're in."

"Well, there's not much we can do about it now."

"True enough, but I wanted to warn you."

"Thanks." Billie settled back in the lounger. "Phew! I still stink."

"We stopped at the store and picked up some stuff to get rid of the smell. Hopefully it'll work."

Seth and Stevie came running into the campsite and stopped short. "Ewww, Mom. You still smell rancid."

"Thank you, son. I love you, too."

"Come on, Stevie, let's grab the poles and catch us some fish."

Billie watched as the boys ran down the path toward the stream until the sounds of rumbling drew her attention to her stomach. "Guess I'd better set up the coffee pot. Did you guys eat?" she asked Fred.

"Yes, but we brought you back some breakfast. Hold on

and I'll get it for you."

Fred retrieved Billie's breakfast from the car while she rose to her feet and stretched her back. Billie accepted the pastries and coffee. "Thanks. I'm here to tell you, that lounger is not the most comfortable bed in the world."

"I'll bet. Oh, here come the girls."

Cat stopped at the car and took out a bag. "Billie, come over here," she said abruptly as she emptied the contents of the bag onto the picnic table.

"I'll get the old milk jug out of the trash," Jen said.

"Trash? Just what are you planning to do to me?" Billie asked.

Cat didn't answer.

Billie watched as Jen cut off the top half of the milk jug to create a plastic bowl, and then rinsed out the sour residue. *I guess I can't smell any worse than I do already*, Billie thought. "So, what are we making?"

Again, Cat didn't answer.

"We're making a potion to make you smell beautiful, my darling wife," Billie provided in a high-pitched voice.

Cat scowled.

Billie took that as a sign that she'd better maintain a low profile while Cat got over her anger about the kayaks.

Cat poured two bottles of hydrogen peroxide into the plastic bowl, along with a quarter-cup of baking soda and a couple drops of liquid dish soap. Billie's eyes widened as the mixture began to fizz.

"Turn around." Cat saturated a cloth in the mixture and applied it to the backs of Billie's legs. "Now the front."

"What now?" Billie asked as she stood there with wet legs.

"Let it set for at least five minutes, then go rinse it off," Cat replied.

"So you are talking to me," Billie said.

Cat scowled again and turned her back on Billie. "Jen, maybe we should go check on the girls at the park."

"Sounds good to me."

Fred and Billie watched them go. "If it makes you feel any better, they haven't talked to me at all this morning either," Fred said. "It appears we're in the doghouse."

"Woof woof."

# Chapter 34

## Drown My Sorrows

The five children were settled in for the night, and the four adults were sitting around the campfire.

"If you're still talking to Seth and Stevie after they burned their tent down, why aren't you talking to us after we wrecked the kayaks?" Billie asked.

"Yeah, why aren't you talking to us?" Fred repeated.

Cat crossed her arms and glared at them. "Because you should know better, you're adults."

"If you use your imagination, maybe," Jen said.

"Do you think we intentionally wrecked the kayaks?" Billie asked.

"You didn't want to come on this camping trip to begin with. Who knows whether it was intentional or not?"

"Really? Do you actually believe I would destroy my own property just to make a point?"

Cat shrugged. "I don't know what to think. Do I believe you did it on purpose? No, I don't, but I'll be damned if I have a clue as to why all this shit has happened to us from the minute we set out on this trip."

"I think it's been a pretty fun time," Fred said.

Jen stared at her husband in disbelief. "You're kidding, right?"

"I admit we've had a few mishaps, but it's still been fun."

"Fred, name one thing that's been fun," Billie challenged.

"Horseback riding."

"Hello?" Jen said. "Does Trigger, Horse from Hell, strike a familiar chord?"

"Okay, how about the beach."

"Nudist colony, Billie going topless, sand castle fight," Cat said with a grimace. "Need I say more?"

"I kind of liked Billie going topless. Ow!" Fred rubbed his arm. "That hurt!"

"You deserved it," Jen said.

"Okay, how about fishing?" Fred suggested.

"Sunburn?" Billie reminded him.

"Oh, yeah."

"Let's also not forget poison ivy, hornet stings, snakebites and, of course, Pepe LePew," Billie listed.

"Don't forget the bear. That's one of my favorites." Fred leaned out of the reach of Jen's swinging hand. "Missed me. Ow! That's no fair, Billie," he said as he rubbed his other arm.

"That's one episode I'd rather forget, Fred," Billie said.

"I guess it has been a rather... unpredictable vacation," Fred admitted.

"And an expensive one at that," Cat said. "One flat tire, two lost cell phones, one melted tent, and two destroyed kayaks. What could possibly happen next?"

"Don't jinx us, Cat," Billie said.

"At least the kids have had fun," Jen said.

"Except maybe when Seth and Stevie burned their tent down," Billie said. "I'm guessing that scared them shitless."

"And I don't think anybody particularly enjoyed the poison ivy," Cat said.

"Well, we only have tonight and tomorrow night left," Billie pointed out. "I am so looking forward to sleeping in my own bed, with no bugs, air conditioning, and a working bathroom."

Cat yawned. "Speaking of bed, I'm ready to hit the hay."

"Me, too. Sleeping on that lounger last night was not what I'd call restful. I'm beat," Billie said.

"You two go ahead, I'll take care of the fire."

"Thanks, Fred. Good night, Jen. We'll see you in the morning," Cat said.

\* \* \*

Cat and Billie cuddled close together on the far side of the air mattress, not because they were being romantic and not because they were cold and wanted to share body heat. They slept on the very edge of the mattress because Seth was sprawled out nearly diagonally across it.

"Cat, you're pushing me off the mattress," Billie complained.

"I can't help it. Seth's hogging the bed."

"Nudge him over."

Cat tried to push her son over a foot and only succeeded in moving him a few inches. "We probably should have bought him and Stevie a new tent instead of letting him sleep with us."

"It didn't make sense to spend the money with only a couple of nights left."

Cat again tried to push Seth over, this time gaining about a foot. "That's better," she said as she rolled onto her back. "Great, just great. Now I need to pee."

"The flashlight's in the corner."

Cat groped around until she found the flashlight. When she clicked it on, it was pointed directly at Billie.

"Hey!"

"Sorry!"

Cat fumbled with the zipper of the tent door for what seemed like an eternity before she finally stepped out into the open air. A cool breeze immediately hit her square in the face. She found her sandals positioned on the mat just outside the tent, slipped them on, and headed down the trail to the bathhouse. The wind seemed to be picking up as she made her way over the small bridge which spanned the stream from which Stevie and Seth liked to fish. Bathroom chores completed, Cat washed her hands. As she dried them, a sudden bolt of lightning lit the sky and a rumble of thunder reverberated through the bathhouse.

"Damn it! I hope I can make it back to the tent before it rains." No sooner had she thrown her hand towel away and opened the bathhouse door, than the deluge began. "Son of a bitch."

She switched on her flashlight and headed down the trail on a dead run. The rain was coming in sheets, and she ran with her head down to keep the stinging droplets from beating against her face. As she ran, the beam from her flashlight bounced off the raindrops, the trees, and the ground, causing a surreal strobe-like effect in the darkness. She lost her bearings and totally missed the footbridge, running headlong into the stream.

"Ahhhh!" Cat screamed as she plunged into the cold water and fell on her face.

She struggled to her feet and stood in the knee-deep water, looking around desperately for her flashlight, only to see it was submerged in the water. She reached into the water and retrieved the light, hoping the flickering bulb would stay lit long enough to get her back to the campsite.

Cat waded to the far side of the stream and climbed the bank, then used what was left of the light to locate the path back to camp. The flashlight died after two steps. She shook it. "Damn you, come back on!" She shook it again, this time with enough force to dislodge it from her hand. A distinct plopping sound told her exactly where it landed.

"Now what am I going to do?" Cat strained to see into the darkness. "Calm down, Cat. Think. Which way did the path go?"

Cat inched her way forward in the darkness, hands stretched before her like antennae to warn her of anything she might be about to encounter. Soon she was able to make out a faint light in the distance and moved toward it. As she drew closer, she realized the light she was seeing was inside their tent. That gave her the courage to move faster. "Thanks for the homing beacon, Billie," she whispered to herself.

"Billie, unzip the flap," she called as she neared the tent.

"Cat, where are you?" Billie called into the darkness.

"Here. I'm here." Cat dropped to her knees in front of the tent.

"What took you so long? I was about to set out to find you. Quick, come inside."

Cat ducked in through the opening.

"Oh my God, you're soaked. Is it raining that hard?" Billie asked.

"I fell into the stream. And I lost the flashlight."

"You what? How the hell did that happen?"

"I lost my bearings. The wind, the rain, I had a hard time seeing the trail."

"Get those wet clothes off, Cat."

"I can't do that. Seth is in here."

"He's sound asleep. Nothing short of food would wake that kid. If it'll make you feel better, I'll hold the blanket in front of you."

Moments later, Cat sat in the middle of the tent wearing a dry T-Shirt and panties. A blanket was wrapped around her shoulders, and Billie sat beside her.

"Listen to that wind howl," Billie said.

Just then, the tent heaved inward, and then expanded like a balloon. Cat flinched. "Oh my God. I hope the tent holds up."

"It sounds like a rocket getting ready for lift off."

"Maybe we should check on the girls."

"They'll be fine as long as they stay in their tent. It's well staked to the ground. I'm more concerned about Fred and Jen's tent staying tied to the trees. I really don't want to spend another night with the Texas Chainsaw."

"Texas Chainsaw?"

"Yeah, Fred's snoring. Oh, that's right—you and Jen were too shit-faced to remember that lovely evening."

Cat clasped her head between her hands. "Oh, God, don't remind me. My head hurts just thinking about it."

A sudden strong gust of wind bent their tent in half, the dome pressing down against Billie and Cat. Cat looked at their son. "I can't believe he's sleeping through this."

For the next hour, they sat side by side, listening to the sound of rain pelting the nylon fly protecting their tent. The pressure gradients gave the tent a semblance of life as it breathed in and out. Finally, the intensity of the storm waned, and they felt safe enough to lie down.

Cat lay wrapped in Billie's arms, her head tucked under Billie's chin. "Thanks for coming on this trip, love. I know it hasn't been much fun."

"No comment."

"I just want you to know that I appreciate it."

"You're welcome."

Cat snuggled in closer and kissed Billie's neck. "Goodnight, my love."

Billie kissed Cat's head. "Goodnight. Sweet dreams."

They were lulled to sleep by the monotonous drumming of rain above their heads.

# Chapter 35

# Happy Trails to You

Billie emerged from the tent the next morning into a campsite filled with sunshine. A slight breeze cooled her skin, and birds chirped cheerily from the branches above.

"Quite a switch from last night," she mumbled as she looked around. A noise from across the site drew her attention. She saw Jen climbing out of her own tent. "Jen, you're up early."

"Correction, I've been up most of the night. Tell me you didn't sleep through that hurricane."

"Not well. I half expected to wake up this morning, and say, 'Toto, we're not in Kansas anymore.'"

"I'm surprised our tent held up. Every time the wind moved the branches around, the tent went with them."

Billie looked around. "Looks like we have a mess to pick up again."

"We should have put the chairs away before we turned in. We'll be lucky to find them all."

"First things, first. I need to hit the bathroom," Billie said.

"Amen to that. I'm with you."


"Mom, we found another one," Seth said as he and Stevie carried one of the camp chairs into the site and placed it with the others around the campfire ring.

"Where was it?" Billie asked.

"We found it in the stream near the bridge. Oh, and we found this flashlight, too. It looks just like the one we have."

Billie took the flashlight from Seth and tossed it to Cat, who gave her a coy look. "That's because it is ours," she said.

"How did our flashlight get into the stream?"

"We'll save that story for another time," Cat said. "So, there's only one chair still missing."

"There it is, Mama," Skylar said.

"Where, sweetie?"

"Up there."

All eyes turned to the branches above Fred and Jen's tent.

"Holy moly!" Fred judged how high up the chair was lodged. "How are we going to get it down?"

"I can climb the tree, Dad," Stevie offered.

"I don't know about that," Fred said. "You might fall— Hey, where did you go?"

"Give me a boost, Seth," Stevie said as he grasped the tree trunk. Within moments, he had dislodged the chair from the branches. "Dad, catch," he said as he dropped the chair into Fred's waiting arms.

Cat shoved a bread wrapper into the trash bag. "That should be the last of it."

"It amazes me how destructive Mother Nature is sometimes. There was trash everywhere," Jen said.

"I'm glad we had the foresight to zip the food tent before we turned in. At least that mess was contained."

"Speaking of food, what do you say we get breakfast started?" Jen suggested.

Cat and Jen worked side by side to set up the camp stove for a brunch of scrambled eggs and sausage. "Would you mind grabbing the milk and butter from the cooler, Jen?" Cat asked. "Thanks." Cat looked at Jen from the corner of her eye as she beat the eggs. "What do you suggest we do today?"

"Good question. We've already shopped, hiked, ridden horses, spent time at the beach and at the park, visited the hot springs. What else is there to do?"

"Yeah. As much as I like being on vacation, by the end, I'm anxious to go home."

"Especially when you run out of things to do," Jen said.

"I wouldn't mind hiking again," Cat suggested.

"Just as long as we stay out of the bushes."

"Very funny, Jen. Really, though, a hike sounds good. We'll take a vote during breakfast."

"Sounds like a plan. Pass me the bread, and I'll make toast."

"Ma, I really don't want to go hiking again," Seth objected.

Tara nodded. "Me, either."

"What do you suggest we do then?" Cat asked.

"The new Transformers movie came out just before we left home. Maybe it's playing in town," Stevie offered.

A round of "yeahs" rang out from the children.

Jen grimaced. "That's not my idea of fun."

"To tell you the truth, hiking doesn't sound that great to me either," Billie said. "How about Fred and I take the kids to the movie, while you two go on your hike? What do you think, Fred?"

"Works for me."

"It's settled then. We'll go to the office for a newspaper after breakfast."

While Billie, Fred, and the kids were at the office, Cat and Jen got ready for their hike.

"I don't know how we lucked out, but a hike with the just the two of us is going to be heaven," Jen said.

Cat leafed through the campground brochure. "There are several trails to choose from. Do you have a preference?"

Jen looked over Cat's shoulder. "Something a little more challenging than the one we went on with the kids."

"How about this one?" Cat pointed to the trailhead pictured in the brochure. "Camelback Mountain, moderate difficulty. It says the hike is about five miles each way, and the trails are well marked."

"I can do moderate."

"Okay then. Sunscreen, ball caps, snacks, sweatshirts, raincoats, bug spray, water. Did I miss anything?" Cat asked as she zipped her backpack.

"How about your cell phone?"

"Why don't you bring yours? If anyone calls us, it'll be Fred, and he's likely to call your cell. Billie's phone was buried at sea, remember?"

"How could I forget? Should we bring a flashlight?" Jen asked.

"I don't think so. We'll be back long before dark."

"In that case, it sounds like a complete list."

"Are you ready?"

"We're not going to wait until the others return from the office?" Jen asked.

"I don't think we need to. Who knows how long they'll be? I'd rather get an early start if that's okay with you."

"At least let me leave them a note letting them know we'll be back before dark."

"Can we stop for a moment, Cat? I need to catch my breath."

"Sure. There's a group of boulders up ahead. It looks like as good a place as any to stop for a while."

Cat and Jen settled onto the path-side boulders and took their water bottles from their backpacks.

Jen wiped the sweat from her brow. "If this is what they call moderate, I'd hate to see what difficult is."

"I have to admit it is kind of challenging. I can't help but wonder if we've veered off track. I haven't seen any trail markers for a while." Cat glanced at her watch. "Sheesh. Where's the time going? It's already four o'clock."

"We left at what, noon? I can't believe it's taken us four hours to get this far. I'm more out of shape than I thought. Maybe we should turn around. At this rate, it'll be dusk by the time we get back to camp."

Cat screwed the cap onto her water bottle. "You're right. Let's go back."

* * *

Billie, Fred and the kids spilled out of the van. "Mom, can we have a snack?" Seth asked.

"You guys just ate three buckets of popcorn at the movies,"

Billie replied.

"That was an hour ago."

Billie shook her head in disbelief. "All right, a snack and a drink for each of you, but don't overdo it. I don't want you to ruin your dinner." She looked at Fred. "Where do they put it all?"

"I hear you. Jen and I would be rich if we didn't have to feed the kids."

Billie retrieved two bottles of pop from the cooler and handed one to Fred. "I wonder if the girls are enjoying their hike."

Fred looked at his watch. "It's nearly four o'clock. I suspect they'll be back soon. I hope so; my stomach is rumbling."

Billie chuckled. "I would hate to have to cook dinner if they're not back in time."

"Correction, Mom, we would hate for you to cook dinner if Mom and Aunt Jen don't get back in time," Seth said from the picnic table.

"Smart ass," Billie whispered under her breath.

Seth waved his bottle of soda in her direction. "I heard that."

"I'm gonna tell Mama you said a bad word," Skylar added.

Billie rolled her eyes at Fred.

* * *

Cat glanced over her shoulder. "Have you seen a trail marker yet, Jen?"

"No, have you?"

"No."

"Do you think we're lost?"

"I'm kind of concerned that nothing looks familiar," Cat admitted. "I would have sworn this was the path we came in on."

"You wouldn't happen to have a GPS on your phone, would you?"

"Yes, I do, but we left my phone at the campsite, remember?"

"Oh, yeah. What time is it getting to be?" Jen asked.

"Holy shit! It's almost six o'clock."

"No wonder my stomach's growling. I ate the last of my snacks back at the boulders."

"Maybe we should call Billie and Fred to let them know we'll be later than expected," Cat said.

"Good idea." Jen retrieved the cell phone from her backpack and dialed Fred's number.

Cat waited patiently. After several moments, she raised an eyebrow in query.

"He's not answering," Jen said. "I've got his voicemail. Fred, this is Jen. It's about six o'clock. Just calling to say Cat and I are running a little late. Give me a call when you get this." She snapped her cell phone closed. "We should probably get moving. I'd like to get off the trail before it gets dark."

A faint rumble of thunder could be heard in the distance. Cat looked through the canopy of trees at the sky beyond. "Great! All we need is yet another soaking. We'd better hurry."

"Which direction?"

Cat looked around. "Hard to tell. Between the dark clouds and the dense trees, it's tough to see a trail."

"There appears to be a break in the trees over there," Jen said, pointing to their right.

"Lead the way," Cat said.

The wind increased significantly as they approached the opening in the trees. "Shit! This isn't good," Cat said. "We may want to stay within the protection of the trees until this passes."

"You might be right, but I want to see what's in that clearing. We might get lucky and actually be near civilization," Jen replied.

"It's worth a look, I guess," Cat said as she followed Jen.

A few moments later, they were within ten feet of the edge of the trees. Cat reached for Jen's shoulder and brought them both to a halt. "That's odd," Cat said. "It looks like there's nothing beyond the trees, just sky."

"I was thinking that very thing," Jen said. "I'm going to take a look."

A strong gust of wind suddenly tore through the trees. "You'd better hurry. The sky's about to open up. I'll look for a place where we can sit out the storm while you check the clearing," Cat said.

"Okay. I'll be right back."

"Be careful."

Cat looked around and found several downed evergreen branches, still heavy with needles, which she was gathering when she heard a yelp from the woods. "Jen? Jen, where are you?" She looked around, but failed to see her friend. "Jen!"

"Fuck! Goddamnit! Help!"

"Jen!"

"Over here. I need help, quick!"

Cat ran toward the clearing and looked around. "Jen, where are you?"

"Over here. Quick, Cat, I can't hold on for much longer."

Cat soon realized the reason they saw only sky beyond the trees was because the ground abruptly fell off a cliff at the edge of the clearing. "Jen, I can't see you!"

"I'm down here. Hurry, Cat!"

Cat approached the edge of the cliff and was startled to see her friend with a tenuous hold on a root protruding near the lip of the drop-off. She immediately dropped to her stomach on the ground.

"Oh my God, Jen! Here, grab my hand." She reached forward as far as she could without slipping over the edge herself. "I've got you. Hold on tight," she said as she anchored Jen's climb over the top of the cliff. When Jen was safely beside her, Cat scrambled to her knees. "What happened?"

"I was walking along the edge, looking for a trail down, and suddenly the ground gave out from under me," Jen said. "Next thing I knew, I was hanging on for dear life."

"Do you know what might have happened if we'd continued along this path in the dark?" Cat asked.

"I hate to even think about it."

Cat climbed to her feet and peered over the edge of the cliff. "You're lucky you didn't fall to the bottom. You would've broken your neck."

"Unfortunately, my cell phone wasn't so lucky."

Cat groaned. "Please don't tell me that."

"Okay, I won't."

A bright bolt of lightning and loud crack of thunder tore through the sky. Cat offered her hand to Jen and helped her to her feet. "Come on. The rain is going to let loose at any moment. We need to take shelter."

\* \* \*

Billie stoked the coals in the fire pit while Fred added another piece of wood.

"It's a good thing we had canned soup," he said. "Kind of hard to mess that up."

Billie glanced at the kids gathered around the picnic table. "They seem to be enjoying it."

A few awkward moments of silence passed before Fred cleared his throat and said, "I wonder when the girls will be back. Those dark clouds look menacing."

"I was thinking the same thing. Have they called your cell at all?" Billie asked.

"I haven't heard it ring."

"Check it anyway. It's possible they've called, and we just didn't hear it."

Fred dug his phone out of his pocket. "Oh, man!"

"What is it?"

"It's off. I forgot to turn it back on after we left the movie theater." The "missed call" chime sounded. Fred opened the phone. "The call is from Jen."

"What time did it come in?"

"It says five forty-eight."

Billie looked at her watch. "That was about a half hour ago."

"She left a voicemail. Here, let me put it on speaker."

"Fred, this is Jen. It's about six o'clock. Just calling to say Cat and I are running a little late. Give me a call when you get this."

"Call her back," Billie said.

Fred dialed Jen's number and waited. "It's going to voicemail."

"Leave a message. Tell them to call us right away."

Fred nodded. "Hi, hon. Sorry. I shut my phone off when we went to the movies and just now turned it back on. Call me back. Love you."

A bright bolt of lightning and loud crack of thunder tore through the sky. "This is not good," Billie said.

\* \* \*

"Jen, grab that bough and drag it over here."

"I think this one should do it," Jen said. She held it in place while Cat used their last shoestring to secure it to the other branches. "Just in time. It's starting to rain."

"Grab your stuff and get inside."

Jen crawled into the triangular space between the large boulder and the small tree limbs Cat had set in place and covered with multiple layers of evergreen boughs. "Where did you learn to make a lean-to?"

"My dad used to take my sisters and me camping in the woods with nothing but our wits. I learned how to build a primitive structure when I was quite young."

"Thank you, Doc."

"Amen to that. I just hope the structure holds. The wind is picking up."

"So is the rain."

"You'd still better be prepared to get wet, Jen. The boughs will keep off most of the rain, but not all of it."

A flash of light and clap of thunder vibrated through the shelter. Jen grabbed Cat's arm. "A little warning would be nice," she yelled into the darkness.

A few awkward moments of silence passed, before Cat said, "You do realize we're here for the night."

"I kind of figured that one out a while ago."

"It could be worse, you know."

Jen grimaced. "Pray tell how?"

"You could be at the bottom of the cliff with your cell phone."

\* \* \*

"What time did you say they left the site?" the ranger asked.

"Around—" A loud clap of thunder drowned out Billie's reply, so she repeated, "Around noon. They said they'd be back before dark. That was at least two hours ago."

"Do you know which trail they took?"

Billie stepped into the ranger's personal space. "If I knew that, I'd be out there looking for them myself instead of asking you for help," she snapped.

"Look, Ms. Charland, I know you're concerned, but our trails are pretty safe."

"Safe? I happen to know firsthand that you have free-range black bear running around here. Don't tell me they're safe."

"Ms. Charland, I'm sure your friends are fine."

"Wives, they are our wives. Get it straight."

"Yes, of course. Look, it'll be nearly impossible to look for them during this storm. I'll take the necessary steps to organize search parties that will start out as soon as the storm is over. Until then, I recommend you return to your site. We'll be in touch with you as soon as the weather breaks."

"You want us to just sit around our campsite and wait? You've got to be kidding me," Billie said. "What if something terrible has happened to them?"

"Putting a search party in danger looking for them is not going to improve their situation any. Besides, as safe as the trails are during the day, the darkness increases the risk that someone else could be hurt in the search. If they're smart, your wives have found shelter and are holed up for the night," the ranger explained. "Now please go back to your campsite and wait the storm out. I promise you we'll begin the search at daylight."

Billie returned to the van where Fred and the children were waiting. "Well?" Fred prodded.

"They said to go back to our campsite and wait.

Apparently, the darkness combined with the storm makes it too dangerous to send out a search party."

"What about Mama and Aunt Jen? Isn't it dangerous for them?" Seth asked.

Billie squeezed her son's shoulder and inhaled deeply to quell her emotions. "Mama's pretty resourceful, scout. Try not to worry about her. I'm sure they'll be okay. The ranger said he'd send a search party out at daylight." Billie glanced over Seth's head to Fred, whose worried expression mirrored her own.

* * *

"Jen, give me your raincoat."

"What? Are you crazy? Why would I give you the one thing that is keeping me at least semi-dry?"

"I'm going to snap our two coats together and drape them over the top of the boughs to block the rain coming through the branches," Cat explained.

"We're going to freeze our asses off!"

"Not if we share our body heat."

"Cat, if you're trying to get me to join the Sisterhood, there are better ways of doing it than this," Jen joked.

"Very funny. Now give me your coat."

"Awww!"

"Trust me, Jen, we'll be warmer if we can stay as dry as possible."

"Fine!"

Jen stripped off her raincoat and handed it to Cat. Cat laid the two coats out across her lap in opposite directions, with the male part of the snap from one jacket and the female part from the other, then she fastened them together to create a makeshift waterproof barrier that was approximately six feet wide and four feet long.

"Let me help you with that," Jen said as she climbed out of the lean-to behind Cat.

With barely enough light to see a foot in front of their faces, they worked together to drape the joined raincoats over the top of boughs, securing them with branches slipped into the sleeves. Moments later they were back inside, cold, but protected from the continuing downpour.

"That's better," Cat said. "We might have lost a layer of insulation, but overall, we'll be warmer if we can stay fairly dry."

"Let's just hope the wind doesn't tear our shelter down," Jen said.

"We're pretty much protected by the trees. Come here. If we huddle together, we'll be warmer."

Cat and Jen wrapped their arms around each other. "How's that?" Cat asked.

"Not too bad," Jen said. "Not toasty, but not freezing either."

"Billie and Fred are probably having kittens right now."

"I'm more worried about the kids," Jen confessed. "Karissa frets about everything. I wish there was a way to let them know we're okay."

"Unfortunately, your cell phone became this camping trip's third electronic victim, so as cruel as it sounds, we're just going to have to wait this one out until morning." Cat felt Jen shiver in her arms. "Are you cold?"

"Not really. I was just thinking about what could've happened if that root hadn't been there for me to grab when the ground collapsed by the cliff."

"Amen to that." A few moments of silence passed before Cat squeezed her friend's shoulders and said, "Close your eyes, Jen. Try to sleep. It's going to be a long night."

# Chapter 36

# Here She Comes... Miss America

"All right, Squad One, you take the south slope of Camper's Knoll. There are three trails to search on that side of the mountain. Squad Two, you've got the north slope. Here's a trail guide. There are only two trails, but they're steep. Squad Three will cover the east side of Camelback Mountain, and Squad Four, you cover the west side. That mountain has some treacherous cliffs and narrow trails, so be careful."

"Ranger Johnson, you haven't assigned us to a squad. Where should we search?" Billie asked.

"You and your family should stay here in case they return."

"No fucking way am I staying here when Cat and Jen could be—"

"Ms. Charland, I understand your concern, but we can't guarantee your safety if you come along."

"Fuck that, I'm going." Billie stomped over to her gear and slung a backpack over her shoulder.

"Ms. Charland..."

"There's no use arguing with her," Fred said. He picked up his own backpack. "I'm going too, and so are the kids."

"Mr. Swenson, I strongly advise against that."

"Well, I strongly advise against your arguing with us about it," Fred said.

"Suit yourself." Ranger Johnson turned to the assembled crowd of searchers. "Let's head out. Report in on your radio every half hour until we find them, and I want everyone to report back here in four hours. If we haven't found them by then, we'll regroup and reassign search areas. Oh, and one more thing. You need to prepare yourself for anything. Our hope is that we find them safe and sound, but—"

"We'll find them safe and sound, Ranger," Billie said adamantly, inclining her head toward the children.

"Ah… yes. Let's pray we do."

* * *

"Jen, wake up." Cat shook her friend. "Jen. Wake up."

"Whaa?"

"It's sunrise. Time to break camp." Cat pushed Jen into a sitting position.

Jen rubbed her eyes. "What time is it?"

Cat looked at her watch. "Exactly five forty-five."

"What is wrong with you, waking me up so early?"

"I have had enough of sitting on the hard ground all night. Time to find our way out of this jungle." Cat climbed out of the lean-to and offered her hand to Jen. "Come on."

Outside, Jen stood erect and stretched her back. "I have to pee."

"My thoughts exactly," Cat said. "You go behind that tree, and I'll go behind this one."

Cat squatted behind her tree. "Be careful what you use to wipe with. We don't need another poison ivy incident, especially on the cha cha."

"You have such a lovely way with words," Jen called from behind her own tree. "I am choosing to drip dry. No itchy coochie for me."

While waiting for Jen, Cat dismantled their lean-to and unsnapped their raincoats. She handed Jen's coat to her. "Here you go."

Cat then retrieved her shoe laces from the tree boughs and re-laced her books.

"Which way do we go, Pocahontas?" Jen said.

Cat looked around. "Well, straight ahead is a dead end, unless we want to take the scenic route over the cliff, so I guess we go back the way we came in last night."

"Lead the way."

* * *

"Billie, are you getting as worried as I am?"

Billie glanced back at the kids. "Don't say that too loud, I don't want them to hear you. But to answer your question, yes, I am beginning to get a little worried. I have this sick feeling in the pit of my stomach, and my heart is doing calisthenics in my chest."

"We've been searching for three hours now," Fred said.

"I just wish they'd told us which trail they were taking."

"When are we gonna find Mama and Aunt Jen?" Skylar asked.

"Soon, sweetie" Billie replied. "Soon." Billie felt a tug on her arm. She looked down at Seth.

"I'm kinda worried about Ma," he said. "I don't want the little kids to get worried, but what if we don't find them?"

Billie stopped and grasped her son's shoulders. "I'm sure they're okay, Seth. Mom is very resourceful. She used to camp with Grandpa all the time. Try not to worry." Billie released her son and watched as he walked down the path behind Fred. She closed her eyes and inhaled deeply, then wiped a tear from the corner of her eye as she followed him.

* * *

"How are you doing back there?" Cat called over her shoulder as she led the way down the path.

"I'm doing okay. Kind of hungry and my back hurts from sleeping on the ground, but I'm holding my own," Jen replied.

"Does anything look familiar to you yet?"

"Not really. Sooner or later, we have to hit civilization. This forest can't go on forever."

"Good point. Let's walk for another half hour, then take a break, okay?"

"Sounds like a plan."

"I can just imagine what's going through Billie's head right now."

"Do you think she's called out the cavalry yet?" Jen asked.

"I wouldn't put it past her. I'm more worried about her than

I am about us. This can't be good for her blood pressure."

"Is it really that serious, Cat?"

"She's apparently been having heart palpitations for several months, which she didn't tell me about, by the way. The last thing we need is for her to go off the deep end from an anxiety attack. She's never going to let me live this one down, you know."

"What do you mean?"

"I told you she didn't really want to go camping, and, quite frankly, with everything that's gone wrong on this trip, I'm beginning to think she was right."

"Enjoy it while you can. I suspect you'll never get her to go camping again."

"My thoughts exactly. Jen, look, there's a fork ahead in the path. Left or right?"

"Beats the hell out of me. Let's toss a coin." Jen fished a coin out of her pocket and flipped it into the air. She caught it easily and slapped it onto the back of her left hand, covering it with her right. "Heads we go left, tails we go right."

"Sounds good to me," Cat said.

"It's tails. We go right."

"Right it is. Do you want to take the lead for a while?" Cat asked.

"No, you're doing a great job."

"All right then, let's go."

A short way down the path, Cat noticed an unusual flower in the sloping brush to her left. "Wow. Look at that flower. It's beautiful. Wait here a sec, I want a closer look."

Cat walked toward the flower, coming within two feet of it when suddenly she lost her footing and fell out of sight. "Ahhhh!" she yelled.

"Cat!" Jen ran toward the spot Cat had been standing and, as suddenly as Cat had gone down, she followed. "Noooo!"

Both women slid uncontrollably down the muddy slope, toppling end over end and losing their backpacks along the way. When they finally reached the bottom, they were covered with dark brown mud from head to foot.

"Oh my God," Cat moaned. "Jen, are you all right?"

Jen struggled to her knees and sat back on her heels. "What the fuck happened?"

"The bank must have been softened by the downpour last night. Obviously, our weight was too much for it."

"Are you saying I have a fat ass?" Jen asked.

"If your ass is fat, then mine is too. I was the first one to fall," Cat said.

Jen shook the mud off her hands. "This is disgusting. We're covered!"

Cat climbed to her feet. "I am so looking forward to a nice hot shower."

"You and me, both," Jen said.

Cat gave Jen a hand up. "Let's go find our packs, then try to locate the trail again."

Jen pointed to the top of the hill. "You're not suggesting we climb back up there, are you?"

Cat looked around. "Look. There's a stream. I bet if we follow it, it'll lead us back to civilization."

* * *

"Dad, what's that shiny thing up ahead?" Stevie asked his father.

"Shiny thing?" Fred said.

"Yeah. On the ground. I'll go get it." Stevie and Seth ran ahead and stopped at the base of a cliff. Stevie picked the object up. "It's a cell phone."

Billie grabbed Fred's arm. "I wonder if it's Jen's."

The two adults took off on a dead run toward their sons. "Let me see it," Fred said. He turned the phone around in his hands. "It looks like Jen's phone. It's pretty damaged. The screen is smashed."

Billie looked around. "There's too much damage to have been caused by the phone simply falling out of her pocket. It's almost like it was dropped, or maybe even thrown from a great height."

"Why would someone throw Jen's cell phone?"

Billie took Fred's arm and pulled him a distance away from

the boys. She spoke in a low voice. "Maybe so she couldn't use it to call for help."

\* \* \*

Jen and Cat walked along in the stream, their hiking boots sloshing in the shallow water.

"Christ, you look like hell," Jen said.

"You don't exactly look like pageant material yourself, right now," Cat retorted.

Jen shoved hard against Cat's shoulder. "Take it back."

"Hey, knock it off."

Jen pushed her again. "I said, take it back."

Cat pushed her back. "Like hell I will. What the hell crawled up inside of you and died?"

"'Look at that flower', she says. 'It's beautiful,' she says. 'I want a closer look,' she says. This is what your closer look got us," Jen exclaimed as she stepped closer and closer to Cat. "Muddy clothes, muddy hair, and we're even more lost than before."

"Chill out, Jen. I don't need you in my face." Cat pushed Jen, who promptly fell on her butt in the stream. Cat's hands flew to her mouth. "Oh, Jen! I'm so sorry. I didn't mean to do that." She reached down to help Jen up and found herself pulled over Jen's head, face first in the stream. Cat scrambled to her knees. "Why you..." Cat pounced on Jen and they tumbled about in the shallow stream, each one alternately gaining the upper hand, until they both fell onto their backs, exhausted. They lay side by side in the stream with the water gently flowing around them. Finally, Cat looked at Jen.

"I'm sorry I said you weren't pageant material."

Jen smiled. "And I'm sorry I implied you had a fat ass."

Cat offered her hand. "Still friends?"

Jen grasped Cat's hand and squeezed. "Always."

"So, as long as we're soaking wet, we might as well clean this mud off of us," Cat suggested.

Jen bolted into a sitting position. "Birthday suit!" she

yelled, removing her clothing.

* * *

"Where did you find this?" Ranger Johnson asked. He turned the cell phone over in his hands.

"At the bottom of Camelback Mountain," Fred replied.

"Are you sure it belongs to your wife?"

"Positive. See those stickers on the front? My daughter gave those to her before we left home for this trip."

"Can you show me exactly where on the map?"

"I can show you," Billie offered. She opened the trail guide and spread it on the picnic table. She tapped the page. "Right here."

"Did you see any other evidence they passed through there, like trampled brush or footprints?"

Billie glanced at Fred. "I didn't think to look. How about you, Fred?"

"Me, neither."

Ranger Johnson folded the map, put it into his vest pocket, and turned to the assembled search party. "Okay, we have reason to believe Ms. Charland and Ms. Swenson passed through the canyon at the base of Camelback Mountain. We head out in twenty minutes."

* * *

"Jen, did you hear that?" Cat stopped in mid-stride on the bank of the stream and listened.

"Hear what?"

Cat placed a finger in front of her lips. "Shh. Listen. There it is again. Did you hear that?"

"It kind of sounds like a dirt bike."

"Or a chainsaw. Come on, let's follow the sound. This could be our ticket out of this jungle."

* * *

"Thank you, Jim. You're a life saver," Cat said as she

climbed out of the cab of the pickup truck.

"Yes, we can't thank you enough," Jen added.

"Will you ladies be okay from here?" their rescuer asked.

"It's just a short walk down the drive to the campground entrance. We'll be fine. Again, thanks for the ride. Are you sure we can't compensate you?" Cat offered.

"No, ma'am. I wouldn't be a gentleman if I expected to get paid for offering my help to damsels in distress."

"Well, it's too bad more people aren't like you. We really do appreciate the ride," Jen said.

"My pleasure, ladies. You have yourselves a pleasant afternoon."

Cat watched Jim drive away, then locked arms with Jen as they limped down the path to the campground. "Home sweet home, or is it camp sweet camp? Are you ready to face the music?"

"At this point, even Fred yelling at me for getting lost will be music to my ears."

"Thank God for Jim," Cat said.

"He was very sweet, wasn't he? I'm thankful he offered us a lift back to the campground instead of just pointing us in the right direction. I'm exhausted. I don't know if I could have walked another step."

"I'm with you. That air mattress is sounding mighty good right now, after a hot shower, that is."

"A hot shower sounds a lot better than the cold dip in the stream this morning. As I said earlier, lead the way, Pocahontas!"

Jen said.

\* \* \*

Cat was awakened by the sounds of arguing.

"How can you call off the search? It isn't even dark yet?"

"It'll be dark within the hour, Ms. Charland. We'll resume the search in the morning."

"Like hell we will," she heard Billie shout at the unseen

man. "I am not going to allow Cat and Jen to spend another night out there alone. She's my wife, for crying out loud. Do you expect me to just sit back and wait for you to get your dead ass moving again in the morning? I'm going back out there right now, and there's nothing you can do to stop me."

*Shit! I'd better get out there.* Cat scrambled to her knees and reached for the tent zipper.

"Ms. Charland, you need to be reasonable. Searching in the dark is dangerous."

"I don't give a fuck. I lost her once, I can't lose her again. I won't lose her again."

A fold of material became stuck in the zipper, making it difficult for Cat to open it.

"Billie, calm down."

That's Fred's voice, Cat thought as she finally freed the zipper and climbed out of her tent.

"I will not calm down, Fred. Our wives are out there. God knows what has happened to them. If you want to stay here, that's fine. In fact, that's a good idea. You stay with the kids, I'm going back out to search."

"Billie," Cat said.

"I'm sure they're fine. You said yourself that Cat is resourceful. No reason to get hysterical."

"Billie," Cat said, a little louder.

"They've been gone over twenty-four hours. I think that's plenty of reason to get hysterical," Billie shouted. "Don't tell me not to get hysterical!"

"Billie!" Cat finally yelled.

Billie swung around and shouted. "What?"

"Ms. Charland, I presume," Ranger Johnson said pointedly.

* * *

Cat and Jen sat side by side in the camp chairs in front of the fire and watched as Billie and Fred paced back and forth in front of them.

"Cat, you scared the shit out of me."

"Ditto," Fred said.

"Give us a little credit. We aren't totally helpless, you

know," Cat replied.

"Yeah, we aren't totally helpless," Jen echoed.

"How did your cell phone end up at the bottom of the mountain?" Fred asked.

"Uh... I dropped it when I almost fell over the cliff," Jen answered. Cat elbowed her in the ribs. "Oww! Why'd you do that?"

"You almost walked off the side of a cliff?" Billie said incredulously. "Great. Just great." Billie picked up one of the camp chairs and threw it across the campsite.

"Cat was there to pull me back up. What's the big deal?"

Fred stopped. "Wait a minute. Cat pulled you back up? That's a little more than almost walking off the side of a cliff!"

"And how did you get so dirty? The clothes you threw into the corner of the tent are covered with mud," Billie raged.

Cat shrugged. "That's from the tumble down the muddy hill, of course. We tried to rinse them off in the stream."

"Oh my fucking God," Billie said.

"Now look who's opening her big mouth," Jen said.

"Well, there's no sense in hiding anything now," Cat answered.

"Should we tell them about the naked romp in the stream?" Jen asked.

"Jesus, Cat, I had all kinds of horrible thoughts about what might have happened to you," Billie said. "What would I have told the kids?" Billie whimpered as she fell to her knees in front of Cat and placed her head in her wife's lap. "I can't lose you again, Cat. I
need you."

Cat rested her head on Billie's. "I need you too, love. I won't leave you, I promise."

Fred was looking at Cat and his wife speculatively. "Naked romp in the stream?"

# Chapter 37

## Enough is Enough is Enough

Cat gingerly emerged from her tent the next morning to find Jen already in the screen tent making coffee. "Good morning, Jen."

"Hiya. Coffee's on."

"Give me a few minutes, I've got to run to the bathroom. Be right back."

"Take your time," Jen said. "I'll get the stove set up for breakfast."

Cat limped her way up the trail to the bathhouse and back. "Girl, you are out of shape," she mumbled as she got back to the campsite and let herself into the food tent.

"Moving kind of slow, huh?" Jen asked.

"I can't believe how much my body hurts today."

"Well, it's not every day you walk through the forest for twelve hours, then throw yourself down a muddy slope," Jen pointed out dryly.

"You've got a point. How do you feel today?"

"Pretty much the way you do. How's Big Guy this morning?"

"She cried for hours last night, and as long as she was awake, she wouldn't let me get more than a foot away from her. Over and over, she repeated that she couldn't lose me again. I guess she was more scared than I even thought she'd be. I was so happy when she finally fell asleep."

"I guess I can understand her fear, Cat. I mean, we knew we were okay, but she and Fred were clueless. They could only think the worst and hope for the best. Maybe her reaction sheds light on some of her odd behavior lately."

"What do you mean?"

"Well, when something scares me, one of my first reactions is anger. Maybe Billie's anger is actually rooted in fear."

Cat sipped her coffee. "I've never thought of it that way. We'll have to talk to Doctor Connor about it at our next appointment."

"I wouldn't wait for your next appointment. Today is Saturday, and tomorrow we pack up and go home. If I were you, I'd call and make an appointment first thing Monday morning."

"I'd never admit it to Billie, but I'm looking forward to going home. I've had as much bad luck as I can handle in two weeks. Getting lost in the woods and scaring the shit out of Billie, Fred, and the kids is not the way I wanted to end this vacation."

"Amen to that."

A crack of thunder rattled the campsite. Cat lowered her chin to her chest and shook her head. "I can't believe it." She looked into the sky. "Can you cut us a break here?"

Another clap of thunder was followed by large drops of water, lots of large drops of water.

"Give it a few minutes. It's coming down so hard, it can't last for very long," Jen reasoned. Her prognostication proved to be correct when the torrential rains let up five minutes later.

"Maybe we should rouse the troops and get them in here for breakfast, in case it starts to rain hard again," Cat suggested.

"Good idea."

Cat and Jen returned to the screen house a few minutes later and began breakfast preparations while, one by one, the rest of their families filtered in and sat at the picnic table. Cat filled the juice glasses, then grabbed the coffee pot. She filled Fred's cup and then Billie's, gently hip checking Billie before kissing her on the head. "Good morning, love."

"Grrrr."

Cat returned to the stove where Jen was cooking scrambled eggs. "It's pretty chilly over there," she said. "I guess, now that she's knows we're okay, it's time to be angry instead of scared."

"You're getting the cold shoulder too, huh? Fred hasn't said two words to me since we went to bed last night."

"I guess I can't blame them for being scared, but they have to give us some credit, too. After all, we are adults, not children."

Another loud clap of thunder filled the morning air. "Not again," Cat said.

"Maybe the rain will hold off long enough for us to eat breakfast and head to the arcade in the recreation hall."

A deafening clap of thunder heralded the torrential rains that once more fell suddenly from the sky.

"Well, isn't this a fine kettle of fish?" Billie said.

Cat tried to suppress the sudden urge to laugh, the sudden urge that often comes on the heels of a tragic event too incredible to be believed. Her eyes met Billie's, and a grin split her face. Billie threw up her hands in frustration. "What's so funny!"

"This. This is so funny." Cat pointed to the rain and their drenched campsite. She looked at Jen and saw that she was struggling not to laugh. Within moments, the laughter could be heard above the pounding rain.

When their merriment subsided, Billie suggested, "What do you say we call it quits a day early and head home?"

An hour later, they had everything on both sites crammed into their two vehicles. It didn't matter that everything was soaking wet; it didn't matter that a layer of mud covered everything.

They were going home.

# Chapter 38

## If It Weren't For Bad Luck, We'd Have No Luck At All

"So, tell me, ladies, why are you here today?" Doctor Connor said. "Your next appointment wasn't scheduled for another week."

Billie squeezed Cat's hand and looked to her for encouragement. Cat smiled and nodded.

"Well, Doctor Connor, we took your advice and went on a two-week vacation."

"Wonderful. What did you do?"

"We went camping, tent camping, with our best friends and their children," Cat replied. "I wasn't aware how much of a sacrifice that was for Billie until after I made the reservations."

"What do you mean?"

"Apparently, Billie doesn't like camping. I know, I know. It sounds downright un-American, but it's true. I was really touched by her willingness to go despite her reservations."

"Camping sounds like a relaxing vacation. How was it?"

"Anything but relaxing."

"Really? Tell me about it."

"Well, the 'fun' started just a couple of hours into the trip with a flat tire on the interstate highway," Billie said.

For the next several minutes, Billie chronicled the nightmarish two-week camping trip for Doctor Connor, explaining in detail every unbelievable misadventure. Cat was amused by the look of shock and disbelief on the Doctor's face as Billie introduced each new catastrophe.

"Okay, stop," Doctor Connor said. "Are all your vacations like this?"

"I swear we must have bad karma," Cat said. "Bad luck followed us everywhere."

"Billie, how did all of this make you feel?" Doctor Connor asked.

"Angry, anxious, impatient. All of the above."

"How about fearful?" Cat suggested.

Billie's eyes narrowed. "The only time I felt fearful was when you and Jen didn't come back from your hike."

Cat took Billie's hand in her own. "I've never seen you so distraught, Billie."

"Wait a minute," Doctor Connor interrupted. "This is important. Tell me more about the hike."

"Near the end of the trip, Jen and I decided to go on a day hike, while Billie and Fred took the kids to the movies, only somehow we veered from the trail and wound up lost. Jen called Fred's phone to tell him we would be back later than we thought, but they didn't get the message until much later. By that time, Jen had ended up almost falling off a cliff while scouting out the area. Unfortunately, her cell phone did fall off the cliff, so we lost our only way of communicating with Billie and Fred. It was almost dusk when we decided to build a lean-to and spend the night in the woods."

"Fred and I joined the search party the next day to look for them. I have never been so scared in my life. We searched all day with no luck. All I could think of was that I had lost Cat again."

"Lost Cat again?" Doctor Connor probed.

"Yes. The feelings of loneliness and anxiety I felt when I woke up after the surgery came flooding back. I felt so alone then. Part of me knew I had lost something very important, but I didn't know what it was. I didn't know until much later, when my memories began to return." Billie wiped tears from her eye. "When they didn't come back from their hike, all I could think about was that I had lost Cat again. The sadness was overwhelming. I've never been so scared in my life."

"How did you react to that fear, Billie?" Doctor Connor asked.

"With anger. I was so angry with Cat, when she did return, all I could do was yell at her and cry. My heart was pounding so hard in my chest that it scared me. I'm so afraid of losing her again."

Cat knelt on the floor in front of Billie and took Billie's face between her palms. "Sweetheart, I'm here. I'm not going anywhere, I promise. I love you with all my heart. Yes, you can be a pain in the ass at times, but there is nothing you can do to make me stop loving you. Please believe that."

Billie wiped the tears from her cheeks. "I'm sorry, Cat. I'm sorry for all the times I lost patience with you, and for all the times I was short tempered. It wasn't you, it was me. I was so afraid of doing something that would make you leave. I can't lose you. I can't."

"Well, you get those thoughts right out of your mind. Like it or not, you're stuck with me."

"I love you, Cat."

"Right back atcha."

Doctor Connor rose to her feet. "So, it appears the camping trip was a successful vacation, after all. Despite your run of 'bad luck,' as you put it, I think you've discovered the root of Billie's anger. It's been fear, all along. Fear is the cause; anger is the symptom. *That* we can work on."

# Epilogue

## Déjà Vu—Not!

Cat and Billie were sitting at the kitchen table, eating breakfast and enjoying each other's company, when the door opened and Jen popped in. "Morning, ladies." Jen helped herself to the last cup of coffee, and then set up a new pot to brew. Cat and Billie looked at each other and smiled as they watched their friend make herself at home.

"Good Morning, Jen," Billie said.

"Want some breakfast?" Cat offered.

"No, just ate." Jen placed a kiss on Cat's cheek and stole a piece of bacon. She circled around Billie, deposited a kiss on her cheek as well, then sat down between the pair and helped herself to a piece of toast from Billie's plate.

"Are you sure you don't want to eat?" Billie asked wryly.

"No. Really, I just ate." She happily chewed on the toast. "What are you two up to today?"

Billie and Cat looked at each other. "Don't know." Cat shrugged. "I haven't really thought much about it."

Jen looked at Billie, who also shrugged. "Boy, you two are bundles of enthusiasm!"

"Why? What are you doing today?" Cat asked.

Billie placed her elbow on the table and rested her chin in her hand. "Yeah, what are you doing today, Jen?"

Jean grinned. "Same thing you are. Don't know."

"Are we in a rut, or what?" Cat commented.

"What's Fred doing today?" Billie asked.

The three women looked at each other and grinned. "Don't know!" they all exclaimed together, laughing.

"Hey, I've got a thought," Jen said. "Since we're all doing the same thing, why don't we do it together?"

"Cool!" Cat said.

"Go for it," Billie piped in.

The back door opened, admitting Fred, followed by Stevie and Karissa.

"Seth and Tara are upstairs, sweeties. Go on up," Cat said to the children.

Stevie and Karissa immediately took off into the living room, while Fred helped himself to a cup of coffee. "Morning," he said to everyone. "What's up?"

"Don't know!" all three woman said at once as they dissolved into laughter.

Fred looked at the three of them as though they were nuts, then into his coffee cup. "Okay, what did you put in the coffee?"

"Have a seat, Fred." Billie pushed a chair out with her foot.

Fred accepted the invitation and joined the women at the table. "Really, what's up?" he repeated.

"We were just sitting here discussing how exciting our lives are these days," Cat said.

"Boring is the word for it," Jen piped in. "We really need to do something to get out of this rut."

"What do you mean boring?" Fred said. "What do I mean?" Jen exclaimed. "Hell, Fred, it's Saturday night and none of us has a date," she said pointedly.

"Huh?"

Jen placed a kiss on Fred's head. "Sometimes you are so dense. Why do I keep you around?"

"'Cause you can't resist my good looks and charm?"

"Oh, please." Jen groaned. "Look, here we are, four healthy adults, five healthy children, and what are we doing? Sitting around pulling lint out of our belly buttons. Sheesh. How boring is that? We need some excitement in our lives, like maybe another camping trip."

"Been there, done that," Billie said dryly. "Gotta admit, it wasn't boring."

"It wasn't so bad, Billie. Your shrink recommended it after all," Jen pointed out.

Billie looked at Cat; Cat looked at Billie. A silent look of agreement passed between them. Billie picked up the half grapefruit from her plate and shoved it in Jen's face, twisting it around, and then letting it fall onto the table.

Astonishment written all over her face, Jen sat there with grapefruit pulp hanging from her nose.

Fred's eyes bulged out.

Cat covered her mouth with her hands to keep from laughing.

Billie leaned toward Jen. "Now, tell me, Jen, was that exciting enough for you?"

"Oh, yeah." The grapefruit pulp jiggled as Jen nodded her head. She reached for a napkin to clean her face. "So, I guess this means no more camping trips, huh?"

The look on Billie's face spoke volumes.

"Okay. I can take a hint... no more camping trips," Jen confirmed. "What would you say to a cruise, or a trip to Disneyland, or... or..."

Billie rose to her feet, a devilish look on her face.

"Billie, I don't like that look on your face. Billie, I'm warning you." Jen rose to her feet.

Jen managed to escape from the house before Billie could reach her. She cleared the porch steps in one jump and was off and running across the yard, trying to escape the madwoman nipping at her heels.

Cat stood to watch the race across the back yard, cringing when Billie made the defensive tackle. She returned to her seat and gave Fred a sympathetic look. "Well, what are you planning for today?"

"Don't know," he replied. "You?"

"Don't know!" Cat answered, sending them both into peals of laughter.

# Happy Campers

Karen D. Badger

Photo Credit: Brad Fowler, Song of Myself Photography

See her author page at www.karendbadger.com

# About the Author

Karen D. Badger is the author of On A Wing And A Prayer, Yesterday Once More (a 2009 Golden Crown Literary Award winner for Speculative Fiction), In A Family Way, Unchained Memories, Happy Campers, Collective Identity Sweet Angel and Relative-ly Speaking (Books I, II, III, IV, V and VI of the Commitment Series), The Blue Feather, All My Tomorrows (sequel to the 2009 award winning Yesterday Once More) and her latest novel, 1140 Rue Royale...all released by Badger Bliss Books, which Karen co-owns with her wife Barbara Sawyer (aka, "Bliss').

Born and raised in Vermont, Karen is the second of five children raised by a fiercely independent mother, who remains one of her best friends to this day. Karen earned her B.A. in 1978 in Theater and in Elementary Education, and in 1994, earned a B.S. in mathematics. In addition to her novels, Karen is the author of many technical papers on photomask manufacturing, which she has presented at numerous semiconductor industry conferences, and is the holder if several technical patents. Karen is currently in her 38th year as a Principle Member of the Technical Staff with a prominent Semiconductor manufacturer in Vermont.

Karen and her wife, Barb (a retired Lt. Col., US Air Force) live in the beautiful state of Vermont—home of Ben and Jerry's. They spend their spare time with family as well as doing home improvement projects on both their homes in Vermont and New Mexico. They also enjoy camping, kayaking, motorcycling and singing Karaoke.

Please visit Karen's author website at www.karendbadger.com, or the Badger Bliss Books website at www.badgerblissbooks.com Also like us on Facebook!

# TITLES BY KAREN D. BADGER

www.badgerblissbooks.com

### *On A Wing and A Prayer*
First edition published by Blue Feather Books, Sept, 2005
Second edition published by Badger Bliss Books – Sept, 2014
Third edition published by Badger Bliss Books – August, 2016
ISBN 13: 978-1-945761-01-0, ISBN 10: 1-945761-01-6

### *Yesterday Once More*
First edition published by Blue Feather Books, July, 2008
Second edition published by Badger Bliss Books – Sept, 2014
Third edition published by Badger Bliss Books – August, 2016
ISBN 13: 978-1-945761-02-7, ISBN 10: 1-945761-02-4
2009 Golden Crown Literary Society Award - Speculative Fiction

### *In A Family Way – Book One of the Commitment Series*
First edition published by Blue Feather Books, March, 2010
Second edition published by Badger Bliss Books – Sept, 2014
Third edition published by Badger Bliss Books – August, 2016
ISBN 13: 978-1-945761-05-8, ISBN 10: 1-945761-05-9

### *Unchained Memories – Book Two of the Commitment Series*
First edition published by Blue Feather Books, Oct, 2011
Second edition published by Badger Bliss Books – Sept, 2014
Third edition published by Badger Bliss Books – August, 2016
ISBN 13: 978-1-945761-06-5, ISBN 10: 1-945761-06-7

### *Happy Campers - Book Three of the Commitment Series*
First edition published by Blue Feather Books, Sept, 2013
Second edition published by Badger Bliss Books – Sept, 2014
Third edition published by Badger Bliss Books – August, 2016
ISBN 13: 978-1-945761-07-2, ISBN 10: 1-945761-07-5

### *The Blue Feather*
First edition published by Blue Feather Books, July, 2014
Second edition published by Badger Bliss Books – Sept, 2014
Third edition published by Badger Bliss Books – August, 2016
ISBN 13: 978-1-945761-04-1, ISBN 10: 1-945761-04-0

***Collective Identity – Book Four of the Commitment Series***
First edition published by Badger Bliss Books – January, 2015
Second edition published by Badger Bliss Books – August, 2016
ISBN 13: 978-1-945761-08-9, ISBN 10: 1-945761-08-3

***All My Tomorrows – Sequel to Yesterday Once More***
First edition published by Badger Bliss Books – May, 2015 Second
edition published by Badger Bliss Books – August, 2016
ISBN 13: 978-1-945761-03-4, ISBN 10: 1-945761-03-2

***Sweet Angel – Book Five of the Commitment Series***
First edition published by Badger Bliss Books – June, 2015 Second
edition published by Badger Bliss Books – August, 2016
ISBN 13: 978-1-945761-09-6, ISBN 10: 1-945-761-09-1

***Relative-ly Speaking – Book Six of the Commitment Series***
First edition published by Badger Bliss Books – March, 2016
Second edition published by Badger Bliss Books – August, 2016
ISBN 13: 978-1-945761-10-2, ISBN 10: 1-945-761-10-5

***1140 Rue Royale***
First edition published by Badger Bliss Books – Sept, 2016
ISBN 13: 978-1-945761-00-3, ISBN 10: 1-945761-00-8

# Happy Campers

Karen D. Badger